Our Dogs

A Politically Inco

By Keith Nobles

ISBN: 978-0-578-42352-4

Contents

Forward

I like history.

Sometimes things happen that we know beyond dispute happened, but by all rational accounting, they should not have happened. Those things have always fascinated and intrigued me endlessly. On a small scale, things such as the Earps and Clantons at Tombstone or Billy the Kid in Lincoln County are things that are completely counter-intuitive and irrational and by all logic should have never happened, but we know without a doubt that they did happen.

On a larger scale, World War I and the American Civil War should have never happened. The American Civil War was completely irrational. I've read hundreds of books on the Civil War attempting to understand the irrational. I have been to the battlefields (even battlefields no one seems to have heard of), even the battlefields in Colorado and New Mexico.

One can look around the country now and see a sprint to the irrational and sense we're about to have something else happen that ought to never happen but will.

I wrote this novel about what that might look like.

The intent of this novel is to extrapolate and portray a plausible near-term future from the path that the United States is currently traveling. Social, cultural, political, geopolitical, financial, and economic conditions were extrapolated out to a logical future point.

This novel is a possible future history if we choose not to change course.

We can be assured that nothing in the future will occur exactly as portrayed in this novel. However, everything portrayed in this novel is plausible. All events and policies depicted on behalf of the *Committee for the Continuance of Government* are actions that have been taken by socialist governments.

The fiction created herein is not in creating the thoughts and actions—for those are all from real life examples—but in the future context in which they're placed when extended out to their logical conclusions.

All characters are fictional other than the references to historical personalities (Trump, Obama, Sanders, von Mises, Marx, Stand Watie, etc.)

The locations described in this novel are real places, and there is adequate information included to find them all yourself if you wish to. Please respect private property.

I would like to thank Stephanie Sines, Tim Ziegler, Adam Siders, Mark McElroy, James Madison, Frank Francone, Jacqueline Harris, Joe Romeo, Kristina Cook, Jimmy Sensenberger, George Dennis Andrews, and Claire Nobles. Joshua Sharf is credited with the cover photo.

1
A most humbling descent

"We have suffered a most humbling descent. We have lost in a few short years more than most will know in an entire lifetime. All of you ask, 'How do we escape this?' We will return to first principles: liberty, liberty, and liberty, with all our energy and with all of our diligence to recover our freedom from defeat. That's our hope. Liberty is the natural state of mankind."

Cindy wasn't sure that she knew what liberty meant any longer. She, along with nearly everyone she knew, listened to the radio broadcast from Mexico every morning. She was doubtful that the broadcast was entirely truthful all the time, but it gave her an additional view of the world that she could no longer acquire anywhere else. She didn't understand all of the concepts that the illicit broadcast preached but found it more compelling than the government telling her what she needed to think. Aside from what she heard from the Mexican-radio broadcast, in the last two years, Cindy had no knowledge of anything in the world outside of the small town where she lived. It was obvious to Cindy that the government didn't want anyone to know what was going on anywhere else.

"All that's the very best of humanity flows from liberty; the worst evil that the world has known has always been a result of the diminishing of liberty.

"Our liberty has been all but extinguished, and as a consequence we have seen the very worst of humanity. We have experienced the evil. We all know the stories; we have all seen it with our own eyes. We have been assured over and over again for decades that the politicians and bureaucrats knew best while also being taught to rationalize away the failures and broken promises. For decades we have had an entire education system predicated on rationalizing away the failures and broken promises for which liberty was ceded. We now know, without any hesitancy, that government did not know best. We know now that no idea was so bad, no lie too large, and no law too odious so long as the state found it to be beneficial to themselves. That the people bore the brunt of this abuse for decades while the government papered over the truth with lies and debt has not been a matter of doubt for quite some time.

"I have full confidence that liberty will be recovered. Liberty cannot be centrally directed, and it cannot be forced. In a country and a world where force has come to be expected and where, for decades our political disagreements have revolved around who will gain the power to command it, liberty becomes a revolutionary concept.

"The efficacy of the state in applying that force has continually waned, and that ever-decreasing efficacy has been made an excuse for ever more force to be applied in order that the futility of the ideology of force not be made obvious.

"Some make the analogy that we have been boiled like the proverbial frog; however, liberty is not done yet. Liberty is the most compelling message the world has yet known because you have the inherent right to live your life as you desire and are not required to submit to others who would force you to live your life in the manner that they desire. You're at liberty to believe as you wish, to worship as you wish, to speak as you wish, to act as you wish, to associate with whom you wish, to buy and sell as you wish, to protect yourself as you wish, to be secure in your property, to be free to exercise your conscience and your judgment. These things are inherent to your humanity.

"Go spread liberty!"

Cindy wondered how anyone could spread an idea as archaic as liberty in the chaos that the United States had become. The country had suffered one body blow after another starting with the pension crisis and subsequent debt crisis just over two years ago. Americans had done what they did so well and latched onto a term, in this case the term was *counter-party failure*. The cable news channels, the few remaining newspapers, social media, and politicians repeated the term, *counter-party failure*, endlessly. She recalled that the counter-party failure began with an Italian bank and spread everywhere instantly.

She was still not sure what exactly that term meant or what had happened, but she understood as everyone else did that the crisis had traveled around the world at the speed of light. The major banks had seemingly collapsed overnight. The governments and central banks tried to save them and not only failed but were dragged into insolvency along with them. The best she could tell was that it seemed as though every bank was counter-party to every other bank, and they all failed simultaneously.

The debt crisis was quickly followed by the war with China. Cindy allowed her thoughts to stray to the horrible day when it was announced that the United States had lost not one, but two, aircraft carriers to Chinese missile attacks. The only option the United States possessed after it became clear that the navy could no longer operate in the western Pacific was to go nuclear, and the President declined to go that route. Consequently, the United States accepted Chinese terms—terms that included the United States withdraw all American military assets from Asia, Europe, and the Middle East; and that the United States military not operate west of Pearl Harbor or east of Puerto Rico.

Cindy put those thoughts out of her mind and focused on the day ahead. It was ration day, and Cindy slipped her ration card into her backpack and walked out of her trailer into the searing sun of Arizona. It was a two-mile walk across Tombstone to the ration center. The ration center had formerly been a hotel, but with the bankruptcies in the wake of the debt crisis, the chain had gone under, and the government saw fit to repurpose the building. She walked purposefully, pulling her little red wagon down Fremont Street and up the incline next to Boot Hill and around the curve to the ration center, and took her place in line next to Lori and Len. Nearly all of the four hundred people remaining in Tombstone were already in line.

"Did you listen to the liberty talk this morning?" remarked Lori.

"I did. I don't know what we're supposed to do with that. We're not much more than cattle lining up for hay anymore, so how do we get from here to there?"

"It's just satisfying that someone set that transmitter up in Mexico; at least we get to hear something other than the government bullshit," said Len.

As if on cue two Apache helicopters flew low and fast over their heads heading for the Mexican border as the line started to move.

"This is all we are anymore, the army patrolling the border and artificial imitation substitute cheese food product hand-outs," remarked Cindy.

"You're young, we're old—don't give up hope yet. By the way, Len killed a rattlesnake this morning, and we'll have it for lunch. Come by and let us make you something fresh," Lori said in a hushed tone as the line stumbled forward.

After Cindy had collected her rations and toted them back to her trailer in her little red wagon, she took the roundabout way to Len and Lori's home. She wandered over to what was left of the Birdcage Theater that had burned the year before, then wandered down Fremont Street to the OK Corral, and then to Len and Lori's—a house that had once been home to Virgil Earp. Cindy had come to Tombstone after college four years before. Upon graduating from college, she had discovered that there was not a significant demand for her History degree and decided that if she was to work a low paying job it should at least be fun, so she took a gig leading tours of Tombstone. Lori and Len had owned the tour company as well as several of the historical buildings. Cindy had enjoyed talking history and explaining to tourist the significance of events and had even entertained writing a book.

That life was gone now.

2
This was not how it was supposed to be

Michael backed the Lexus out of the garage of the house on Gilpin Street with his wife Joy in the passenger seat.

He thought that he had lived life the way he was supposed to.

He had attended a premier college and built a solid and lucrative career as a software executive. He had successfully paid off the mortgage on a large house in an elite Denver neighborhood populated with other successful, liberal professionals. He and Joy had raised three children, and they had the financial wherewithal to send them to private schools and good colleges, and all three were professionally successful in their own right as adults. He and Joy now had grandchildren.

Michael and Joy had built a large retirement fund with the notion that they would have the time and ability to visit the grandchildren, travel the world, golf at the Denver Country Club, and lunch at their favorite Cherry Creek bistro.

That was all before the hard times.

Michael now drove the Lexus on the short but dangerous journey to collect their weekly rations at what had formerly been the Cherry Creek Mall. *This was not how it was supposed to be*, he thought, damning the world.

He drove south on Gilpin and as he neared 4th Avenue, he noticed the road ahead blocked by vehicles and men with guns. Michael turned east on 4th in order to avoid the bandits. Many of the streets in this section of Denver had been one-way, but no one paid attention to that anymore. On what used to be busy streets, there was now so little vehicle traffic that it typically didn't matter if it was designated a one-way street or not.

Michael contemplated an alternate route and decided to go south on Race. Slowing the Lexus sedan as he approached the intersection, he saw men with guns in his peripheral vision and continued on 4th, rapidly accelerating.

Why are there no security agents? he thought angrily. *Everyone knows that this is ration day and the bandits are out in force stealing ration cards.* Michael glanced at Joy, her apprehension and fear was visible.

The first time that he and Joy had their ration cards stolen at gun point, Michael had journeyed to security headquarters in Lakewood to report the theft and complain. Not only had the security agents refused to accept his report, they had nearly laughed him out of the office. They had explained, while giggling, that ration card thefts were not their responsibility. Michael quickly discovered that ration card theft was no one's responsibility. He and Joy were on their own.

For the first time in his life, he had wished he had owned a gun.

This was not how it was supposed to be, Michael thought.

He made an abrupt right turn onto Vine knowing that University was often blocked by bandits. Michael and Joy crossed over 3rd and could see 1st Avenue. They were only blocks from the mall now.

Michael accelerated the Lexus as Joy clasp her hands together in relief.

As the Lexus approached 1st Avenue a pickup truck backed off of the lawn of a house and blocked their route. Michael braked violently to a stop only to have another truck block the escape route behind them. Six men with handguns approached the Lexus from all angles. A man rapped the barrel of his gun against the driver-side window. Michael complied and rolled the window down.

"Ration cards!" the man with the gun demanded.

Michael handed the man their ration cards as Joy sobbed uncontrollably.

"Out of the car! You give us the car, too!"

This was the second week in a row that Joy and Michael had been robbed of their ration cards.

3
The asylum

John sat in his designated seat as a senator in the Colorado state senate and thought back to Douglas Adams briefly mentioning a character in a couple of his books named, Wonko the Sane. Wonko named his home *Outside of the Asylum* and every place else was *Inside the Asylum*. Wonko decided that he could no longer live sanely in a world where toothpicks needed instructions. Wonko had the instructions for toothpicks mounted in an area outside where he could see them and thus be discouraged from ever going back into the Asylum.

John was one of only seven senators present this day. The senate had not had a quorum in over a year. Initially senators from the western slope and southern Colorado had been unable to find transportation to Denver, and when it became obvious that this situation was permanent, other senators that could possibly attend stopped doing so due to the futility and absurdity of the situation. John listened as fellow state senator, Cassie Roseman, droned on about a school bill that she wished to pass and that reaffirmed for John that this was the Asylum.

There would not be a quorum to vote on this bill and, if there were and it passed, there would not be the funds to implement it and, if somehow funds were miraculously discovered, there would be no personnel to execute the actions the bill called for. *Insanity*, John thought.

Still here the seven senators sat pretending that what was so was not so.

John decided at that moment that he could no longer pretend and that the Asylum no longer had a future. He took his portfolio out of his briefcase and thumbed through looking for a speech he had delivered six years before. He had found, through all of the turmoil, that rereading this speech had often kept him grounded.

"I get that people on the Left commonly believe that they're inaccurately portrayed as more friendly to totalitarianism than they believe they actually are. Let us look at that and why that is.

"I understand that most people on the Left are not advocating for Stalinism. Most people on the Left do have some idea in their minds of what an ideal society looks like. My observation over the past years is that folks on the Left are outcome-oriented. They have in their minds an outcome that they desire, an outcome for an ideal society, and the process for reaching the outcome is much less important than the outcome itself.

"To the Left the desirability of the outcome outweighs the process of obtaining the outcome. That has been true since 1848, and, to be frank, it's made the Left the scourge of humanity.

"To the Leftist, this outcome that they foresee is so desirable that when others consider them a scourge, they automatically assume these other folks are in opposition to their outcome rather than their process.

"Here is where the rubber meets the road: Leftism in all of its versions is predicated on the required use of force.

"This is the scourge of Leftism.

"Leftism is predicated on applying whatever force is required in order to obtain that desired outcome. Simple truth. It doesn't matter if whom you choose as your example of Leftism is Marx or Lenin or Castro or Bernie Sanders. They all advocate for force in order to obtain their desired outcome.

"At this point in time, the romanticism that of necessity must accompany Leftism can only be maintained via fantasy. We simply know and understand too much. We know and understand that everything that Leftist proclaim that they want they can obtain voluntarily—yet Leftist worldwide despise the voluntary. To be blunt, Leftist must work themselves into an emotional and mental state where they do truly believe that they're superior beings. We see it with the phrase, 'are you woke?' which has nothing to do with devising a monetary policy that would be fair and everything to do with justifying the use of force against other human beings—based on having reached this emotional and mental state whereby *woke* indicates some level of understanding unique to themselves that entitles them to use that force.

"Many Leftist at this point say something akin to, 'But we don't want to use force!' The response to that is, 'Do you want to take other people's stuff? Do you want to make people behave as you believe is fair? Do you want to control what they say and communicate so they don't say things you deem *hateful*? Do you want to control who they can't associate with and force them to associate with whom they don't wish to associate?'

"Of course, you do. That's all part and parcel of Leftism. What's more, that's all force.

"Let us go back to Stalinism and being outcome-oriented that I mentioned a bit ago: Other than Stalin and his cronies, no one in Russia advocated for Stalinism. No one in Cuba advocated for Castroism. Last night I was reading about Leningrad in the 1930's, the Stalinist purges and trials. Leftists point to Stalinism as the extreme example, but is it really? Was Stalinism unique? Once you abandon process in exchange for outcome, you release hell, and it doesn't matter where you are on the globe when you do that. Once you abandon process, that means you have also abandoned principle.

"The principles of liberty are that you have rights from your creator that are inherent to your humanity. Among those are the rights to communicate, worship, associate, provide for yourself, manage your own affairs, and decide what you will do with your own property. Liberty-based systems are those in which the government protects these rights that are inherent to you. In liberty-based systems, the laws are oriented toward protecting your life and property, protecting your right to speak and associate.

"All Leftist systems are collectivist. All collectivist systems, of necessity, require these inherent rights to be forsaken in exchange for what *those at the top* consider best for the whole. Collectivist systems are always predicated on there being those at the top; that's a feature, not a bug, because force requires someone to apply it—otherwise it would be voluntary and not collectivist. You can't be both collectivist and voluntary—you must make a choice between the two. If you choose collectivism, then you choose force, and if you choose force, then you will have people at the top who will wield that force—and because it's outcome-based and eschews process and principle, those people at the top will wield that force in whatever manner they believe brings about the desired outcome.

"The fantasy required to maintain the romanticism of the Left is that this is not so. Leftist always maintain that those at the top won't wield power without principle or process and will respect inherent human rights—they believe that right up until they meet prison or concentration camp or firing squad. We see this every day in Venezuela. How many people must be starved, how many must be killed for the good of the collective? This is not ancient history; this is the morning news. The inherent right to associate, to speak, to provide for yourself, have all been removed from the people in Venezuela, and removed by force. To violate the dictate of those at the top—even when you're starving—will bring upon you force from the state up to and including death.

"Recently a young woman made a speech calling for the removal of rights that are inherent to your humanity and did so while wearing the flag of Castro's Cuba. Many people have made the remark to the effect of 'she was simply celebrating her heritage by wearing the Cuban flag.' Shall we examine that argument? If her parents had come from Germany, would you be rationalizing away her wearing a swastika? Now, Leftist will say that Nazi Germany was different, up to and including the absurdity that Nazi Germany was not socialist or collectivist or Leftist, even though Nazi is an acronym for National Socialist Workers Party. It's not as though the Nazi's tried to hide the fact that they were socialist or anything; it's simply a shared delusion among the Left that the Nazi's were not socialist.

"Let us compare this young woman wearing the communist Cuban flag to her wearing a swastika. Did Nazi Germany throw people in concentration camps due to their religious beliefs? Yes. Does Castro's Cuba throw people into concentration camps due to their religious beliefs? Yes. Did Nazi Germany have separate opportunities based on race? Yes. Does Castro's Cuba have separate opportunities based on race? Yes. Did Nazi Germany throw people in concentration camps if they were gay? Yes. Does Castro's Cuba throw people into concentration camps if they're gay? Yes. Did Nazi Germany throw people in concentration camps if their political beliefs were not what the state approved of? Yes. Does Castro's Cuba throw people into concentration camps if their political beliefs are not what the state approves of? Yes.

"I could go on and on and on here for many thousands of words demonstrating that the exact same things that would get you thrown into a concentration camp in Nazi Germany will get you thrown into a concentration camp in Cuba today. Suffice it to say that drawing some moral difference between wearing the flag of Castro and the flag of Hitler is a tortured exercise unless you engage some shared delusion that what is, is not.

"There's a choice to be made here—you can choose between a system of liberty, where the proper role of government is in protecting those rights that are inherent to your humanity (even if some people choose to say or believe things that you find abhorrent), or you choose collectivism, where all of those rights inherent to your humanity are sacrificed to what the few at the top believe is best for the collective.

"Choose wisely..."

John thought back to the many times he had read *The Road to Serfdom* without ever realizing that the road ended in a cul-de-sac. John had been elected to the state senate from a district that was not known for electing liberty candidates. He was able to pull off the surprise victory by the narrowest of margins when it became known that his incumbent opponent had a persistent habit of hanging out in the ladies' rest room.

John had naively thought he could be a rational voice for natural rights and liberty, but it was simply too late in the game. The country was already well on the way to tearing itself apart, and nothing he could say or do was going to change that outcome. He had spent his time in the senate attempting to defend liberty with his votes while watching the world he had known dissolve into chaos.

Back then, he and his ideological comrades had debated if the future they were heading into would more closely resemble *1984* or *Brave New World*.

They didn't seriously contemplate that it would be *Lord of the Flies*.

4
Twenty-two days without food

Michael rested on the bed as he watched his wife, Joy, totter about the bedroom. He had the desire to assist his wife, but the lack of nutrition inhibited the commands sent from his brain to his body. He knew his body was no longer capable of complying with his conscience.

Michael had been a robust man, but he now had to use a cane just to get to the bathroom.

For the tenth time in the two years since the Committee had begun issuing ration cards, Joy and Michael had been robbed of those cards at gunpoint. Now they had been robbed two weeks in a row. Because the Committee made no provision for lost or stolen ration cards to be replaced, this meant an entire week without rations each time their cards were stolen. In the latest theft Michael and Joy also had their car stolen, they now had no means to get to the ration center at all.

It had now been twenty-two days without food.

Each time they had to go without food became exponentially more difficult for them at their age.

They had attempted to cobble together a reserve, but it was never enough. This was certainly not how they had imagined retirement would be. The first three times that their ration cards had been stolen they had used what valuables they had to buy food on the black market, but they no longer possessed anything worth trading.

Michael closed his eyes as Joy left the room. Twenty-two days without food affected the mind as much as it did the body.

Joy decided to try to sleep in the living room. Her mind was as exhausted as her body, but sleep would not come to her. She worried about all that was left undone and her inability to competently complete even a simple task. She lay down on the couch before being overwhelmed by the memory of her friend Vera dying on this couch.

In an effort to escape the memory of Vera's death, Joy rose from the couch—her nutrition-deprived brain had learned to hate even the elementary aspects of existence. She walked feebly to the front door and with great effort opened it. She was consumed with a terror she had never before experienced as she wandered to her neighbors' car parked at the curb. With all of her strength, Joy tried to open the car door but could not. Panic gripped her before she experienced a fleeting moment of clarity and realized that she had no idea why she was in the street at all.

Joy looked about in the dark at the overgrown lawn and fallen fences and decrepit state of her once prosperous neighborhood and was again gripped by an irrational terror. She thought of her children that she had not seen in two years. Through the fog that was her mind, she was overpowered by the blunt realization that she would never see her children or grandchildren again.

Joy staggered back to the house and into the living room. She had an urge to be with Michael and went to the bedroom, lying down on the bed next to him, weakly grasping his hand.

"What shall we do?" Joy mumbled in a barely audible voice.

"It's all nonsense, dear, all of it. All nonsense," Michael replied.

With that they each closed their eyes, never to open them again.

5
Essentials of life

People were filing into the Kennedy Senate Caucus room on the third floor of the Russell Senate Office Building as the Committee members took their places at the head of the room. The Kennedy Senate Caucus room was now the permanent home for the *Committee for the Continuance of Government*, a committee comprised of career bureaucrats and former cabinet members whose seniority stretched back before the hard times.

The meeting was brought to order by the gavel of Ted Harris. Harris had been the very last Secretary of the Department of Housing and Urban Development under the old government and before that the Governor of Connecticut. After the debt crisis, and on the eve of the war with China, it was Harris who had convinced the President to sign the Executive Order creating the Committee for the Continuance of Government and empowering the Committee to devise and execute a method to provide whatever the Committee deigned were the *essentials of life* to the American people. Harris had prevailed upon the President to allow Harris, himself, to choose the Committee members and draft the Committee rules. Harris had populated the Committee with his own ideological and political allies, save one committee member that the President had insisted upon. In drafting the rules Harris had allowed for a simple majority in order to vote a member off of the Committee. The exception to this rule was the Chairman, and his position required a supermajority with all members present in order to replace him.

Harris ruled the Committee with an iron hand, and the Committee ruled America with an iron fist draped in shredded velvet. Indeed, Harris had chosen the Kennedy Senate Caucus room precisely because it had hosted the Watergate hearings and the Iran-Contra hearings. The room, itself, exuded power.

The Committee had taken unto itself the right to ration all of those *essentials of life*. They had created a ration card system, and the bureaucracies that answered to the Committee busily spent their days determining how much food was available, where it would go, and who would get it. They also rationed medicine, fuel and bandwidth—and determined what traveled across that bandwidth. Most of the bandwidth was dedicated to providing content for the virtual reality centers that the Committee had opened in great number throughout the major cities. Other than the government and their chosen friends, internet and cell access was closed to the public.

The meeting opened, as it often did, with the one person that had been selected to the Committee by the President criticizing the virtual reality centers. Dr. Ann Hubbell had been the last Surgeon General and the token member of the opposition party to be included in the last administration. The President had insisted on her being made a member of the Committee for the Continuance of Government both due to her public health expertise and to give the impression to a dying political system of continued bipartisanship.

Dr. Hubbell opened with her typical complaint, "The virtual reality centers are not psychologically efficacious. There are more than five hundred of these theaters in forty cities, and they're not helping the American people. More than half a million people a day are attending these facilities just in New York City, another half a million in Los Angeles, another half a million in the Bay Area, even in Denver it's close to a hundred thousand people a day, and these people are often spending unhealthy amounts of time in virtual reality. Ten, twelve, fourteen hours a day or even longer is common."

"It's been almost two years now that these centers have been in operation, Dr. Hubbell. The Committee agreed then and the Committee agrees now that it's paramount for the government to provide the people accurate information. The technologists suggested that the most efficient method to communicate that information and make it stick is via virtual reality. The Committee has determined that the most effective use of our limited resources, after food and medicine, is to assure that citizens no longer fall prey to fake news and that virtual reality is the most effective means of accomplishing that goal," replied Harris.

"The only thing we're accomplishing is to create psychopaths that can no longer differentiate between reality and virtual reality, Chairman Harris."

"Did you not read the Committee report from March on just how effective these centers are, Dr. Hubbell? Now, we need to move on to discussing counterfeit ration cards being used by the resistance."

"Did you not read *Animal Farm*, Chairman Harris?"

Ann Hubbell knew with that remark that she had terminally overstayed her welcome on the Committee for the Continuance of Government. Without further comment she stood up and clutched her purse and exited The Kennedy Senate Caucus room. Unsure of the consequences of her actions Dr. Hubbell decided not to go to her government car and driver on First Street, N.E. Thinking quickly, she decided to use the tunnels to the Dirksen building and then disappear into Washington.

Dr. Hubbell took the stairs next to the rotunda down from the third floor of the Russell building and passed through the tunnel to the Dirksen building. As she exited the tunnel two large men grabbed her by each arm and forced her outside into a white van that still bore the faint lettering, Bureau of Land Management.

6
Get in!

Dennis and Kris waited behind the deserted coffee shop in Parker. They each had a suitcase and a shoulder bag.

"Think he's really coming?" Dennis asked, seeking reassurance.

"Oh yeah, he'll be here," Kris responded.

Kris ran through a quick checklist in her mind. Brody had told her it would be expensive to leave the country. They had to pay Brody, pay Mexican smugglers on the other side of the border, and then pay Mexican officials in order to stay once they were there. The dollar was now worthless, so the payment had to be in tangible goods—preferably gold, silver, or jewelry. Dennis and Kris were in their late twenties and well educated. Dennis had a degree in Civil Engineering and Kris a degree in Computer Science.

They both believed that they no longer had a future in the United States. They both wished to do something meaningful with their lives, and the United States no longer afforded that opportunity.

They thought their best chance was in another country.

Between the two of them, they had three gold coins and two old silver quarters. What the shoulder bags contained was jewelry. Their mothers had each given all of their jewelry to finance this trip. Friends and other relatives had supplied even more jewelry.

Dennis and Kris felt a responsibility to the people who believed in them enough to give them their most valuable belongings in order that they could escape the United States. It meant even more knowing it was quite possible that they would never see these friends and relatives again. Unless something dramatically changed, they would never again be able to communicate with them.

"Maybe he's not coming," Dennis remarked.

Kris certainly felt vulnerable in the dark parking lot, but she was not yet ready to bolt.

After another two minutes of doubt, a Ford Expedition pulled into the parking lot. The headlights faced directly at them, and Dennis and Kris froze in fear until they heard the voice of Brody yell, "Get in!"

Kris and Dennis got in the backseat and Dennis said, "How are you?" then instantly regretted it. Brody was a smuggler and Dennis and Kris were about to do something quite illegal. "How are you" struck Dennis as a juvenile thing to say.

"I'm fine," responded Brody. "We have to pick up another passenger."

"You said it would only be us," said Kris.

"I take as many as I can fit. Besides, you will feel safer in Mexico with another man in your party."

Kris was unsure but realized she also had no choice. To bail out now was not a step she was prepared to take. Kris didn't want her husband, Dennis, to know the things Brody required of her just to arrange this.

"We'll pick him up down past Franktown, his name is Tony. You'll like him. He's a dentist. Then we'll hit I-25 south, drive all night. We'll take you to the border down by Columbus, New Mexico. Fernando will meet you at the border and take you into Mexico. Did you bring enough to pay?"

"Yes."

"Okay, you can pay me when we get to the border. You will pay Fernando as soon as you step over the border. You made the right decision. This country sucks now. If I had a real skill like you, I'd go myself, but I have always just been a gopher. No other country wants me."

The Expedition traveled south on Parker Road, past Franktown and continued past Castlewood Canyon. Immediately after crossing the bridge over the canyon, Brody made a hard-right turn. They proceeded up a curving road for two hundred yards and Brody parked.

"Might as well get out and stretch a bit, this will be your last chance for hours."

Kris and Dennis rather reluctantly exited the Expedition. Their nervousness was enhanced by the thought of another passenger, and stopping to pick him up drove their anxiety off the charts.

Kris and Dennis stood closely together at the rear passenger side of the Ford while Brody walked slowly about scanning the darkness.

"Is that him over there?" Brody whispered while pointing behind Kris and Dennis.

Kris and Dennis turned around to look, and Brody quickly shot each of them in the back of the head.

7
200 units of insulin

Jo Roth began to emotionally prepare herself. This was Wednesday, and every Wednesday and Saturday she had to go pick up insulin for her father's insulin pump. Twice a week Jo had to pick up 200 units of insulin at the medical ration center.

Since the hard times had hit, the focus of Jo's life had become acquiring the insulin that her father required in order to stay alive. This meant that twice a week she had to walk the three miles to the medical ration center and trade sex for insulin. She was repulsed by having to perform sexual acts for George Thompson, who was nothing more than a minor functionary at the ration center, in exchange for the life of her father.

Jo was disgusted with herself.

She chose the clothes that she knew Thompson wanted her to wear, feeling her skin crawl as she did so. She had grown to genuinely detest life, detest what was required of her in life, and detest herself. If not for her father, she felt that she would have no reason to live.

After dressing, Jo walked out of her room and into the living room seeking her father.

Not seeing her father in the living room, she peaked into the kitchen. He was not in the kitchen either. Jo strode down the hallway to his bedroom and knocked lightly on the door before pushing it open just a bit and saying, "I'll be leaving soon."

No response.

Jo pushed the door completely open and saw her father lying on his bed. She walked to her father, sat down on the bed and repeated, "I'll be leaving soon," while gently grasp his hand.

She immediately noticed how cold his hand was.

Jo surprised herself in that she didn't feel grief. She didn't feel relief either. What she felt was a craving for vengeance. Jo craved vengeance for the degradation and humiliation that she had suffered in order to prolong the life of her father, a life that was now over.

The craving for vengeance overwhelmed her and crowded out other emotions.

She rummaged through her father's closet and dresser. Finding what she sought, she decided she would indeed go to the medical ration center that day and see George Thompson.

As Jo entered the medical ration center, she bypassed the throng of people lined up for medicine and knocked on the office door of George Thompson.

"Come in," was the response.

"Oh, good to see you, Jo," Thompson remarked.

Jo knew what Thompson expected. She turned her back to him and faced a chair. Nearly one hundred previous times she had removed her clothes and placed them on that very chair, but this time she removed a snub-nose .38 from the purse she was grasping. Thompson didn't know that Jo had the gun until she spun and pointed it directly at him. Jo fired twice, the first round striking Thompson in the right arm and the second missing him entirely. She took a few steps toward the screaming Thompson; she was now almost on top of him. She pulled the trigger again, a bullet smashing into the top of Thompson's head. She then turned the gun on herself as security agents burst through the door to Thompson's office.

8
The Indian forces of Stand Watie

Brian Vann stood at the back of the cemetery in Gore, Oklahoma with his hat in his hand. He had been coming to the cemetery all of his life. Brian stood over the grave of his wife Elizabeth. She had fought cancer for two years until the hard times had closed the hospitals, and the doctors had nothing but a little pain medicine to provide her. Brian and Elizabeth's son, Petty Officer Third Class Isaiah Vann, had gone down with the USS Gerald Ford in a Chinese missile barrage in the South China Sea. The cemetery had given him much needed perspective. He stood near the graves of Eliza Holt and Dr. William Wallace Campbell. He thought of the missing grave, that of William Holt. William Holt had been the Captain of Holt's Squadron in the 2nd Cherokee Mounted Rifles. Knowing the United States Army was approaching the Indian forces of Stand Watie encamped at Webbers Falls, Holt had decided to swim the Arkansas River the night before the battle. Holt warned his family at his home on the other side of the river and then swam back across the river that night to command his squadron. Holt became the first Cherokee killed in the battle of Webbers Falls the next morning. His family fled south to the safety of the Choctaw Nation but never saw their husband and father again.

Vann stood nearest the grave of Dr. William Wallace Campbell. Dr. Campbell had completed the Cherokee Seminary then attended medical school in Nashville. Completing his education in 1863, he was incapable of returning to the Cherokee Nation due to the Civil War. He instead volunteered for service and became the only Indian to serve as a medical officer to a non-Indian regiment in the Civil War.

Brian thought of Rich Joe Vann and his steamboat.

These were his people, his kin. William Holt had founded Gore, known then as Holt's Landing, as a Cherokee Old Settler in 1830. The family had operated a farm and a ferry across the Arkansas River to Webbers Falls and also a general store. After the Civil War, the community had come to be known as Campbell's Landing as Dr. Campbell ran all of those enterprises plus a medical practice in Webbers Falls.

Brian thought of his great-great-grandmother who had taught school at Webbers Falls after having attended the Cherokee Female Seminary, only to die at a young age shortly after his great-grandfather was born.

He thought how these folks had seen good times and terrible times, but he was certain that he was living in times just as irrational as those his ancestors had experienced.

Among the irrationalities was that he had ration cards for fuel and food; but the ration card for fuel required him to go to a gas station in Sallisaw twenty miles east. His ration card for food required him to go to the high school in Checotah, twenty-five miles west. That was ninety miles of round-trip driving on a ration card that only entitled him to three gallons of fuel a week.

Brian Vann had 320 acres but no way to farm it. The land around Gore and Webbers Falls was some of the best farmland anywhere on the planet, but the government made no allotment for the fuel necessary for it to be farmed. Brian had a garden as most around there did, but the ability to grow enough food to really make a difference was denied him and everyone else that he knew. It was tempting to think that some beltway bureaucrat was simply unaware of how good the land along the bend in the Arkansas was. Brian dismissed that thought because he knew the truth was that the farms owned by corporations received all of the fuel and fertilizer. The corporations were an integral part of the Committee for the Continuance of Government, as they made clear in the days immediately after the Committee was formed.

Interestingly the Committee for the Continuance of Government had issued press releases the first few weeks that they were empowered then nothing after that. The only way that Brian knew they were still running the country was due to the television and the visits by the government folks twice a year. The first year the government people showed up, they demanded that everyone turn over all of the produce from their gardens. The government men had guns and presented the justification that people in places like Tulsa were starving so it was "only fair" that they take the garden produce.

The folks in Gore and Webbers Falls were suspicious of the proclamations of the government men. The suspicions were confirmed when the citizens offered half of the garden produce to the government men, and if the men insisted on taking all of it, then the good citizens would not bother to plant gardens again the next year. The offer was accepted. The people of Gore and Webbers Falls knew full well that their produce was not being used to feed the hungry people of Tulsa.

The government men now showed up once in the spring to confirm the gardens were planted and again later in the year to collect half of the produce and infrequently at other times of the year.

Brian wondered why he and his neighbors had stood for this for so long.

9
Let's discuss this over a meal

Ted Harris gaveled the Committee for the Continuance of Government to order.

"What's our security situation, Mandy?"

"Cheyenne has flared up again, a rally on the steps of the state capitol there yesterday. It was well attended, our agents on site reported two thousand people or more."

"What is it with that town?" Matthew Giles said. "Bunch of redneck racists."

"What do you propose, Mandy?" Harris asked.

"We have additional agents from Denver driving up there today. These agents will assist in apprehending the ringleaders of the rebellion at their homes tonight. We have them all under surveillance; we know where they'll be."

"I make a motion that we suspend rations for a week for Cheyenne and alert them that if this continues, we'll suspend rations for another week. All in favor?" Harris responded.

"Aye," was the response in unison.

"The, 'ayes,' have it. George, make it so," Harris said looking at George Sandrop.

"I will see that the message is broadcast this evening," Giles added.

"Very good. What's wrong with those people? This is the third time we've had a similar problem in Cheyenne," Harris remarked.

"A quick note. Denton will be really pissed that we cut off food to Cheyenne again. Warren Air Force base is there, and it really hits the families of the military hard," James Ramsey interjected.

"Admiral Denton is responsible for feeding those people, it's his problem," Harris replied.

"Who cares about the Air Force whores. Let them and their little brats starve," Giles added.

"We should have a plan for presenting this to Denton," Ramsey said in an attempt to return the conversation to a rational basis.

"Perhaps we can use this example to turn Denton into an active participant in the rebuilding of the country. It's outrageous that he won't cede the power of the armed forces to us," Sandrop said spitefully.

"We should just take the military from him," Giles said. "Denton personally selected all those men, and only men, to replace the officers that the President had placed on the Joint Chiefs of Staff. He's a sexist reactionary."

"Denton is a reactionary who has no interest in building a progressive equitable society," Harris observed. "However, for the time being it is what it is. Those men he selected are loyal to him, and he knows they'll not be playing politics with him or betray him. They're a solid front. The Pentagon has more than its hands full with mutinies and trying to feed their people. At the moment they're no threat to us, so we should focus on more important issues that are more immediate."

"It's becoming ever more clear that we need our own military. We need to identify those that are loyal to us and arm them," Sandrop said.

"We could put the resistance down in a day if we were to do that," Giles added. "It's what Che would've done."

"How exactly would we identify those who are and are not loyal to us?" Mandy Ford asked knowingly.

"Why can't you get on board with solutions?" Sandrop asked angrily.

"All you ever point out are problems and never solutions!" Giles asserted.

"Let's move on now. Mandy, what else?"

"Ration card theft combined with counterfeit ration cards is a growing issue."

"That problem is overblown. You just keep bringing it up so you can have more power. This is just factionalism!" Giles yelled at Mandy Ford.

"Once we removed the capitalist incentive, we removed the incentive for crime. We simply have to keep hunting down want-to-be capitalist, and when we remove them from the scene, we have also removed the criminals. They're one and the same," George Sandrop advised.

"Catch the men that are angry over having lost their privilege, and we'll have caught the criminals!" Giles screeched. "We must have justice for all!"

"Every time a ration card is stolen the anger and discontent grows," Mandy Ford replied.

"Let us assume that ration card theft is a tactic of the resistance to delegitimize us, Mandy. If we continue to apprehend members of the resistance then we'll also reduce ration card theft, no?" Harris quizzed.

"Ration card theft has more to do with hunger than privilege," Mandy asserted.

"We provide adequate calories," Sandrop defended.

James Ramsey thought to himself, *This has all become so surreal.*

"What else do you have, Mandy?" Harris said.

"In general, discontent is growing. A part of that is hunger, but the larger part is the lack of improvement in people's lives. There's a sense that what it is now is permanent and that feeds the discontent," Mandy reported. "For example, ration cards are the most valuable currency out there. There's a belief among many that the only available means to improve your situation is by taking from others. Now, I'm not defending that, but so many people believe it is, so it's a problem."

"That's ridiculous. That's simply a leftover remnant of supremacy. We're providing food, housing, medicine—there's no need for anyone to improve their lives above the life of their neighbor. Only people who think like the privileged wish to improve their lives past what their neighbor has," Giles asserted.

"Well Matthew, it's an interesting opportunity for you. Why don't you develop a series of television broadcasts on the need for us to all rise together? You can show how everyone being equal is superior to striving for the next dollar. You're in charge of media, view this as a teaching moment for the public and teach them why there's no longer a need to steal or feel the need to be better than their neighbor. Everyone in the country can relax now that the Committee is in charge. Keeping up with the Joneses, let alone surpassing them, is a thing of the past. That was a product of the oligarchy, and we have eradicated the oligarchy," Harris suggested to Giles.

"I have the sense that we simply are not taking what Mandy says to heart," Ramsey interjected.

"Of course, we are!" Sandrop snapped.

"You were never really one of us!" Giles accused.

Ramsey gave Giles a look of disbelief.

"James, time is on our side. As more and more people recognize that their lives are now free of the daily pursuit of food, shelter, and medicine and they're now free to pursue their passions, then society will continue to change for all the better," Harris said.

"If time is on our side, then why is discontent growing?" Ramsey asked.

"Those damned supremacist!" Giles screeched.

"This is the last-ditch effort of the resistance," Sandrop added.

"James, we knew that progress would not be linear," Harris said.

"I'm not at all convinced that discontent is growing," Sandrop rebuked.

"The people are on our side. We should simply liquidate all of the malcontents," Giles suggested.

"You're missing the critical path here. Take Denton and the military for example; barracks mutinies are not just a threat to them but to us. Large numbers of well-trained young men operating in coherent groups with high quality weapons is the greatest potential domestic threat that we have. From a foreign policy point of view, Denton being able to continue to convince the world that the nuclear weapons are secure and that there's not a rogue element that has the potential to fire those weapons is the most significant reason that China and Russia have not already used nuclear weapons on us. Repeatedly denying food to Cheyenne, where many of the nuclear weapons are controlled from, is unnecessarily tempting fate. These are bad ideas," Ramsey interjected.

"James, there are people out there who want what we're doing to fail. They resent having lost their privilege; they resent having lost their place in the oligarchy. This is an historically unique opportunity that we have to remake society from the ground up in the principles of equality, unity, fairness, justice, and peace. We knew that there would be resistance, and Mandy is doing an excellent job ridding us of that resistance."

"I want to address liquidating the malcontents," Giles requested.

"Go on," Harris replied.

"I make a motion that we direct the security agency to identify and remove from society all malcontents," Giles moved.

"Do I hear a second?" Harris asked.

"Seconded," Sandrop responded.

"Wait a minute—exactly how would I do that?" Mandy interrupted.

"You figure it out. It's what you're on this committee to do!" Giles asserted.

"Vote?" Harris asked.

"Aye," was the response of everyone on the Committee save Mandy Ford and James Ramsey.

"The, 'ayes,' have it."

"Now, Matthew, let's talk about the message we're giving the people," Harris continued. "You had your television show for all those years. How do we improve our messaging in order that people understand what advantages we have given them?"

"I think our messaging is spectacular and the people are very happy with where this is going. All of the data we have shows that the people are solidly on our side. Our programming is educational, and people are learning from it daily as to why the oligarchy was their enemy and how we have set things right. People crave an equitable society," Giles replied.

Ramsey buried his head in his hands.

"Do you have an issue with that, James?" Harris asked.

"People are hungry, and it's not improving. Life is not improving. We can't feed Hawaii at all, they're forever under martial law by direction of Denton. Maybe two hundred thousand people have starved to death in Hawaii in two years? No way to get enough food to Hawaii to feed everyone. Many of those people were tourist there when the war broke out. Not an inconsiderable number of these tourist who were originally stuck there were Chinese. Denton allowed Japan and other countries to evacuate their nationals, but he would not allow Chinese ships to approach. China had to contract out to other countries to evacuate their nationals. You know how hard it's running a foreign policy when the military acts independently? China threatened to invade Hawaii! Alaska, they might as well be in the 19th century. In the lower forty-eight, it's become a dog-eat-dog world. We have no idea what the actual mortality rate is. People are dying from hunger, murder; we don't even have hospitals open. People are afraid to leave their houses..."

"You lie!" Giles interrupted. "Our data shows that most of these communities are recovering nicely. People are as happy as can be expected. The only problem that we have is with the malcontents spreading vicious rumors and resenting the loss of their privilege. Round them up and shoot them is the answer!"

"Feeding people leads to a lot more contentment than shooting people," Ramsey retorted. "I don't know where you think you're getting that data from."

"Now, now," Harris said. "How about we have lunch brought up, and we discuss this over a meal?"

10
A sea of little tents

John Tribell exited the state capital building at mid-afternoon, looking from the capitol steps out onto the sea of little tents that now populated the state capitol grounds, Civic Center Park, and the grounds of the Denver City and County building. Many of the virtual reality addicts no longer bothered to go home, they slept in little tents and abandoned cars near the virtual reality centers. It was a warm sunny late spring day, so state senator John Tribell decided to take a walk and perhaps reminisce about what was no more. He walked west on Colfax and on to 15th then to Glenarm. Here he paused as he watched people enter into and exit out of one of the oldest theaters in Denver, a theater that had been converted to a government virtual reality center.

John wondered how many people were in the building and how long they had been in there. The virtual reality centers were now open twenty-four hours a day, seven days a week. Wicked rumors persisted that some people never left, they simply remained until they grew too weak from hunger to leave and eventually died there. John wondered if those rumors were true.

"Senator Tribell?"

Only then did John notice the pretty young lady standing next to him.

"Yes, I'm Senator Tribell. Have you ever been inside one of these?"

"No, I have not."

"Would you like to?"

"No, I don't think I would. I'd like to know you though."

John found the prospect of getting to know the pretty young lady more enticing than satiating his curiosity about virtual reality.

They walked to 15th and Welton where there was a short brick wall circling what had previously been a parking lot and now was home to abandoned cars being used to sleep in.

John and the young lady, who he quickly discovered was named Robin, talked for hours sitting on the brick wall. Robin talked about her studying biology at CU until the hard times closed the school. John talked about his unlikely path to the state senate and his sister in Tombstone.

The next afternoon they met again and talked for hours once more, on a bench near 14th and Grant.

The afternoon after that they met yet again on a bench in front of the former Colorado History Museum on Lincoln. After that meeting John took her home, but only after coining the phrase dystopian dating.

Only on the day after their first night together did Robin confess, "I lied to you. I have been inside virtual reality theaters. In fact, I was hooked. It's stronger than any drug. If you don't want to see me anymore, I understand."

John was not letting her out of his grasp. "Of course, I still want to see you. Don't be silly. Why didn't you just tell me then?"

"I didn't want you to know I was so weak, that I was a VR junkie who escaped the life."

"Is it really that addictive?"

"Yes, people stay in there until they die. They don't want to leave. It's pleasure in a world with damn little of it. It's also the death of your ability to tell reality from virtual reality. They control your mind."

"Why did you break from VR?"

"I didn't want to die in there, and I would have."

Robin went on to explain in great detail her escape from the VR addiction and all about those who helped her.

Only after exhausting every detail did Robin drop the bombshell, "I'm part of a group that wants to get rid of VR. A revolution if you will."

11
The death of culture

Chris Malone sat in his favorite chair fretting in the dark. The electricity was now off more often that it was on, and he had long ago run out of candles and batteries. He recalled something he had read that Aleksandr Solzhenitsyn had written, "We didn't love freedom enough." He fretted while thinking about what to do if the entire country was a gulag. He indeed burned as he watched his daughters play on the ragged living room carpet. He certainly believed that the country deserved all that had happened. We simply didn't love freedom enough.

For many years Chris had written history and had published four books on the Stalinist era of the Soviet Union. He was working on a dystopian novel when the hard times hit.

He recognized from history everything that was happening around him and felt powerless to change it. He fretted over his daughters' futures and the world they would grow up to inhabit. He worried about his wife, Jennifer. She seemed to have aged twenty years in the last two. He had regressed from dealing with first world problems to third world problems overnight.

Chris contemplated resistance. As a father, as a husband, he trembled at the risk. If he was caught, the penalty would not just be on his head but on that of his wife and daughters. He weighed that against the knowledge that he could not live with his conscience if this was the world that he left to his girls.

He reflected on the changes they had experienced. Just two years ago it was believed that the world was on the verge of curing cancer and ALS and Alzheimer's disease. Now people waited in monstrous lines on the appointed day hoping to get a small packet of allergy medicine. It had been two years since they had seen fresh fruit or fresh vegetables or meat that was not processed. He tried to recall the last time that any of the ration was not processed food. Seventeen months ago, a small can of unsalted mixed nuts. He considered that a can of mixed nuts was a highlight of the last two years. He knew that his daughters remembered the can of nuts like it had been Christmas.

Chris contemplated that the ration and lack of medical care was symptomatic of the real problem—the death of culture. The Committee relied on brute force to remake society into the model they desired. Now all of society had become nothing more than brute force. Robbery of ration cards, arson, rape, murder—all common events in daily life. The Committee had used brute force to create a zero-sum society while punishing any collaboration that people voluntarily engaged in to improve their individual lives. Consequently, the Committee unwittingly communicated that using force to take what you desired from others was the only means of improving your situation.

He reflected on how the culture had died—each side had asserted a position of ever-increasing moral superiority thereby justifying the emotions that they wished to experience in regard to the other side. Each side had used government power to inflict their version of superior morality on the other. Society had become nothing more than two teams vying for power in an all-or-nothing proposition without possible retreat or compromise.

He contemplated that the Committee was the only outcome possible from a competition such as that.

The television and radio stations endlessly asserted that with the Committee providing food, housing, and medicine everyone was freed from the tyranny of employment to pursue the beauty in life—but there was no beauty in life. There was no art, no music, no literature, no theater, no sports, no cinema, no picnics, no recreation. People were so afraid to leave their homes that socializing was a rare and risk-filled event. There was only hunger, the hope that you would not get sick, and fear that when you left your home you may be robbed or killed. What was missing from life was any grace, forgiveness, or room for error.

Life was nothing more than a small group of people inflicting their morals and vision of the future on everyone else. Chris thought that history may not repeat, but it certainly rhymed.

He thought of his friend, Rick, an economist and author in Texas. Rick had warned him prior to the debt crisis and had instructed him on how to protect the small amount of wealth he had acquired. "Time is your enemy when debt is growing and revenue can't keep pace," Rick had told him. *A lot of good that did*, Chris thought. Now he hadn't heard from Rick for two years, and there was no more private wealth, large or small. Chris wondered how Rick was doing. There were rumors of internments camps for those who had advocated for freedom and free markets. He hoped those rumors weren't true

12
This is going the wrong way

Ted Harris left the Kennedy Senate Caucus room via the door at the back of the room. The door entered to a dimly lit hallway historically used by senators wishing to escape the microphones of the press in order to make their way back to their senate offices. Harris alone now reserved the right to use this hallway along with whom he invited to walk with him. It was a sign of favor and power to be chosen to walk with Harris.

On this day Harris invited the woman he had placed in charge of internal security for the United States, Mandy Ford.

"What's our situation?" Harris said curtly.

"It continues to go the wrong way, not quickly, but the wrong way. There's growing discontent. People are asking why, after two years, we can't do better? There are resistance cells that have formed in most major cities, but the real threat is in the rural areas where the control of food is less efficient and communities are more coherent."

"Aren't your people seizing privately grown food?"

"Yes, to some extent. Our agents are very susceptible to being bribed with food. The fuel limits are the major inhibition in the cohesiveness of the rural cells. We have done an excellent job of infiltrating the urban cells of opposition, but we cannot know what we do not know."

"Wasn't, 'we cannot know what we do not know,' a phrase used by a former Secretary of Defense? You better do a better job of knowing than he did."

"Every week the trust in the government recedes. Barely enough food to stay alive and three gallons of gas a week is not cutting it. Americans who used to be understanding of the limits as a matter of circumstance are no longer understanding. By the way, Dr. Hubbell was correct in that the virtual reality centers are creating psychotics."

Harris shot a stern look at Ford and asked, "Where is Dr. Hubbell and her staff?"

"She's been taken care of by Hunley. Look, I will be blunt with you. This is going the wrong way, and we must find a way to reverse it. These cells are attempting to connect with each other; this radio transmitter in Mexico is blasting out a liberty message to most of the western United States, and someone in California that people are calling the Oracle of Rocklin is producing large quantities of flyers calling for free markets. We have found these flyers as far away as Phoenix. We don't even know if this Oracle of Rocklin is a person or a group or what. We don't even know if they're actually in Rocklin. We don't even know if they refer to themselves as the Oracle of Rocklin, but their followers do refer to them as that. The same measures used to control the citizens also limit our ability to know what's going on. We have blind spots, and if we don't give people some hope of improvement, a spark could set this off. We're only able to maintain the status quo because the people who oppose us don't appreciate how weak we are. Our security is increasingly akin to someone that pretends to look larger than they are when approached by a wild animal. We use a reputation for viciousness to overcome our weakness. Once people figure out that we're not as large or powerful as we have pretended to be, then we're likely to be devoured, and if we don't make changes, they'll figure that out. We had three agents killed this week, but more troubling, six others are unaccounted for. We hope they're also dead because defectors would be fatal to our projection of power."

"What about the reports that Giles provides the Committee, that things are going well?"

"Giles is an inveterate liar, and those reports are horseshit. Pure fiction, he makes them up."

Harris pondered what Ford had told him and responded, "We can't go back to what we were. We can't go back to the political divisions, to the constant political investigations. Factionalism. Remember when people figured out that they could almost entirely shut down television networks, government departments, and businesses by calling in never ending bomb threats? Remember there were just enough bombs to make the threats real? Remember when congress passed the Loyal American Gun Act, and we sent the BATF and FBI out to seize all of the semi-automatic rifles? Remember how we couldn't find any agent willing to do that after the first week? It destroyed the credibility of the government. Remember street fighting in Atlanta and Columbus and Orlando? Of course, you do. We were on the razor edge of out and out civil war. We can't have that again. You know that. We have to control this, or the American people will be at each other's throats again."

Mandy Ford pondered that the Committee had shut down television networks, government departments, and businesses that they had not approved of, and silently wondered if what Harris really meant was that if the American people were not controlled, they would be at the throat of the Committee.

"Shall we lunch in the cafeteria? They're serving chicken parmesan today. It's not terrible," asked Harris.

13
Forks of the Platte

Jerry Sandoval sat next to his backpack in the dirt parking lot next to the Forks of the Platte. He had left his home in Littleton before sunrise the morning before and walked southwest following the Platte through Chatfield State Park and up Waterton Canyon to the Colorado Trail. He had spent the previous night in the forest downhill from Lenny's Bench then arisen before dawn again to complete the hike to the Forks. He was exhausted.

Jerry was a defector.

As he sat exhausted, he thought of what had brought him to this point. He reminisced about joining the Marine Corp right out of high school followed by his career as a policeman until the hard times hit. The city government had become insolvent along with his career as a policeman. Jerry had jumped at the opportunity to become an agent for the Committee for the Continuance of Government. He had believed in the mission to restore order and assure that the *essentials of life* were fairly distributed to everyone.

Over the last two years, Agent Sandoval had gone from being frustrated at the inefficiencies of the Committee to disillusioned to believing that the Committee intended for minimal weekly rations of food and fuel to be a permanent situation used for ongoing control of the population. As a Marine he was proud to defend his country. As a policeman he was happiest when he felt he could protect the innocent. He loathed knowing that as an agent for the Committee, he was an oppressor of the helpless.

Jerry could hear a vehicle approaching from the south and he stood up. The moment of truth was a 1970's vintage International Harvester Travelall with massive rust holes.

"In," was the barked command of the man in the driver's seat. Jerry climbed into a passenger seat that had holes in the cloth upholstery, taking careful note of the man with an M1 carbine in the backseat. They rode silently next to the South Fork of the South Platte River. Just past the spot known as Nighthawk, the driver turned onto a rutted driveway going up the hill away from the river. Jerry wondered where they got the gas to run such a vehicle, trying to calculate if the Travelall might have consumed an entire three-gallon ration in just this short trip.

They arrived at a dilapidated cabin nearly hidden in the trees. Jerry noticed the other vehicle present at the cabin was a Jeep Wagoneer of similar vintage as the Travelall.

Inside the one-room cabin were three other men, two wooden chairs, and a table.

"Presuming you're armed, why don't you set your weapons on the table until we get this sorted out?"

Jerry removed the Springfield XD from his waistband and the Smith & Wesson M&P Shield from his ankle holster and placed them on the table.

"Good people have vouched for you and vetted you. If you screw us over, you know what the penalty is."

"I'm not here to screw you over."

"Why are you here?"

"Because the Committee for the Continuance of the Government has to go away. It's evil. The VR centers have to end, and we have to have a country that's more than weekly rations controlled by bureaucrats."

"Tell us what the security department has?"

"Much less than you probably think. No drones. No electronic surveillance. Fewer agents than you may think, and most are only doing the job for rations. The majority of agents are used to protect the corporate farms and factories and the transportation of the fuel and rations, along with protecting government and corporate personnel. The number of agents available for combatting cells like yours is remarkably small, but some cells have been infiltrated. Your cell has not been infiltrated."

"What about the military?"

"The military is dedicated to defending the borders. They still have nukes, and that's why China has not taken Hawaii and Russia has not taken Alaska. The agreement with the Committee was that the military would not interfere in domestic matters. For the most part, the military is focused on feeding its personnel and quelling barracks mutinies. Two years ago, the Pentagon agreed not to discharge any personnel; the last thing the Committee wants are well-trained young people being released into the population in cohesive groups. The Committee exerts control by preventing cohesiveness from occurring; that's why no one ever receives more than one week's worth of rations and why the rations are so skimpy that it's almost impossible to save any and create a reserve. The thought process is that any revolt would go hungry after a week. It's the same thought process with the fuel ration. There's still a refinery operating in Commerce City for example. The fuel ration doesn't reflect the quantity of fuel available, but it's limited in order to prevent a cohesive opposition. Once the ISPs and cell companies went under and those services were nationalized, the Committee was able to only allow the government and their friends to use those services. Prevent communication, limit movement, prevent a reliable source of food outside of what the Committee chooses to provide, and you will prevent a cohesive opposition from organizing or a rebellion from gaining traction. That's the logic."

"What's the end game?"

"The Committee views this as the opportunity to rebuild society, a society where everyone is materially equal. Well, where the masses are materially equal. The Committee and their friends are certainly more equal than others. Of course, the Committee, itself, has no means to produce anything, so certain corporations that they were friendly with were granted committee-directed monopolies. The Committee and the chosen corporations work hand in glove. The goal is something resembling communism with this Fascist twist of corporate monopolies producing the goods that the government dictates, without competition. The Committee believes that the root of our problems was a material inequality combined with free speech being used to convince people to vote against what the Committee considers was their own interest. Consequently, they're committed to material equality no matter how meager as well as controlling what people believe using the VR centers. It's the twenty-first century version of *bread and circus*. The Committee is unlikely to voluntarily reach the conclusion that they're in error. They view this as an historical opportunity to remake society premised on absolute equality and uniform social consensus that originates with government edict, even though that edict is communicated by virtual reality and presented as entertainment. The ideal end-state that they envision is so wonderful that the misery, poverty, and death that they create in pursuit of this ideal end-state is rationalized as a worthwhile price to pay. Any failure is the result of treason or capitalists or racism or anything other than themselves."

"Tell us about the security agents?"

"The agents basically fall into two groups, those like me that were former police or military and don't like playing the role of oppressor but like starving even less. Generally, we believed the 'restore order and make sure everyone receives the essentials of life' story when we signed up. We didn't realize at the time that we were signing up to use force to remake society from top down using food and medicine as a weapon. The other group are the true believers; they really believe in this new world they're trying to build and have no issue of conscience in whatever it takes to bring that new world to fruition. Most of the true believers are being deployed to infiltrate cells of resistance or people under suspicion. They don't task them with guarding fuel deliveries and such mundane tasks very often. The true believers have all of the morals of the NKVD, and Mandy Ford takes full advantage of that. Sometimes the infiltrators don't infiltrate an existing cell, they recruit people they suspect into a fictional cell and see if they'll bite. Ford calls them fantasy cells. They appeal to peoples' fantasy of resisting, and it enables security to entrap and liquidate potential resistors before they actually resist."

"Is it safe to assume that the agents guarding food and fuel and such won't put up much resistance if someone were to try to take that food and fuel?"

"Hard to say, but they are definitely not motivated to sacrifice their lives for a fuel truck. There are agents I trust and vouch for that are willing to help from the inside."

"What's the security hierarchy?"

"It's pretty flat. You have captains, of which I was one until yesterday morning, and a state director. That's Matthew Herzfelt. Then you have a regional director, Josh Hunley. Hunley is Beria. Give him the man, and he'll find the crime. Killing anyone suspected is easier than truth and justice to him. Above that, Mandy Ford, who does whatever the Committee tells her to. Herzfelt is an animal. He has men detained for no other reason than to extort sex out of their wives or daughters in exchange for freeing them."

"As we have been told. Do agents get better rations? Perks?"

"A little better food and a little more but not much. Agents are in a position to be bribed and to steal, and that's how they do better than most. Some agents extort the black market."

"How does the security department communicate?"

"The government and their friends are the only people left with cell phones and internet access. For the government, it's just like 2019."

Jerry reached in his shirt pocket and pulled out a thumb drive.

"This has a dozen logins and passwords, including for admins, to access the entire security system. Other data you might find useful as well. The Committee's concept of cybersecurity consists of keeping people they don't like off of the internet, once inside, the system is almost wide open.

There's also a list of all of the infiltrators that I know of, but it's their real names, not the names they use to infiltrate. That I don't have. Could be quite a task to connect the real names with the identity of the infiltrators. They go deep undercover. The infiltrators have even been known to kill fellow security agents in order to prove their bona fides to the resistance cell. True believers."

"Jackpot on the data. Tell us about security headquarters in Lakewood."

14
A toast to the creation of an equitable society

"I'm glad we can gather for a meal and discuss matters in a less formal environment," remarked Ted Harris.

"Indeed," replied Matthew Giles as he devoured calamari.

"We need to move on putting people back to work," suggested George Sandrop as he poked at the remains of a pork chop on his plate.

Ted Harris stood up, raised his glass of port and said, "A toast to the creation of an equitable society!"

"Here, here!" was the unanimous response as each person at the table stood and raised their glasses before sitting again.

"We agreed two years ago that rooting out the opposition was necessary before we launched an employment program. We have not yet completed that effort," Harris stated.

"Two years has been plenty of time to root out opposition," George Sandrop remarked, casting a glance at Mandy Ford. "It's important that we implement Intersectionality as societal and employment policy and not just theory; otherwise, the people will lose faith that we're creating an equitable society."

"Be that as it may. We have not achieved our initial objective quite yet," Harris said in an attempt to return the conversation to his chosen subject.

"We should revisit the calories we're issuing. Are eight thousand four hundred calories a week sufficient?" Harris asked.

"I'd think so," said Giles.

"The experts told us that it was sufficient," Sandrop agreed.

"I suspect you're slow walking us to an epiphany, Mr. Chairman," Mandy Ford said knowingly.

"Would it be effective in suppressing the resistance if we were to increase the weekly calories, give people hope of improvement?" Harris replied.

"I wouldn't think so. The resistance would use additional calories to build a reserve and use that against us," asserted Sandrop. "The heart of the resistance is male capitalist, supremacist. Increasing calories won't alter that. However, a jobs program focusing on giving the premier positions to marginalized communities will do a great deal to combat that."

"What would we pay them with? The dollar is worthless. What if people are not qualified for those plumb positions?" Ford asked.

"Are you implying that marginalized communities are inferior, Ms. Ford?" Giles shot back.

"No, I'm not. I'm asking practical questions," replied Ford.

"Those are valid questions; however, we agreed that we would not move on jobs until we suppress the opposition," interjected Harris.

"If we returned to a more traditional law enforcement model it might help suppress the opposition. Crime is rampant in most of the cities, especially the theft of ration cards. This puts a tremendous burden on people who have their cards stolen," Ford suggested.

"That problem is overblown, and a return to the previous model of law enforcement has racist and elitist overtones. These communities do a fine job of policing themselves. The last thing we need are police cars patrolling the communities of those who have historically been marginalized and persecuted by the police," Giles responded.

"Many of those communities are where the resistance appears to be growing most rapidly," responded Ford.

"Horseshit," Sandrop blurted.

"What do you mean growing? I thought we were close to stomping the opposition out! Which is it?" Giles said venomously.

"Now, now, gentlemen. Let's make this a productive time," Harris said.

Sandrop sat back in his chair, red faced and scowling at Mandy Ford.

"Another round of port," Harris called to the waiter.

"The people are with us. The opposition is comprised completely of those who resent having lost their privilege. Well, I spit on their privilege. Round them up and shoot them. Che Guevara was right!" Giles asserted.

"I will have the tiramisu," Sandrop told the waiter filling his glass.

Ted Harris again stood up, raised his refilled glass of port and said, "A toast to the end of privilege!"

"Here, here!" was again the unanimous response as each person at the table stood and raised their glass before sitting again.

15
Something useful to help combat the Committee

State Senator John Tribell sat in the Chevy Suburban next to Robin and fidgeted nervously. John was not nervous because that evening he would be introduced to the resistance cell that Robin was a member of, but because he had invited five of his friends to also join the cell. John had abandoned his state senate duties a month ago in favor of recruiting for the resistance with Robin at his side.

John had carefully considered his recruiting plan, his pitch, and those he hoped to recruit. They had all been friends and acquaintances from long ago in the liberty movement. John now worried that his five recruits would be where they were supposed to be. The driver of the Suburban was a burly man with a beard that John had never met before. He had introduced himself as Gary.

Gary steered the Suburban into the abandoned gas station parking lot on highway 85 just south of 470. Braking to a stop, the occupants of the Suburban scanned the parking lot for a full minute until the five men walked out from behind the dilapidated carwash building. Gary flashed the headlights as the five men made their way to the Suburban.

Gary, John and Robin, and the five recruits proceeded south on highway 85 without talking, John now giddy that all of his recruits had followed through. He was excited to do something tangible to oppose the Committee, and he was even more excited that he and Robin were doing this together. Life had become much brighter since he had abandoned the senate in favor of full-time resistance with Robin. Gary turned off of 85 at Sedalia onto Jarre Canyon Road and accelerated the Suburban toward the Rampart Range.

John thought about meeting the cell in just a few minutes and considered if they could do something useful to help combat the Committee. Robin had told him in detail about each of the thirteen members in the cell. The leader was named Dave, and he was a former Army sergeant. Dave was training the cell members in sabotage. Robin had explained how the missions could be carried out individually rather than as a large group so as to minimize the visibility of the group. Robin had told John how cautious they were of infiltrators. As a consequence, John had to provide Robin with detailed information about his recruits including their family members and friends in order for Dave to be able to approve them joining the cell.

The Suburban slowed as it rolled through the abandoned village of Sprucewood. The Rampart Range had been almost entirely depopulated due to the distance required to travel to a ration center. Gary veered the Suburban to the right and they descended Douglas County Road 40 through the short, steep canyon to the Platte River. At the bottom of the canyon Gary parked the Suburban in a dirt parking lot between the road and the river, and all eight of the passengers exited into the darkness. Robin wandered away from the car, straining to see the groups' accomplices.

"This is where we were supposed to meet, right?" Robin said to Gary.

"This is the place, I'm sure," Gary responded.

John and his recruits followed Gary and Robin through the dark parking lot like puppies.

"Why don't you go that way down the river, and I'll go this way and see if we can find them?" Gary said to Robin.

"Sounds like a plan."

"Do you want us to go with you?" John asked.

"No, you all stay here. When we find Dave, it will be easier if everyone is together."

With that Robin and Gary walked off into the dark. John debated sitting on a rock, but before he could arrive at the decision, John and the recruits were lit up by flashlights followed immediately by short burst of automatic gunfire, the bullets ripping through their chests.

Six men with M4 carbines walked up from the riverbank to where the lifeless bodies lay in the dirt. Gary and Robin approached from the north and south.

"God, these people are stupid. Sleep with one of them and tell them you're in the resistance and they all think they're Patrick Henry or something. 'Give me liberty or give me death' shit. Alright, let's go," Robin said as she kicked the corpse of John Tribell and walked back to the Suburban.

Jerry Sandoval winced at the sound of the M4's four hundred yards down the hill from him. Jerry had only been at the cabin for seven hours and he was glad the cell observed noise and light discipline. The first vehicle had arrived half an hour ago, and the little group at the cabin had taken defensive positions outside. They didn't often see vehicles along this section of the Platte, and it was even more rare to see a vehicle after dark. When the second vehicle arrived, the hair went up on Jerry's neck as he wondered if security had somehow tracked his location.

The gunshots ended that speculation.

"This is what happens when a cell is infiltrated," Jerry whispered to Ray his interrogator after the vehicles had departed.

"NKVD indeed," Ray whispered back.

Jerry, Ray, and the other three members of the team spent the remainder of the night working their way down the hillside to the massacre site. Slowly, silently, stopping to listen for long periods. It took them five hours to cover the four hundred yards.

In the pre-dawn Ray recognized the face of state senator John Tribell.

"I saw him speak a few times back in the day. He was a liberty guy. Sad," said one of the team members.

Ray reached into his jacket pocket and removed a cell phone. He powered the phone on and noted he had 18% battery left. There was no cell service available for the public, but the camera came in handy for reconnaissance work. Ray started snapping photos of the bodies, emphasizing the face of John Tribell. He made sure that Tribell's face could be recognized.

"Let's go," Ray said.

"Where are we going now?" Jerry asked.

"Denver, but we're taking the long way."

16
A series of dead drops

Leah plugged the thumb drive into her tablet. Leah worked with the resistance through a series of dead drops that she hoped would protect her. She had checked first thing in the morning on the abandoned car around the corner from her apartment, and the passenger side window was rolled down. This was a signal to check another abandoned car several blocks away where she found a small stone visible on the dashboard and this sign indicated that there was something for her lying inside of a dismounted tire behind a house that had fallen victim to fire. Inside the tire, Leah found a Ziploc bag containing a thumb drive and handwritten instructions.

Leah downloaded the contents of the thumb drive: photos of six men who had been shot with a particularly explicit photo of one man's face, a press release describing the death of these men with emphasis that one was a state senator, and login credentials to the Committee for the Continuance of Government security system.

The handwritten instructions included a list of websites and social media to post the photos and press release to, as well as email addresses to send them to. While the United States no longer had public internet access, most the rest of the world certainly did. Leah was to do all of this work using the login credentials of a specific agent. There were further instructions to send messages from the accounts of different agents to yet other agents at precise times each of the next two days.

Fortunately for Leah, the security headquarters at the Federal Center in Lakewood carelessly allowed their Wi-Fi signal to reach beyond the fence surrounding the perimeter. She could do all of this from the comfort of her car parked outside the Federal Center if she was discrete.

Ray hadn't slept in two nights, he knew that much was to be done and that it had to be done with precision. Ray was a mystery to everyone in the cell he had created. Not only did no one know his last name; no one knew that Ray was not even his actual first name. Where he came from and what he did before forming the cell no one knew, and Ray intended to keep it that way.

He understood that the information that Jerry Sandoval had provided him combined with being an eyewitness with photographs of the assassination of John Tribell provided the best opportunity yet for the resistance to bring the Committee for the Continuance of Government to its knees. Perhaps even topple the Committee.

Ray had spent the pre-dawn hours working the dead-drop system that he had devised for his cell. Dead drops were old-school, Cold War, pre-digital age spy craft, but they were effective, and the security agents didn't have the manpower to puzzle them out. The first part of Ray's plan for the day had been successful, and twenty-armed cell members were with him in Greenland. He looked at his watch, 2:00 PM. If the other part of his plan worked, there would be three unescorted fuel tankers approaching the Greenland exit at about 2:20 PM. They would be unescorted because their security escorts would have received seemingly legitimate messages to return to the Federal Center about the time they passed through Castle Rock.

The plan was very simple. When the tankers approached, they intended to block the southbound lanes of I-25 with vehicles. When the tankers stopped, they would place additional vehicles behind them to block any escape route. Men would rush from the ditches and remove the drivers of the trucks from the cabs. Three of Ray's men would then drive the tankers to the Lone Rock campground near Deckers, where Ray was confident they had little chance of being discovered. They would leave the drivers by the side of the road unharmed.

Ray glanced at his watch, 2:15. He looked up and saw three tankers on the horizon. Unescorted.

Like clockwork.

17
We have to move on housing

Ted Harris sat in his office in the Russell Senate Office Building attempting to mollify committee members, George Sandrop and Matthew Giles.

"We have to move on housing," Sandrop started.

"It makes no sense to have two people living in a three thousand square foot house and six people living in eight hundred square foot apartments. If we're going to have an equitable society, we have to match people's needs to the homes they live in," interjected Giles.

"Things are fragile. You have to understand. We don't presently have the logistical capability to force tens of millions of people to trade homes and half of them would be doing that against their will. We'll face significant resistance in forcing people to move from their three thousand square foot home to a six hundred square foot apartment. Telling them that it's in order to develop an equitable society won't be a well-received argument at the moment," Harris retorted.

"We agreed to move on this last year, right George? Maybe we can start in one city, say Philadelphia?" said Giles.

Giles didn't complete his sentence before Mandy Ford opened the office door and burst into the room proclaiming, "We have a problem."

"Well, what is it?" replied Ted Harris.

Ford glanced at Sandrop, and Giles then looked to Harris.

"Just tell us," said an exasperated Harris.

"The international media is reporting on the death of John Tribell. He was a state senator in Colorado. No one ever heard of him unless you were a politico in Colorado. He was a nobody. However, it's reported that there were eyewitnesses, and there are photographs."

"Why does this matter to us?"

"We enticed Tribell into a Honey Trap, recruited him and some of his friends into a fantasy cell, and liquidated them. This was done in a remote part of Colorado about forty miles from Denver. We believed it had been depopulated."

Harris shot a look at Giles and Sandrop, and they interpreted it as a demand to leave.

"When did this happen?"

"Yesterday."

"Yesterday!" Harris screamed, "How did photographs get out of the country?"

"It gets worse. The resistance may have hacked the security system. The Tribell story and photographs, with eyewitness accounts, was sent to foreign media and posted in forums using the account of one of our most loyal agents in Denver."

"Are you sure he's loyal? How do we know he didn't do it?"

"We're, um, questioning her thoroughly. However, this afternoon we had three fuel trucks that were going from Denver to Colorado Springs that were hijacked. Shortly before the hijacking, the security escort was recalled to headquarters by a message sent from the account of yet another agent. We're interrogating that agent as well, but the coincidence of two agents in the same office so egregiously misusing the system to essentially commit treason is too much to ignore. It's looking more likely that we were hacked. Additionally, one of our captains from the Denver office disappeared three days ago. We're thinking that he defected."

"Fix this! Do you understand? Until it's fixed, and we know it's fixed, I want you to send the order that all messages directing an agent to change their assigned task are to be ignored. Understand? Get all those logins and passwords changed! We can't have hackers sending our agents wherever the hackers want them to go."

"I'll send the order out immediately."

"On your way out, tell Ramsey to get in here. I want to see him right away."

"Yes, Mr. Chairman."

Harris buried his head in his hands until the door opened again, and James Ramsey walked in and sat down. Ramsey had been the last Secretary of State in the old government and was in charge of foreign affairs for the Committee.

"How bad is this Tribell thing?"

"Horrible. The overseas media are portraying us as running death squads. Massacring political dissidents. Comparing us to Stalin and Pol Pot. This is the kind of thing media frenzies are built on—state senator is shot from ambush by agents working at the behest of government, eyewitness accounts, photographs. This story has it all."

"Can't we get our side of the story out?"

"Chairman, death squads are our side of the story. What do you want me to put out to the media? That he was opposed to what we're doing on principle, so we lured him into a trap and killed him? I told you long ago, you had to rein these security people in. They have been throwing matches at gasoline for two years now."

"Well get something out there. Say he was a drug dealer or that he died in a battle with other rebel factions. Anything."

"Mr. Chairman, I think you're failing to appreciate the situation. Twenty-four hours ago, no one outside his district ever heard of this guy. Now his death is international headline news. The top of every website, the lead story on every broadcast. You would think we had killed Gandhi or something. Anything we say along the lines that you suggested will just make us look incompetent. What we need to say is that we have launched a full investigation and we'll get to the bottom of this, find the criminals, and hold them accountable. Now no serious person in the international community will believe that we'll hold anyone accountable but saying he was a drug dealer or killed by rebel factionalism will just make us look pitifully inept."

"I will remind you who you're talking to, Ramsey."

"Chairman Harris, it's time we stopped pretending. The United States sparked a debt crisis that gravely damaged the world economy, defaulted, then lost a war while walking away from every military ally and financial obligation that we had, and now we have closed what was previously the world's largest market to all but a very few select imports. To top it off, the rest of the world now believes that we murder dissidents. We have no friends in the international community, but we do have a great many enemies that would like this committee to become a footnote in history. Other nations are seeking regime change if for no other reason than they want a United States that's economically vibrant in order that they may sell products here and try to restart the global economy. These nations will use the Tribell affair as an excuse to interfere. I wouldn't be surprised if some foreign intelligence operatives already coordinate with the resistance. That's the extent that this committee is hated by the rest of the world. In the last hour Japan and the UK have called for an international investigation into atrocities committed by the Committee. This is not a trite matter that will be going away by telling a few lies about the fellow who was killed."

"Go tell the world we'll investigate and that we'll hold the perpetrators accountable."

18
Naco

Cindy awoke in her Tombstone trailer and tuned her radio to the morning liberty broadcast from Mexico.

"The world has been shocked by the murder of Colorado State Senator, John Tribell, and five of his companions. Eyewitnesses say Tribell was ambushed and shot by the security forces of the Committee for the Continuance of Government..."

Cindy felt as though she had been kicked in the chest. Her brother was not just dead but murdered by the Committee for the Continuance of Government. She slumped back on her bed and cried until there was a knock on her door and the voice of her friend Lori calling her name.

"We heard on the radio. We're so sorry," Lori blurted out as Cindy opened the trailer door. Lori and Cindy embraced while Len stood outside in the sand looking uncomfortable. "Why would they kill him? Why?" Cindy blubbered.

After spending the day crying, accusing, and being comforted Cindy, Lori, and Len found themselves sitting in folding camping chairs outside of Cindy's trailer at dusk.

"What can I do? What should I do?"

"Go to Mexico," Len replied.

"Mexico!" Lori and Cindy exclaimed as one.

"Yes, Mexico. You will be safer, and you can tell your brother's story. If what we heard this morning is true, this is a worldwide thing. People will want to hear your story, and they'll listen to you; you can expose what this country has become."

"Mexico," Cindy mumbled.

It's not that Cindy had not thought of it before. Several dozen people from Tombstone had left for Mexico over the previous two years. There was no way to know if they made it successfully and if they did, what their life in Mexico was like. The rumors were that Mexico was not allowing Americans to cross the border and that if you crossed illegally and were eventually caught the consequences were most unpleasant, particularly for women.

"Do you have photos, letters, documents showing he was your brother?"

Cindy nodded her head affirmatively.

"Get everything you have together, and first thing in the morning we'll go to Naco."

Cindy sat in her room in the Gran Hotel Ciudad de Mexico reflecting on the previous 48 hours. The border crossing had happened exactly how Len had expected. She was first told that no Americans were being accepted into Mexico. Len politely explained that this was the sister of murdered Colorado State Senator, John Tribell. The Mexican customs official raised an eyebrow, and she was invited inside the small customs building. The officials examined her photographs and documents and made phone calls. More officials arrived and also examined her photographs and documents and asked her questions and made more phone calls. Six hours later officials from Mexico City arrived and examined her photographs and documents and asked her more questions. Once they were satisfied that she was indeed the sister of John Tribell and that she wished to tell her story to the world, the Mexican Federal officials chaperoned Cindy as she was whisked off to Mexico City and provided a room at the Gran Hotel Ciudad de Mexico.

It was certainly nicer than her Tombstone trailer.

The Mexican government had issued a statement to the world that they had granted asylum to the sister of John Tribell before Cindy had even climbed into the king size hotel bed at the end of the day.

Just as Len had predicted, she was a thing.

Reflecting came to an end with a knock on the door of her hotel room. She peaked through the peephole to see a government official she recognized from the previous evening. She opened the door and the official said, "The BBC is downstairs and ready to interview you for television. Follow me please..."

19
Satisfaction

Brody relaxed in his recliner with the satisfaction that life had never been so good. All of the years he had spent endeavoring to fulfill his penchant for killing without getting caught and all the years of barely scraping by as a petty criminal had come to a glorious end the last two years. People willing to pay almost any price to escape the country in secrecy had provided him the perfect cover for his avocation. For Brody the best part was that no one would miss them. The Committee had so inhibited communication that his victim's families would assume their relatives were leading a prosperous life in Mexico rather than having been shot in cold blood on the great plains of Colorado.

He held between his fingers the pendant he removed from the young lady that he shot the night before. He kept a souvenir from each of his victims. Brody pleasantly scanned his apartment studying his souvenirs and reminiscing. He'd been killing at a pace of two to eight people a week for almost two years. Ted Bundy had nothing on him. He felt satisfied that he was the greatest ever.

He held the pendant and relived in his mind the unique satisfaction he felt holding the Makarov 9mm behind the head of the unsuspecting young lady and pulling the trigger. Brody loved his Makarov. He had paid less than a hundred dollars for it years ago without any paperwork and had purchased a case of 9 x 18 Makarov ammunition at a gun show for less than three hundred dollars for a thousand rounds. He still had half of the case remaining.

He relished the powerlessness of his victims and lived for the moment he was able to pull the trigger. The entire game of posing as the smuggler who would get them out of the country safely, winning their confidence, having them in his old Expedition, the misplaced apprehension that he knew they felt, culminating in pulling the trigger—it was all so perfect.

Brody was living his dream and he could live it without fear of getting caught. The security agents were focused on finding people who may overthrow the system, and Brody loved the system more than the Committee could ever imagine.

He reflected on the irony that the most significant threat to getting caught was that he was not rail thin as were the people living on rations. He convinced his victims to bring all of the valuables they could muster, and he subsequently used those in trade on the black market. He had fresh meat, fruit, vegetables, liquor, beer, and candy.

It was perfect.

20
A portrait of the United States as a living hell

"What the hell? His sister did a BBC interview from Mexico?" Ted Harris stormed at the Committee for the Continuance of Government, "Seriously, what the hell? We don't allow this! Who fucked up here? Who let her out of the country?"

The Committee members sat in stone silence. They had never heard Ted Harris use that word before.

Mandy Ford meekly broke the silence, "We depend on other countries not allowing Americans in. We rely on giving the impression that we don't allow people to leave. That's how we control this; but Mexico let her in. The Committee has never issued an actual order to prevent people from leaving the country. It's the other countries not wanting to be flooded with American refugees and the refusal to let Americans in that we have counted on."

"How bad is this?"

"It's bad. She paints a portrait of the United States as a living hell. Communications are restricted, movement is restricted, starvation rations, government agents seizing food for themselves, neighbors disappearing in the middle of the night, all that stuff. She's also convincing people that her brother was a harmless intellectual dedicated to improving people's lives and that he would never hurt a fly. That damn picture of she and her brother backpacking in Colorado juxtaposed against the photo of his face after he was shot is killing us. It's on every website and TV station in the world," replied James Ramsey.

"Damn!" screamed Harris.

"That transmitter in Mexico repeated the BBC interview verbatim to everyone in the western United States who happened to be listening, and that would appear to be most everyone," Ramsey added.

"People are very angry, both outside the country and in the west where they heard the Mexican broadcast," Ford chimed in.

Matthew Giles injected, "Why should they be angry? I think we're blowing this out of proportion. We assured everyone a place to live and food to eat, not just the privileged few getting the spoils as it used to be.

We should stand on what we have accomplished and not be fearful of these right-wing racists. The people are with us!"

Ramsey stared at Giles with his best "you're a dumbass" look while Ford involuntarily shot Giles a disbelieving glance.

"Five years ago, there were homeless people in San Francisco that were getting more calories and better-quality food out of dumpsters than the average American gets today," Ramsey retorted.

"This is a tinder box," Ford added.

"Squash the malcontents," George Sandrop contributed. "We're not going to give up on an equitable society simply because some miserable woman in Mexico did an interview with the BBC. What's the life of one disgruntled state senator in the grand scheme of what we're trying to accomplish here?"

"Squash them with what exactly?" Mandy Ford asked.

"The Chairman should go on television and radio this evening. Wrap him in the flag, tell the people we're saving the United States and that foreign agitators are intent on destroying the country for the gain of foreign powers. Explain that things have been tough but that we wanted to make sure that everyone got enough to survive. Tell them we're working on making it better for everyone. Tell them we'll all rise together, fairly and equally," Sandrop responded.

"That's not a bad idea," Harris said.

"The question is how many would watch?" asked Mandy Ford.

"Not many I'm afraid," responded Ramsey.

"Our programming is useful, popular, and educational," interjected Giles.

"Prime time last night was a three-hour long Introduction to Critical Theory. Trust me, no one watched. No one," shot back Ramsey.

"I think that television is a good idea, but it must be followed up with action," Harris remarked.

"Such as?" asked Mandy Ford.

"Can we organize some rallies and marches for tomorrow?" Harris suggested more than asked.

"We have to rally the people!" exclaimed Giles.

"We put prohibitions in place in order to prevent a resistance from cohesively organizing. Those same prohibitions are a hindrance in our ability to organize the masses, especially on short notice. The risk is that the Chairman goes on television tonight and not many watch because not many will know. We organize rallies for tomorrow and, because we face the same challenges in getting the word out as the resistance, the rallies could be small. This could lead the people to conclude that we're weak," Ford replied.

"The people are strong!" Giles proclaimed.

"I have had about enough of you. I understand that between being a cable news star and producing internet documentaries on fracking that you acquired a terminal case of the make-believe, but this is the real world. We're not strong. We're extremely weak. This is fragile, and this is dangerous, and if we're not smart, this could slip away from us quickly. The people are not on our side, mostly because we have spent the better part of two years keeping them on the edge of starvation while boring them to death with academic Marxist theory and punishing them if they attempted to improve their lives," Ford said to Giles in her best FBI voice.

"Here, here," chimed in Ramsey as Giles exited the Kennedy Senate Caucus room in a huff.

"Can we communicate this using the virtual reality centers instead of television?" Harris asked.

Everyone on the Committee turned to look at Geoffrey Snider, the chief technologist for the Committee for the Continuance of Government.

Before Snider could respond, an aid handed Ramsey a note.

Ramsey glanced at the note and said, "The ambassadors from Japan and the United Kingdom are requesting an interview this afternoon."

"Tell them we're working through the complexities of the issue," Harris ordered.

"Geoffrey?"

"Virtual reality can't work that quickly on the mind. Yes, we can certainly communicate this evening via VR that there will be rallies tomorrow, but we can't be certain about how many people that would prompt to attend those rallies."

While Snider answered the question, Mandy Ford was gazing at her phone.

"There are large groups of people forming in Seattle, Phoenix, Cheyenne, San Diego, Boise, Tucson, Colorado Springs, Tulsa, and in all of the major Texas cities. Many are armed. They're shouting 'Remember Tribell.'"

"That has to be organized, it can't be spontaneous," remarked Harris.

Harris' response prompted Ramsey to roll his eyes.

"Do you have a problem with that?" Harris shot at Ramsey.

"I do. This committee has increasingly existed in some Trotskyite bubble where it's removed from the material and social reality of life in the United States. What started out as the promise to make sure that everyone received the basics to live in hard times has morphed into preventing people who wish to improve their situation from doing so and preventing them from improving their life because it might not be equitable for other people who decline to or are unable to improve their own situation. If you think people have to organize to hate you, then you're mistaken. That hate is completely spontaneous and genuine. Do we have the ability to counter these groups?" Ramsey said as he looked at Mandy Ford.

"No."

"Then it's time that we begin to discuss an exit while that opportunity might still be possible," Ramsey said slowly.

"That is absurd. We're still in control here and we still hold all of the cards," rebutted Sandrop.

"What Tribell represents to the American people is that not only will the Committee prevent you from improving your situation but that we'll kill anyone who might have a better idea of how to improve the lives of the people. It doesn't matter what Tribell actually thought or did or believed. What matters is what he now represents. The paradigm has changed, George, and the balance of power is changing with it," Ramsey replied to Sandrop.

"I don't believe the situation has changed that significantly," said George Sandrop.

"You should have paid more attention to that whole Berlin Wall thing in history class."

"Jim, you're panicking. We'll cut off the food and fuel, and these criminals will be begging us to come back in a week," Ted Harris said, looking directly at Ramsey.

"Mr. Chairman, if you cut off the food and fuel, you will convince them of how right they are. You will merely be confirming what many already believe to be so and encourage additional people who don't now believe how inept and ridiculous we are to begin believing it," said Ramsey while silently pondering why this was not obvious to Harris and Sandrop.

After a moment of silence, Ramsey continued, "Anyone who knows history knows that now is the moment to start planning how to get the hell out of Dodge."

"We can survive this, we still have lots of cards to play. It's not that bad," was the rebuke from Sandrop.

"Mandy, cut off food and fuel to the places that have rebellions forming," Harris directed.

"Mr. Chairman, it appears that the entire state of Texas is now in rebellion. Certainly not everyone in the state is rebelling, but there's rebellion across the entire state. Do you want me to cut off food and fuel for the entire state of Texas?"

"Yes."

"That is insanity," Ramsey interjected. "Let me explain what's going to happen. The people of Texas will open the border with Mexico. Most of the food and fuel Texas consumes originates in Texas. They'll seize the production facilities of both food and fuel, and there'll be no 'cutting them off.' You won't be destroying the rebellion. You'll be giving them a base of operations with access to foreign assistance."

Harris looked at Mandy Ford and said, "Mandy, do it. Cut them off. James, I'll take your views into consideration. We'll table all of the other suggestions for now. Meeting adjourned, we'll meet again tomorrow morning at ten."

James Ramsey exited the Kennedy Senate Caucus room pondering exactly how he would ask the ambassador from the Court of St. James for asylum and if the United Kingdom would help spirit him out of the country. The pondering came to an end when two large armed men grabbed him by each arm and forced him outside and into a white van. The van bore the faint lettering "Bureau of Land Management."

21
Aligaliyvhi

Brian Vann stood in the bed of a pickup truck looking out on the crowd. It was mid-afternoon in Gore, and he had started spreading the idea of a community meeting just that morning. It seemed that nearly everyone from Gore and Webbers Falls and the surrounding countryside was here. Brian wondered if his voice would carry far enough. He had considered having the meeting in the parking lot of the diner in Gore but had instead decided to hold the meeting in the park below the bridge across the Arkansas, where the old ferry landing used to be. He realized that turned out to be a good decision.

"I hope y'all can all hear me."

Heads in the back of the crowd nodded up and down.

"Osda. 'siyo. A lot of you probably heard on the radio from Mexico yesterday that a state senator from Colorado by the name of Tribell has been murdered by the Committee. Most of you probably heard what Tribell's sister had to say this morning. We all know the security agents come here and steal our food from us. We have all been threatened if we don't give it to them. We all know the Committee won't allow us to have the fuel or fertilizer to farm our own land. We all know that the Committee won't even let us have a good way to talk to or see our kin even if they're only twenty miles away. Some of you have not heard from your folks or brothers or sisters or children in two years, even if they're only in Tahlequah or Tulsa or Durant. What we learned this morning removed any doubt that the Committee does this on purpose. They don't want us talking to each other, even if it's family. It's not that the Committee doesn't have the ability to make that happen, it's that they stop it from happening just like they stop us from having fuel and fertilizer. Now we know they kill people who might have a better idea. They just want to control us. They're afraid of us. Well, I'm done with them and this. I suspect most of you are too.

"Here's what we'll do if y'all are willing: we won't let those government folks in. If they show up, send them away, chase them away. Don't hurt them unless they're going to hurt you but send them away. Give them nothing and agree to nothing. What we got told this morning and yesterday is that there are a lot fewer of these agents than we may have thought. There are a lot more of us, and we all have guns, too. So just send them away. Now here is the hard part. The Committee can stop sending us food and fuel. If we're going to do this then we have to take care of each other like we did in the old days. If you have food to share, then share it with people that don't have enough. If you can spare a gallon of gas for someone who needs it then do so. Care for each other, check in on each other. No one is going to come and take things from you. You just have to do this yourself for others.

"Gadugi. A good number of you here are Tsalagi, and you know what I'm talking about. If you aren't Cherokee, you will learn what gadugi is. West of us are the Muscogee, to the south are the Choctaw. They have their own gadugi; they'll get it right quick.

"Spread the word. Go home and tell the people around you about this, spread it out and tell the ones you tell to tell the people beyond them what this is. Explain gadugi. If everyone tells their neighbors on the far side about gadugi and to chase the security agents away, it will reach the people who make the fuel and fertilizer and food. The government has no power if we won't give it to them. We aren't going to give them power just so they can use it to starve us and steal from us and keep us from our families and kill us.

"If you have had enough like I have, then go tell your neighbors and tell them to tell their neighbors.

"Gadugi. Di-tsa-da-s-de-li-s-gi i-tse-he-s-di. That is how we will do this. Aligaliyvhi!"

Brian stepped down out of the pickup truck bed hoping that he was not leading people into disaster while recalling what Stand Watie had long ago said, "If I commit an error, I do it without bad intention."

22
What's the password?

Ray stood outside the northeast corner of the Federal Center perimeter with twenty members of his cell, all carrying rifles. Sandoval had informed him that there was no video coverage on this approach to the security headquarters due to lack of maintenance on the cameras. Jerry had even drawn a map of how to execute the takeover of security headquarters with the least amount of potential surveillance of the approach. Jerry had also informed Ray of the time when there would be the fewest agents at headquarters.

Ray quickly cut the chain-link fence and slipped through the cut, and as each additional team member went through the cut, they sprinted in a straight line to the building that housed security headquarters. Once the last member had arrived at the building that housed the security headquarters, Ray peered quickly around the corner of the building. Once they turned this corner, they would be on video surveillance; hence speed was critical. Ray took a deep breath and said, "Go!" The team sprinted around the corner to the glass door. Just as Jerry Sandoval had explained, there were landscape logs bordering the sidewalk near the door. Team members quickly picked up the landscape logs and used them to smash the glass in the locked door. They then charged through, breaking off into smaller teams to seize rooms that Jerry had drawn out on a map for them.

In the communications room Agent Colson watched the breach occur on the video monitors. He instantly sent out a message for assistance, informing all agents in Denver that headquarters was under attack and for all agents to come to their aid. He was already a captive when another message went out three minutes later directing all agents to ignore the previous message and informing them that the attack message was due to a hacker.

Ray charged up the stairs leading a team to the office of state security director, Matthew Herzfelt. When Ray burst into Herzfelt's office, he was stunned that not only was Herzfelt in the office, so was regional security director, Josh Hunley.

"Hands on the back of your head! Drop to your knees!" Ray shouted at Herzfelt and Hunley. Two team members frisk Herzfelt and Hunley, removing the pistols from the holsters on their belts and ankles. Ray picked up Hunley's cell phone that was lying on the desk. "What is the password?" Ray demanded of Hunley, pointing a 1911 at him.

"seeyou then numeral 2."

"Seriously?"

Ray unlocked the phone. Opening the camera app, Ray snapped a photo of Hunley and Herzfelt on their knees with their hands on their heads. Scrolling through the contact list in the phone Ray selected Mandy Ford and Ted Harris and attached the photo of Hunley and Herzfelt in a text message along with the words, "pwned! All your base are belong to us."

That ought to get a reaction, Ray thought.

23
Addled

Ted Harris was awaiting the arrival of Admiral Denton when his cell phone buzzed. Harris' reaction was instant ill humor. He had issued explicit directions that he was never to be sent text messages. The thought passed through his mind that someone is in big trouble as he retrieved the phone from his desk. What Harris saw in the text message genuinely shook him.

At that moment Admiral Denton entered his office. Denton had never seen Harris so addled.

"Mr. Chairman."

Harris looked up, sweat beading on his forehead, and said, "Please sit, Admiral."

Denton tried to recall if he had ever heard Harris use the world, please, before.

"We need the help of the Pentagon."

"Mr. Chairman, we have had this conversation before. The military will not interfere or intervene in domestic affairs on your behalf."

Denton thought that Harris just might be so obtuse as not to realize that he was not popular with the rank-and-file of the military. Harris was seemingly oblivious that his policies were all but starving the military families. It was all Denton could do to rein in the military from going after the Committee. Having the military participate in the oppression of their own families was a non-starter.

"Please Admiral, we need a show of force to restore order in certain small parts of the country."

"Like Texas you mean? I know what's going on, and the answer is no."

Mandy Ford burst into the room.

"You're excused Admiral."

Denton exited the room, thinking the curtness of the dismissal was more in line with the Harris that he had come to know. Denton knew from the tone of the brief meeting that he had important decisions to make in the coming hours.

"What's going on, Mandy?" asked Harris?

"The resistance has taken over security headquarters in Denver and regional director Hunley and state director Herzfelt are apparently hostages. They sent a text message and—"

"Yes, I saw it."

"—it gets worse. That photo as well as a press release is being posted in forums all over the world and presumably is being sent to international media using our communications system at Denver headquarters. That's not even the worst news. They're also posting our most confidential files on these forums. Reports of infiltration activities, executions, that sort of thing."

"How bad is that?"

"How bad are internal reports of our executing resistance members? I have two dozen embassies that have tried to contact me in the last hour inquiring as to why they can't get in touch with Ramsey."

"Direct them to Giles."

"Sir—"

"Okay, Sandrop."

"I don't know if a report was filed on Tribell yet or not. If there was and they find it, it will be very bad."

"What about the rest of the country?"

"Texas is nearly gone. Crowds are growing in many cities. Our agents are being chased out of everywhere they try to go in eastern Oklahoma, and it's now spread to western Arkansas. That's new this afternoon. At the speed it's moving it'll cross the Mississippi tonight and be in California by morning."

"Can we retake the Denver headquarters?"

"Doubtful. Messages were sent by the occupiers directing our agents to go all over Colorado. Communicating with them, marshaling agents in any numbers, and coordinating a counter-attack will take time, and that's probably what we don't have at the speed this is moving. The agents have no way of knowing what are and are not legitimate messages."

"I hold you responsible."

"I thought you might."

Mandy drew a Smith & Wesson M&P Shield from the holster behind her back and fired two shots into the chest of the chairman, waited a moment and fired one into his forehead.

Mandy Ford knew exactly what Ted Harris intended when he said that he held someone responsible.

Mandy left the Russell Senate Office Building at a gait that approached a trot. She went directly to her waiting car and directed the driver, "To Dulles."

24
Rapid changes

"Rapid changes occurring in the United States. Let's go through these quickly because there are many."

Ray listened intently to the liberty broadcast from Mexico after a sound night of sleep and while seated with his feet resting victoriously on the desk of state security director Herzfelt.

"Mandy Ford, who had been in charge of internal security in the United States for the Committee for the Continuance of Government, was detained as she arrived in Toronto last night. Ford claims that she shot and killed the Chairman of the Committee, Ted Harris, yesterday afternoon. Ford released a brief statement claiming she shot Harris because he 'was a murderous tyrant.' Meanwhile Ford will remain in custody in Canada and will be investigated for her role in the atrocities that are becoming ever more widely known.

"George Sandrop and Matthew Giles of the Committee for the Continuance of Government have issued a statement that the Committee will continue and that nothing has materially changed. The statement also named Ford and fellow committee member James Ramsey as traitors.

"In Denver, the resistance has occupied security headquarters and taken regional director Hunley and state director Herzfelt prisoner. The resistance has posted numerous files from the security headquarters documenting murders and atrocities committed by the agency. Included in those files posted early this morning was a report on the murder of state senator John Tribell. It documents in detail how Tribell was beguiled by a female agent and lured into an ambush by the security agents of the Committee.

"In Texas, every major city is engaged in rebellion against the Committee. There are reports in many western states of the security agents for the Committee giving up and even joining the rebellion..."

The entry of Jerry Sandoval into the office broke Ray's focus on the broadcast.

"What do you think?" Jerry said.

"I think we need to find the infiltrators. If these radio reports are true, we also need to think about how we might feed people, or at least whom we need to think about giving the power for how to feed these people to. At this point putting that power in the hands of a government committee will not be a compelling suggestion."

"Ever read Hayek? Von Mises? Rothbard?" asked Jerry.

"Well, yes, as a matter of fact I have."

"Well? What would they say to do?"

"I've been thinking about that. I read once that, in the couple of years right after World War II, the workers at the Volkswagen plant produced cars and traded them for food. No one in Germany had the money for cars, but farmers had food, and farmers wanted a car, and workers had to eat."

"That's a hard thing to scale," Jerry remarked.

"Indeed. So many things need to be done. Stand up a government that's representative and a currency that's not worthless," Ray responded.

"Let's focus on what we can do today. The infiltrators are still out there, the true believers, and they'll be dangerous. Nothing like watching the government that you murdered innocent people for collapse before your eyes and the people you intended to murder come out on top. They'll be motivated to violence."

"You know what files we should look at. Let's get started," Ray suggested.

25
Let's just go now

"Isn't this wonderful Dana? The whole thing is collapsing. Harris is dead. There's hope for freedom again!" Charlie said exuberantly as they listened to the broadcast from Mexico.

"Yes, it is," responded Dana. Unbeknownst to Charlie, the woman he knew as Dana had gone by many names. Most recently she had been known as Robin.

"The terror is over!"

"It's wonderful," the woman exclaimed.

"What shall we do to celebrate?"

"Dear, I have to go out for a bit. I'll be back."

"Really? What do you have to do?"

"Just run a few errands and go see my friend, Leslie. Really, I'll be back soon. Leslie's been sick, and I need to check on her."

"Ok," Charlie replied dubiously.

The woman Charlie knew as Dana took her purse and left the apartment. Once she got in her car, she slid open the compartment under the passenger seat and removed her cell phone. Trying to remain calm she drove a few blocks to a strip mall parking lot. There she made a call.

"Gary?"

"Hey, Katie. Bad day."

"No shit. What're we going to do? Where are you?"

"I'm in Thornton. Where are you?" said Gary.

"Aurora. We have to get out of town. We have to get out of the country. They'll be looking for us hard. They occupied headquarters. They have all the files! They know everything!"

"I know. Calm down. Meet me in the parking lot of Community College of Aurora. Know where that is? I can be there in an hour."

"Yes. Get there fast."

Katie drove to the Aurora City Hall that was now being used as a ration center. The parking lot was crowded with cars, and she could hide in plain sight. She stayed in her car in the parking lot for fifty minutes until making the short drive to Community College of Aurora.

Not seeing Gary's Chevy Suburban, Katie pulled into a parking spot but left the engine running in case she needed to get away quickly. She glanced at her fuel gauge, half a tank. One of the perks of being an agent was getting all the fuel that she cared to burn. Katie looked about nervously, filled with anxiety. Katie had never considered the possibility that the resistance could win. She had never prepared for the moment that she could become the hunted rather than the hunter.

After what seemed to Katie an eternity but was in truth only a few minutes, Gary's Suburban entered the far end of the parking lot then parked next to her. Gary sprung out of the Chevrolet and got in the passenger seat of Katie's car.

"Let's just go now, head south, get to Mexico, right this minute," Katie pleaded.

"That's a bad plan. They either do have or will soon have our license plate numbers and a description of our cars. They have our names and photographs. To make a run for the border in one of our cars is exactly what they think we'll do, and they'll be looking for us. That makes the odds bad."

"What then? Hide out here forever? They'll never stop looking for us because of that damn Tribell. Maybe the Committee can pull this out and save it?"

"No chance of that I'm afraid. Harris is dead, Ford is in Canada under arrest, and Sandrop and Giles seem like idiots. Who knows where Ramsey is? No, I know of a fellow, a smuggler, named Brody. I always figured he could be a source and that I could take him down whenever I wanted. We can use him for cover, but we need money for Mexico. Gold, silver, jewelry, things like that. I don't have any of those things, and I'm guessing that you don't have much?"

"I don't have any of those things," Katie responded.

"Well then, we better go get those things. Where's your gun?"

"In the spare tire space in the trunk."

Gary opened the passenger side door while Katie popped the trunk lid from inside the car. Gary went to the trunk and retrieved Katie's Glock G43 9mm. Returning to the passenger seat Gary said, "Let's start robbing."

26
How unnecessary it all was

Ray recited Shakespeare silently to himself in an attempt to counter the growing rage. For the first time in two years Ray allowed himself to feel anger. He and Jerry had spent the previous six hours digging through the files of the Denver security headquarters and had reviewed episode after episode of people being persecuted and killed for nothing more than believing in what the United States was intended to be, or sometimes simply because they had an attractive wife or daughter.

Ray and Jerry had pieced together the names of the government infiltrators that worked out of the Denver headquarters, complete with photographs and even vehicle make and model with license plate numbers. Jerry had departed headquarters to take that information to the radio station and TV station, both of which had fallen to resistance cells earlier that day.

Ray looked at the photographs of Katie Davis and Gary Weiss. He then paged through the photographs of the six shooters from the Tribell assassination.

Ray felt the anger burn through him. He could feel his quickening heartbeat and the arterial tension. He felt pressure in his neck and the energy surging to his forearms and hands. Ray felt the tightening of the muscles in his feet and legs and he could hear his pulse pounding in his right ear.

He was angry at how unnecessary it all was.

Damn them all! Ray thought before catching himself. Ray knew that emotions would lead to mistakes and that he could not afford to make a mistake. He consciously slowed his heart and began thinking through how he might catch Davis and Weiss in particular. He considered that broadcasting the photos may lead to their apprehension then reconsidered and whispered, "They're headed to the border."

Jerry pulled the Wagoneer into the parking lot at the television station on Speer, south of downtown Denver. The resistance cell that had taken over the television station was one that Jerry knew had been infiltrated. *This should be an interesting conversation*, Jerry thought.

He met the two well-armed men at the door to the station with the greeting, "I have names, photographs, and vehicle license numbers for the government infiltrators. We need to get this information broadcast over and over until we find these people."

The two sentries looked at each other, looked at the packet in Jerry's hand, and the older one said, "Come with me."

27
We have a moral obligation

Admiral Denton looked each of the officers seated around the table in the eyes before he began to speak.

"I have fought against military involvement in domestic politics my entire career. However, at this point in time the United States no longer has domestic politics or domestic anything. What we have is chaos and as inept and treacherous as the Committee has been, what we're looking at in the near future will be a debacle unless something is done to stave off humanitarian disaster.

"This is what I'm proposing: that the military remove the remaining members of the Committee from power, take over the distribution of food and fuel, do what we can to expand the production of that food and fuel, do what we can to open up public communications again, and, most importantly, announce that there will be a constitutional convention in six months.

"We have a moral obligation not to allow people to starve, but this cannot be a long-term role for the military. We need to hand this over to a representative government quickly. Let the future convention decide what to do nationally and how to do it going forward.

"We'll swear our oath of loyalty to the convention.

"Questions? Thoughts? Objections?"

No one sitting at the table was surprised by the Denton proposal.

"What about atrocities and crimes that have been committed? Do we take on the role of law enforcement to investigate and apprehend?" General Helfrich asked.

"I think our role is in assisting with the logistics of reconstituting state government and leave law enforcement to the state governments. The state governments can then determine how they wish to go about law enforcement and what prosecution methods they care to adopt," Denton replied.

"If I'm understanding correctly, the task is to assure the continued flow and distribution of food and fuel while simultaneously restoring local and state representative government?" General Baumgartner asked.

"These states all have an elected governor and an elected state legislature. That some of these entities may not have met in two years or more and certainly have not exercised their duties in two years doesn't equate to their no longer existing. I'd think the proper course is to find these elected officials in each state, get them all back in the same room at the same time, and hand back to them their legal authority and make them responsible for reconstructing their states and for developing a political process for moving forward. I want to be very careful that we don't take on more than we can handle and that this is not perceived as a coup and a military dictatorship. It's critical that we be forthright and transparent with the state governments and the people of the United States. We must guard against expectations that would be over-optimistic for the situation and our capabilities."

"What about civil disturbances, uprisings, that sort of thing?" asked Admiral Andersen.

"I think the rule of thumb must be protecting lives. I think being forthright about our situation and intentions will hopefully nip those sorts of things in the bud along with our restoring state government. I'd imagine that the most likely cause of civil disturbance would be rumors. I could be wrong, but I'd think the idea that someone else is getting more than their fair share would be the root of insurrection. We can make an effort to stop rumors before they start by being transparent."

General Helfrich added, "Keep it simple."

"Yes, by all means, keep it simple and get representative civilian authority in charge as rapidly as possible. Hand off the responsibilities to the state governments quickly. This will inevitably look different in New York than, say, Arizona, but we have to get this done and off our hands as soon as practicable. Facilitate transportation for state legislators, focus on the logistics of restoring state and local government, and don't over-promise."

"What shall we communicate in regard to a constitutional convention?" asked General Nash.

"I'm hoping that the promise of a constitutional convention is a carrot to incentivize people to behave appropriately. The convention may re-adopt the old constitution or modify it or draft a new constitution. That is up to them. The message is that each state will have a vote and a say in the new constitution. Each state should send two representatives to the convention and each state will select their own representatives in whatever manner the state government decides. The delegates can come up with their own rules for the convention. It's important after the last number of years that everyone has input into how things will work going forward. There will not be unanimity, but we do want comity. Communicate that the intent of the convention is to reconstitute a Federal government that does things for them instead of to them."

"What if some states decide that they want to secede? Based on the recent past, they may view that as the preferred option," asked General Helfrich.

"They may indeed. Tell them to send representatives to the convention anyway. Let them know that the convention is the proper venue to discuss secession, and before any state makes that decision, we require that they meet with all of the other states to discuss and make known that intent. Let them know that there are no pre-determined outcomes to the constitutional convention and that their grievances may be addressed without having to leave the union. Also, and this is critical, inform them that the military is neutral on the issue of secession but that declining to attend the convention is not an option."

"If they still decline to attend?" responded General Helfrich.

"Be as firm and persuasive as possible but don't force the issue. We will not compel them to attend if they're resolute. Civil war is not the goal. We have plenty on our plate already."

"What about resistance from those that are loyal to the Committee?" asked Admiral Andersen.

"We're all trained to deal with the unexpected. I don't perceive that there's very much loyalty to the Committee in the general population, but there may very well be pockets of resistance. We have to be cognizant of the fact that, due to the transmitter in Mexico, the people in the western half in the United States generally possess a great deal more information than the people in the eastern half of the United States possess at the moment. This could be problematic. We have to be very careful. The people in the west obtained the information in somewhat of an organic manner. If the military informs the people in the east of all that has occurred, they may very well view it as propaganda that we're presenting in order to justify a military takeover of the country. That is probably our worst-case scenario. General Martinez, I am assigning you to devise a means for people in the eastern United States to obtain access to international media as soon as possible."

"Yes, Admiral," responded Martinez.

"General McNeil, I am tasking you with going to the Russell Senate Office Building and detaining incommunicado the remaining members of the Committee. You will additionally assign sufficient staff to supervise the bureaucrats in order that the food and fuel continue to flow. You will determine what bureaucrats will be replaced without inhibiting the efficiency of the work and replace them as quickly as practicable. Those bureaucrats don't all have clean hands. Most importantly, turn that damn virtual reality off."

"Yes, Admiral," responded McNeil.

"Furthermore, General McNeil, you will also have a team take Federal Correctional Institute, Petersburg. Accomplish this by whatever means is required. We know with relative certainty that this is where the former Speaker of the House, various senators and congressman, talk radio hosts, and media personalities are being kept. What's more, we believe that this is where the President, First Lady and Vice President were sent when the Committee determined that they were to be detained. It's doubtful that they're still there. If they're not there then use whatever means are required to locate where they are. Understand, General McNeil? It's critical to our credibility that we show the Committee was lying when they claimed that the President had retired to upstate New York."

"Yes, Admiral," responded McNeil.

"Additionally, former members of the Committee for the Continuance of Government are also being held in Petersburg. Not everyone held there is an innocent victim.

"Admiral Wright, you will take charge of international communications and relations.

"You all have a packet on the table in front of you. Admiral Webb, you should have received your packet," Denton said as he glanced at the Admiral in Hawaii on the video monitor.

Admiral Webb nodded affirmatively.

"Open your packets now. These are your orders. You have each been assigned geographic boundaries that are your responsibility. You will have command of all personnel, regardless of service branch, within your assigned boundary. Pay particular attention to the timelines. If you have any questions or issues now is the time. Once we leave this room this operation is a go."

The officers studiously read their orders while Denton glanced about the table reading the officers body language for clues of discomfort. Denton noticed Ziegler touching his neck with his fingertips.

"Do you have a question, Admiral Ziegler?"
"No, sir."
Denton stared doubtfully at Ziegler but let it go.
"Are we good to go?"
"Yes, Admiral," the officers replied in unison.
"Meeting adjourned."

28
Jagged little what if

Brody was apocalyptic in his unhappiness. All that he had found perfect was sliding away, and there was nothing that he could do about it. Rebels had taken over security headquarters, and now the television and radio were broadcasting the names, descriptions, and even the vehicles of the infiltrators. The rebels were promising to restore normalcy. Normalcy was the last thing that Brody wanted. People outside celebrated while Brody panicked. What if the bodies were found? They were sure to be; there were over four hundred of them. What if they could be identified? What if they notified the next of kin and his name came up? True, Brody was not his real name, but still, what if they figured out who he was?

Brody's mind was overwhelmed, and he could not act. His mind was pierced with jagged little "what if" interruptions to such an extent that he was incapacitated.

"*What if they come here and see the souvenirs*?

"*What if the black-market sellers get cornered and pin the jewelry and coins on him?*

"*What if he had the last white 1998 Ford Expedition still running in Denver?*

"*What if he had the only Makarov out there*?

"*What if they found all of the brass he had left at the murder scenes*?

"*What if his fingerprints were on the brass*?

"*What if they still had fingerprint records*?

"*What if someone saw him carrying suitcases into his apartment*?

"*What if someone saw him carrying suitcases into his apartment several times a week*?

"*What if they find the bodies*?

"*What if they identify the bodies*?

"*What if they tie the bodies to him*?

"*What if the relatives explained the smuggling*?

"*What if he was the only human smuggler in Denver?*"

Brody fell into his recliner consumed with the panic of what if. He knew that time was of the essence and that he should be doing... something. He fought with futility—his mind that was engaged in the never-ending loop of what if.

His heart nearly came to a stop when he heard voices in the hall outside of his apartment.

The voices quickly moved on, neighbors loudly celebrating the vanquishing of the Committee, but the fright restarted Brody's focus.

The thoughts of what to do rushed into his consciousness.

I have to leave.

Where?

Mexico.

Not Mexico.

Another city.

Another state.

Another name.

Another car.

What state?

What city?

What do I take?

A knock at the door brought Brody's heart to a complete stop.

The next knock prompted him to reach for the Makarov.

With his left hand, Brody opened the apartment door ever so slightly while his right hand clutched the pistol behind his back. Standing outside the door was a man that Brody recognized as a security agent. Brody's heart stopped again.

"We need to go to Mexico and we need to go now," Gary whispered to Brody.

Brody visibly exhaled. Standing behind Gary was a woman that Brody didn't recall having seen before. Brody quickly regained his composure.

"Be in the parking lot downstairs at ten tonight."

"No, we need to go now."

"Ten tonight. We go when I say we go, or we don't go at all."

Gary was visibly annoyed but quietly responded, "See you at ten."

Brody shut the door.

As Brody turned away from the door, he realized the woman standing behind Gary was the woman that he had seen in the photograph on television that morning. He had failed to recognize her because in the television photograph she was a blonde, while the woman at his door had black hair.

Brody whispered to himself, "This could be perfect."

The security agents were desperate to get out of town. Brody realized the priority of the rebels was to hunt down the security agents. No one would be investigating him for quite a while, even if the bodies were found. If he took out the agents, he could just keep indulging his passion.

If bodies were found and tied to him at any future point, he could claim that he was a hero. He could say he was simply killing collaborators and agents. Brody had the thought that there would certainly be more security agents wanting to escape, and killing even more agents that desired to escape would only bolster his story that he was a hero.

Perfect.

29
Treason and deception

George Sandrop gaveled the daily meeting of the Committee for the Continuance of Government to order in the Kennedy Senate Caucus room on the third floor of the Russell Senate Office Building.

"We have suffered treason and deception by members of this committee and the assassination of the Chairman. We will not be deterred. This committee has the opportunity to create a just and equitable society, and to assure a material equality and an equality of outcome and to remedy the injustices of the past. This vision is too important, and the moment for implementation is historically unique. We will not be dissuaded by betrayal. We will counterstrike and put down the traitors. The people are with us. The people demand a society of complete equality."

"I nominate George Sandrop as Chairman of the Committee for the Continuance of Government!" shouted Matthew Giles.

"Seconded," responded Geoffrey Snider.

"Thank you. The first order of business is the retaking of the states and cities that are in rebellion. Mr. Giles, I place you in command of the security agency. Put down the rebellion."

"Yes, Mr. Chairman," replied Giles.

"You will immediately inform me when the radio and television stations have all been brought back under our control so that I may address the nation. The people need to know the level of treachery that they have suffered. The people will rise up against the rebels once we explain that the rebels stand for a return to the inequalities of gender, race, privilege, and oligarchy. By the way, immediately after this meeting I will be traveling to Fisher Island to attend my daughter's wedding. I require you to keep me abreast of all developments and progress while I am away."

"Yes, Mr. Chairman. I will be weekending at Tybee Island. I will issue the appropriate orders and keep you informed," replied Giles.

"Geoffrey," Sandrop said while looking at Snider, "We're depending on you to get the appropriate message out via the virtual reality centers. It's critical that the people know that we're on their side."

"Yes, Mr. Chairman. We're already working it. I will be at Chincoteague this weekend and will have full access."

"It's good that you all get out of this bubble in D.C. and have some peace and quiet. I am glad to see that you're availing yourselves of that opportunity. The work of the Committee is of critical importance, and you're all vital to the success of the country. This is very stressful work, and you all need to get away and relax as often as possible. Mr. Faulkner, give us an update?" Sandrop said glancing at Dennis Faulkner. Faulkner was the Committee member representing the corporations that were chosen to continue production.

"We have had a considerable amount of production capacity taken from our control in the last forty-eight hours. More than thirty percent of raw food production, twenty percent of manufacturing—"

"Mr. Giles will restore that capacity to the control of the Committee very quickly. Nothing to worry about in that regard; a temporary situation," Sandrop asserted.

"Yes, Mr. Chairman," Faulkner replied while secretly wondering how he could get out of the country undetected.

The attention of the Committee was drawn to loud voices punctuated by two gunshots outside of the Kennedy Senate Caucus room. As Sandrop and Giles rose out of their chairs, Marines burst into the Kennedy Senate Caucus room brandishing weapons.

A Marine Corp Colonel approached the table at the head of the room where Sandrop and Giles were now standing and assertively enlightened the Committee, "The Committee for the Continuance of Government is now dissolved. You will all be detained until a legitimate Federal government is created, and the new government will then take custody of you. Come with me, gentleman."

Less than five miles away Admiral Denton sat at his desk in the Pentagon reviewing the updates as they arrived.

The Committee for the Continuance of Government was in custody with only one casualty, a security agent who drew his sidearm on the Marines.

Denton had over six dozen additional reports from various cities in regard to security headquarters being taken, television and radio stations coming under military control, and broadcasts being made to explain what was happening and why. Now they could add to the broadcasts that the Committee was dissolved and in custody.

Facilities that had been occupied by resistance groups were being handed over peacefully once it was explained to them what was happening. The key to resistance cooperation had been, as Denton anticipated, the promise of a constitutional convention. This was not to be a military coup or dictatorship but a restoration of representative government. All reports indicated that those loyal to the Committee were fleeing rather than resisting. Very little resistance was being met and very little bloodshed. One dead in Boston, two in Los Angeles, and one in Phoenix. Denton could live with those numbers. He was pleased that there were not yet any pitched battles.

Denton awaited the report from Federal Correctional Institute, Petersburg. It was the situation at Petersburg he deemed most critical. Exposing that the last President, First Lady, Vice President, and Speaker had not retired quietly as the Committee had claimed but had been imprisoned was key to the public and international understanding of the action he had taken today. Denton had no intention of returning the President or Speaker to power, they were the people who had agreed to cede power to the Committee in the first place, but he understood that exposing their imprisonment would be a powerful tool in the battle for hearts and minds. To expose the secret imprisonment of the leaders of the last elected government of the United States would delegitimize the Committee in the eyes of all but the most hardcore true believers.

"Admiral, here is the update from Petersburg," an Army Major announced while striding to Denton's desk. Denton took the update from the Major's grasp and, with a deep sigh of anticipation, read the report.

"Federal Correctional Institute, Petersburg. Mission complete. Resistance was brief but violent. Suffered two dead and three wounded. Most of the prison personnel surrendered along with a few suicides. No prisoners remain. Repeat: no prisoners remain. All prisoners executed by the Committee. Informed that the President, Vice President, First Lady, and Speaker were executed eighteen months ago and are interred on a farm SW of Petersburg. Sending team to verify and exhume."

Denton suppressed his emotions and ordered the Major, "I want immediate confirmation on the fate of the President. Additionally, I want to know the moment the virtual reality feed is cut."

30
Who else is here?

George Wesley lounged in the recliner watching his name and photo being displayed on the television. Wesley was correctly identified as one of the six shooters in the Tribell massacre, and he presently relaxed in the safe house that he had prepared, awaiting the arrival of his five accomplices. One by one the television had shown the names and photos of his fellow shooters as well as a description of their vehicles and license plate numbers.

Wesley had foreseen the possibility that the Committee could lose power and had spent months preparing the safe house; stashing away enough food to last seven people a month, he had acquired weapons, ammunition, all the ingredients required to manufacture Molotov cocktails plus extra fuel for vehicles. Wesley was not only preparing to hide out but to participate in a counter-counter-revolution.

A light knock on the door drew the attention of Wesley and his girlfriend, Sheri, away from the television. Sheri arose from the couch and looked through the peephole, then opened the door. A tall thin man in his mid-twenties entered the room as Wesley said, “Glad you made it.”

“Who else is here?” the man known as Will said.

“Just us so far,” replied Sheri.

Will settled onto the couch.

“You followed the protocol?” Wesley asked.

“Oh yeah, I ditched the company car down by Sheridan and Twelfth. Stole a van, ditched it in Broomfield, stole a Toyota and dropped it two miles from here,” Will responded.

“Good man,” Wesley said proudly.

Another knock on the door and Sheri got up to go to the peephole again. Opening the door an older stockier man entered.

“Howdy,” said Jay.

“Welcome,” replied Sheri.

“Are we it so far?” queried Jay.

“So far,” responded Wesley.

Wesley, Sheri, Will, and Jay sat in the house for another three days before concluding that the rest of the team had either found alternate refuge or been apprehended.

31
The hood of the Wagoneer

Ray and Jerry leaned on the hood of the Wagoneer that was parked on Alameda in front of the Federal Center.

"Restoring state government and a constitutional convention was probably the best we could have hoped for," Jerry remarked, looking over his shoulder at the security headquarters that was now teeming with air force personnel that had arrived from Buckley Air Force base.

"Glad somebody has a plan. Hopefully it works and they mean what they say. With any luck this place doesn't turn into Baghdad," Ray responded.

"A hint about where you came from?" Jerry asked teasingly.

"Maybe. Guess I should've said Mogadishu."

"I noticed it wasn't Damascus."

"No, it wasn't, was it," Ray laughed.

Ray had dismissed the rest of his cell just minutes before, telling them to go home and care for their families and neighbors. Ray was feeling the bittersweet emotions of knowing that the cell that he had so carefully hand-picked, trained, and led for more than eighteen months had flawlessly performed their mission and that they most likely would never be called on again.

Ray wondered how one could appropriately recognize and thank those who risk everything with no promise of success? Hopefully a shot at renewed freedom would be enough thanks for them. Ray understood it always would be and always had been this way, the few who risk everything in relative anonymity in order that all may benefit.

"What now?" Jerry asked.

"I'm of a mind to go find a couple of infiltrators named Katie Davis and Gary Weiss. I appreciate the sentiment of the military in standing up a state government and letting them handle who is deserving of what justice, but those two having additional time to get away doesn't sit well with me," Ray replied.

"That will be like looking for a needle in an infinite number of haystacks," Jerry advised.

"Yeah, it will be difficult, but I detest the notion that they'll get weeks or months of a head start. It took fifteen years to track down Eichmann. Mengele never was brought to justice. I'm not saying that these two rise to the level of Eichmann and Mengele, but it took years to find the big names, or they were not found at all. Most of the actual shooters of the Einsatzgruppen simply walked with no justice at all. I suspect that even with all of the attention paid internationally to the Tribell murder, the enthusiasm to find these two will die quickly. I'd prefer they get some justice rather than living their lives out in Brazil."

"What do you think?"

"I think they'll be heading to Mexico. I-25 is the straightest line to get there, at least until you get past Las Vegas, New Mexico. Even then, I-25 might be quicker than state highways to the border, or at least they might think it is. Then again they might assume the military is patrolling I-25 so...."

"I'm in if you want me. What are we going to do for fuel?"

"Perhaps the question to ask is what will they do for fuel? We figure that out, we might figure them out," Ray responded.

"I know someone who might be of assistance," responded Jerry.

"Let us go talk to the Chair Force guys again and see if they can help us out at all," Ray suggested.

32
My sister in Canon City

Brody finished loading his suitcases into the Expedition. He had packed his remaining valuables, souvenirs, ammunition, and a few clothes. Seven suitcases. Upon further consideration he had decided that relocating to a new city was the wiser course. He had no intention of ever returning to his apartment in Englewood.

"Are you going somewhere?"

Brody turned to see elderly Mrs. Larson. Brody had always found her nosiness to be a particular tweak to his ego. In fact, he had often fantasized about shooting her.

"I'm going to see my sister in Canon City. Since things have changed, I'm hoping to be able to find her."

"That's a lot of luggage," Mrs. Larson observed.

"Well, I have some of her stuff to get to her."

"What about gasoline?" Mrs. Larson asked curiously. "That's a long ways."

"Well hopefully the kindness of others will help me out," Brody replied.

"Huh," snorted Mrs. Larson derisively while walking away.

Brody had acquired the skill to be convincing in the style typical of accomplished serial killers.

He closed the rear gate on the Expedition and moved to stand in the shadows to await the arrival of his passengers.

It was only a few minutes later that his passengers walked into the parking lot. Gary was carrying a suitcase and Katie a backpack. Brody thought to himself, *Traveling light*, as he emerged from the shadow.

"Let's go," whispered Brody to their backs as the two turned around to face him in the dark.

Gary placed the suitcase in the back and he, Katie, and Brody got into the Expedition, Katie in the front seat beside Brody and Gary in the backseat directly behind Brody. Brody thought to himself that was an odd seating arrangement.

They pulled out of the parking lot of the apartment building near Belleview and Broadway and headed west on Belleview then south on

Santa Fe. It was on US 85 just south of 470 that Brody said, "I have another passenger to pick up on the way."

"No, no way. We're it!" stormed Gary.

"We take who I say we take, and I have another seat open," Brody responded calmly. Brody was practiced at this conversation.

"Not acceptable, don't do it," Gary said firmly.

"We really don't want another passenger. We'll pay more," Katie said.

"I don't go to the border without a full car," Brody responded.

"No," said Gary.

Brody turned west at Sedalia onto Jarre Canyon Road, and Katie and Gary held their breath. This was the route one would take to where they had killed John Tribell. Katie and Gary both wondered if they were being set up, if they were being taken to where they killed Tribell in order to be executed. Could Brody be part of the resistance?

Gary silently drew his Sig P938 and held it closely against his leg in the dark SUV.

Katie and Gary held their breaths as Brody drove through Sedalia and only exhaled when Brody turned south on 105 after crossing Plum Creek.

"It's just a short distance to where we'll pick her up," Brody said.

"Her?" Katie and Gary said almost in unison.

"We don't want another passenger. Don't do this," Gary said once again.

"She won't be a problem for you, trust me," Brody responded.

"Don't do this," Gary reemphasized.

Brody sped down the two-lane 105 only slowing when he approached Wolfensberger Road and then turning right onto the dirt path into Bear Canon Cemetery. Brody drove to the southwest corner of the old cemetery behind the church and parked.

"She should be here somewhere," Brody remarked and as he exited the Expedition he called to Gary over his shoulder. "You two might as well get out and stretch your legs, this'll be the last stop for a long time."

Gary and Katy looked at each other before Gary opened the car door and got out.

Brody had wandered behind the car a good distance and drew his Makarov while hidden in the darkness and pretending to look for his passenger. When he turned around, he noticed that Gary and Katie were both standing at the back of the Expedition but on different sides of the car. In the several hundred times that Brody had done this, it was the first time a couple didn't stand next to each other.

Well this will make it more difficult, Brody thought.

"I think that's her over there," Brody said pointing behind Gary and Katie while walking toward the car.

Brody was perturbed that only Katie turned to look.

Brody knew this would be much more difficult. He was accustomed to leisurely shooting his victims in the back of the head. He was now shaking but knew that he was committed.

Brody leveled his Makarov at Gary and fired a round that missed to the left. Brody quickly went to pull the trigger again, and it would not pull.

Gary raised his Sig and fired once, hitting Brody in the xiphisternum. Brody went down immediately.

Gary walked to where Brody bled out on the ground and kicked him lightly. Gary bent over and picked up the Makarov.

"Looks like the second round failed to load, probably the magazine spring." Gary commented calmly.

"What an idiot. Did he really think we'd pay him to take us to Mexico?" Katie remarked.

Gary walked to the Expedition and leaned in the door and turned the key. The instrument panel came to life and Gary thought, *Damn, we need gas*.

In their home across the road from the cemetery, Wilma and Jeff heard the sound of a vehicle, voices, and then two gunshots. Jeff and Wilma had lived in this house for twenty years before the hard times, and it had been idyllic: a large home on thirty-five acres in the West Plum Creek valley at the foot of the Rampart Range. Once the hard times hit, their horses had been stolen and presumed eaten, their dogs had disappeared, and they lived on rations and a garden. The neighbors had all given up and left, hoping for something safer and easier in the city. Now Wilma and Jeff sat in the large house in the dark, frozen by the sound of gunshots so near.

Jeff quietly arose and took his Winchester Model 70 off the gun rack on the wall. He opened and closed the bolt quickly to confirm it was loaded.

He stood in the dark living room and listened.

"Help me, help me please," Jeff and Wilma could hear the voice of a woman calling out.

"Oh!" Wilma exclaimed.

"Help me," the female voice cried.

Jeff opened the front door as quietly as he could and stepped out on the porch. He and Wilma could now hear the voice quite clearly and the voice was close.

Jeff and Wilma took a few steps toward the voice that continued to cry out and then stopped and listened. They repeated this process until they arrived at the gate of the cemetery.

Jeff whispered to Wilma, “Stay here,” while he flipped the safety off on the Model 70. Jeff took half a dozen steps into the cemetery and just passed a large cedar tree when a bullet pierced the side of his head at close range.

Wilma shrieked in horror as a man stepped from behind the cedar tree, pointed the gun at Wilma and said, “We need gas.”

33
Are you going to hunt them down?

Ray and Jerry pulled up in the Wagoneer in front of the Ken Caryl Ranch home of Diane Andrews.

"So, she knew Katie Davis and Gary Weiss?" Ray asked.

"In the early days of the Committee, she interfaced with those two on infiltration Then Diane realized, as so many of us in security did, that this was not about restoring order and the 'essentials of life' and asked for reassignment. Diane knows these two better than anyone else friendly to us," Jerry responded.

After knocking on the door and being invited in, Jerry got right to the point.

"We're going to find Gary Weiss and Katie Davis. What can you tell us that could help us find them? What do we need to know?" Jerry asked.

"Seriously, you're going to hunt them down?" Diane queried back.

"Yes."

Diane got a faraway look in her eyes and then furrowed her brow.

"I'm going with you then. Let me pack a few things and I'll be right down. I can tell you all about them while we drive."

Diane returned quickly with an overnight bag and said, "Let's go."

Ray steered the Wagoneer to the on-ramp for 470 as Diane began to speak.

"I worked with them both the first six weeks of the Committee. I quickly recommended to Herzfelt that they not be used. I was dressed down for that recommendation, and I asked for a transfer. I ended up guarding a food ration center in Arvada. They're both true believers, but Gary is smarter than Katie. Katie is the more beguiling. I don't know that Katie has ever been out of Denver or Boulder in her life other than to assassinate people. She genuinely believes that if you go ten miles outside of Denver everyone is a Klansman and they're all racist, sexist, homophobes and they all deserve to die. That's how she thinks. She's bought into the whole Progressive socialist justice warrior bullshit and has no moral issue extrapolating that ideology out to its logical end. She views herself as an avenging angel for racism, sexism, you get the idea—and in her mind the definition of a racist or sexist is anyone who disagrees with her.

"Gary has travelled a bit. He's more opportunistic and more likely to go with the flow, be that good or bad. He's probably not willing to die for the ideology as Katie is but Gary is certainly willing to kill for self-preservation. He was more reticent to kill when he started, but he quickly developed a taste for it. Katie was eager to kill."

"We figure they're heading to Mexico. Sound right to you?" Ray said.

"Oh yes, especially because Gary will drive that boat," replied Diane.

"Any hints on how to track them?" Jerry asked.

"Follow the bodies," responded Diane.

"Anything more substantial than that?" Ray asked.

"They'll be like fish out of water in southern Colorado and New Mexico. Assuming they can't acquire large amounts of gasoline at any one time, they'll have to stop and acquire gasoline often. People will remember them. There's no tie between these two, other than the desire to survive. Conceivable that they could turn on each other if they're put in a situation where selling the other one out meant that they would survive. Do we know what vehicle they're driving?"

"Probably not. We know what vehicles they had, but based on what you just told us, there's probably already a body lying somewhere next to the car they started out in," replied Ray.

"Do we have any help in this endeavor?" Diana asked.

"Marginal. The military isn't wanting to get involved in law enforcement, they want to stand up the local and state governments and hand law enforcement off to them quickly. After a protracted negotiation before we got to your house, we did convince the Air Force to send the photographs of Gary Weiss and Katie Davis out to all of the forces in the regional command along with an explanation of who they are and an agreement to continue to show the photographs on television. We convinced them that letting the killers of John Tribell slip out of the country would be a bad start for them. They saw the logic in that. We were also able to sufficiently convince some Air Men of the importance in what we were doing so they gave us a full tank of gas," Jerry said.

"If Weiss and Davis get a full tank of gas they could be in Trinidad or farther by morning," Ray commented.

"Wolverines, baby," responded Jerry.

"Let's see what the radio has to say," said Ray.

34
We aren't sightseeing

"... and the Committee for the Continuance of Government has been detained. Citizens are asked to continue to be on the lookout for Gary Weiss and..."

Gary reached over and turned the radio off as the Expedition rolled south on highway 105 toward Palmer Lake.

"We need to figure out some gasoline. We got like three gallons at that house. We may not even have a hundred miles worth in the tank," Gary said.

"Chances of finding a place to even steal anything but a few gallons from this late at night are pretty much zero," replied Katie.

"The farther we go south the less there'll be," Gary said.

"I've never been this far before. We have to be close to the Ludlow Massacre, right?" Katie asked.

"I think that's quite a ways yet," Gary responded.

"Well we have to stop there. We have to pay our respects. The capitalist and the army slaughtered innocent people. We have to stop there," Katie demanded.

"Ummm, we're on the run for our lives. We aren't sightseeing," Gary stammered.

"No, we'll be stopping when we get there," Katie asserted.

Gary gave up on arguing and started hoping that Katie would go to sleep or something.

They sat in silence while the Expedition entered the town of Palmer Lake and came to a stop sign at a T intersection. Gary turned right and continued on 105 into Monument and onto I-25 south.

"What's the plan?" Katie asked.

"Find some gas to steal, maybe a small town farther south. If we only get one or two or three gallons at a time, it will be tough to make it to Mexico," Gary replied.

"That's not much of a plan," Katie criticized.

"Do you have a better one?" Gary retorted.

"I just figured that since you said you knew what you were doing you had a plan is all," replied Katie sarcastically.

"I do have a plan, I plan to get to Mexico alive," Gary exasperatingly responded.

"That's a goal, not a plan, don't you know the difference?" Katie said opening the wound she had inflicted on Gary's ego a bit wider.

"I know the difference," Gary shot back.

"Well then what's the plan?" Katie retorted.

Gary sat and steamed in silence.

As the Expedition rolled south on I-25 Katie saw the road sign for the now closed Air Force Academy.

"Bastards," Katie muttered.

"You need to get in the back seat and lie down," Gary said as he steered the Expedition to an off-ramp.

"What the hell?" Katie shot back.

"Colorado Springs has, like, three air force bases and an army base, and if there are patrols looking for us anywhere, this is the place. They're looking for a man and a woman, and if they only see a man, we have a better chance."

Katie climbed between the front bucket seats and laid down on the floorboard in the back as Gary guided the Expedition down the off-ramp.

"You suck."

Gary exited I-25 and headed east and then south through Colorado Springs, working his way down side streets and boulevards. The effort took nearly an hour and a half, wandering through neighborhoods until they re-entered I-25 at Fountain.

"Okay, you can get back up," Gary informed Katie when he returned to I-25.

"You suck," Katie repeated as she climbed back into the front seat.

They drove in silence until after they passed through Pueblo and Gary noticed the fuel warning light started to flash on the Expedition.

"We'll need gas soon," Gary remarked.

Katie rolled her eyes.

"You have no plan, do you?"

Gary ignored Katie and drove down the interstate looking for a likely spot to steal gasoline. When he saw a road sign for Colorado City and Rye, he decided that was his best bet, and he exited the interstate.

Gary and Katie found that Colorado City seemed to be nothing more than abandoned buildings and abandoned cars. Gary noticed on his left an abandoned gas station and behind that an old motel with a parking lot populated with what looked to be abandoned cars.

Driving slowly through the motel parking lot, scanning for a car that still had the gas cap in place, a Camry came in to view that Gary thought was a good bet for gasoline. He pulled up next to the Camry and turned the Expedition off, leaving the key in the ignition. Exiting the Ford, he opened the tailgate and unzipped his suitcase and removed a rubber tube. He removed the gas cap on the Expedition, pried open the door over the gas filler on the Camry, and then removed the gas cap. He inserted the tube into the gas filler of the Toyota.

Gary turned to Katie, who had exited the Ford, and said, "Hopefully—"

Before Gary could finish his sentence, a gunshot broke the calm of the night, followed immediately by a second shot. Katie ducked below the Camry, turned and ran the few steps to the passenger door of the Expedition as the second shot ripped through Gary's shoulder.

Katie scrambled over the passenger side and into the driver's seat, turning the key in the ignition before she even sat down. As Katie was shifting the Expedition into reverse Gary was crawling into the passenger door that Katie had not bothered to close in her panic.

Gary was screaming as Katie rammed an abandoned Pontiac behind the Expedition. Slamming the transmission into drive, the luggage in the back of the Ford spilled out of the open tailgate and into the motel parking lot as Katie accelerated the short distance onto Colorado 165 and then south on the interstate.

Gary was screaming for help and a doctor and swearing as Katie was in full panic mode. It wasn't until she reached the Apishapa River that Katie began to get her wits about her. She looked at the dash and it registered that she must be nearly out of gas. Katie then looked at the speedometer and realized she was going ninety miles per hour. She let off the accelerator and allowed the Expedition to slowdown. Next, she looked at Gary. He was holding his left hand on his right shoulder and there was blood everywhere on his side of the car. He was moaning and screaming and cursing and calling for his mother.

Katie was attempting to discipline herself sufficiently to formulate a plan when she passed the road sign for the Ludlow Massacre Site.

Katie thought, *This is it*. The romantic in her kicked in. She's out of gas, and Gary's shot. They'll make a last stand at the Ludlow site. Katie thought she'd be honored to die in a blaze of gunfire at the Ludlow site. How appropriate. Her heart swelled. Katie took the exit and headed west on a narrow, neglected two-lane county road. The sun was just rising behind the hunted pair as she viewed the sign, "United Mine Workers" with "District 15" in faded red below.

She turned into the parking lot behind the sign. In the first light of dawn she saw a chain link fence with a gate surrounding a pavilion and a building and what seemed to be placards. Katie parked and turned the ignition off.

"Where are we? What are you doing?" Gary moaned.

"We're at Ludlow!" Katie exclaimed.

Gary was momentarily silent in his shock and disbelief.

Katie got out of the Expedition and walked the fence until she arrived at the gate. She entered and began reading the placards one by one, then paid homage to the monument. She stared at Water Tank Hill, where the Colorado National Guard had long ago placed a machine gun in order to rake the tent village where the striking miners and their families lived on this very spot. Katie could hear Gary moaning in the Ford, and it annoyed her.

Evil, evil, evil, Katie thought. *How could the army and the capitalist slaughter innocent men, women, and children? How could they do that? They all deserve to die.*

Her focus was broken by a white Chevrolet pickup truck pulling into the parking lot. Katie walked toward the Chevy as the driver of the truck parked and exited.

The man driving the truck called out, "Can I help you? I can give you a ride to Aguilar," as the moaning from the Expedition drew his glance.

It was at that moment that Katie shot him.

Katie then strode toward the Expedition and opened the passenger door.

Gary looked up at her, grasping his shoulder.

"You were weak," Katie said accusingly as she shot Gary.

Katie them mumbled, "What idiots," as she walked to the Chevy pickup.

35
Arguing over who will get to abuse power

Admiral Denton looked each of the officers seated around the table in the eyes before he began to speak.

"It's been a month since we dissolved the Committee for the Continuance for Government. You all have the data, but we need to discuss what is happening and what we do next. There have been pleasant surprises and less pleasant surprises. What is the latest on the virtual reality addicts?"

"As you know, Admiral, when we cut the feed to the virtual reality centers the people inside the theaters remained, as though they were waiting for the feed to return. In some locations more people showed up, and they waited. We physically closed the centers, and they lined up outside to wait, as though the centers would be reopening. While the trend has been edging downward in terms of numbers, there are still people lined up outside the virtual reality centers as though they expect them to reopen. Informing them that the outcome they anticipate will not materialize has little effect. God help these people. I don't know what the states will do with them," replied General Baumgartner.

"Incredible," said General Nash.

"What are your updates, Admiral Wright?"

"We're slowly normalizing relationships with the rest of the world. The United Kingdom, Japan, Mexico, Canada, and India have proposed contributing to the recapitalization of an American banking system. Taking into consideration the political situation, I think we move on that offer immediately. The world is by and large sympathetic to our goals and supportive of our means. China and Russia and their vassals are the only countries protesting."

"The political side of it's the headache. We've reassembled the state legislatures and governors in all of the fifty states now, and most of them have simply picked up where they left off as though the last two years never happened. All they do is bicker, and most of the bickering is nothing more than arguing over who will get to abuse power to their own advantage. They're just as divided and ineffective as they were two years ago. We've handed over responsibility in a handful of states—Arkansas, Idaho, Wyoming, North Dakota, New Hampshire—but the rest don't want the responsibility. Well, except New York, and they want to form something akin to their very own Committee for the Continuance of Government," said General Nash.

"All these state legislatures care about are grand gestures and moralizing. The concept of rebuilding their states fills them with dread. Other than the handful mentioned, they have no interest in rebuilding whatsoever," General McNeil asserted.

"If the hope was that we'd find a Jefferson and Adams out there, then we have struck out so far," remarked Admiral Ziegler, "We don't even have a Hamilton. Just a bunch of Burrs."

"These state legislatures have no skin in the game. They're perfectly happy if we continue to provide food, fuel, and medicine and they can spend their time dicking around with things that don't matter but that make them feel important and eventually put cash in their pockets," chimed in General Baumgartner.

"They spend their time figuring out how they can individually gain power and prosperity instead of how to rebuild their states," said General Helfrich.

"The state legislatures have fallen into thinking that we're their bureaucracy, that we'll feed people while they make speeches," General Baumgartner added.

"Why don't we give them skin in the game then?" asked Admiral Denton.

"It's a major risk to require these legislatures to be responsible for food, fuel, or medicine," said General Martinez. "In many cases it will require interstate cooperation."

"We'd be courting significant peril. It's not possible to overstate the hubris, incompetency, and rent-seeking of these state legislatures. I can't see to trust them with the delivery of food, medicine, and fuel," Admiral Andersen commented.

"I wouldn't trust their ability to pour pee out of a boot if the instructions were written under the heel," Admiral Ziegler added.

"What other choices do we have, gentleman?" Admiral Denton asked, "Shall we not require them to sink or swim?"

36
Whirlwind of hope, emotion, and disappointment

Chris Malone found himself on the west steps of the capitol in Denver ready to address the crowd.

The last month had been a whirlwind of hope, emotion, and disappointment for Chris. The dissolution of the Committee had relieved him of the fight with his conscience over resistance and filled him with hope that his daughters could inherit a better world. He cried when the military announced a constitutional convention. That had all been followed by the disappointment of the Colorado state legislature. The legislature was so ineffective that his neighbor called it a goat-rope.

The goat-rope comment had been the start. Following that comment Chris discussed with his neighbor the history of the United States constitution and what it was intended to accomplish. He explained the role of the Colorado state constitution to his neighbor as well. The neighbor then relayed the conversation to other people, and those people came to talk to Chris. It then snowballed, people from other neighborhoods came to talk to Chris. People were eager to understand what the schools had failed to teach them, and they understood how this information was applicable to their current situation.

What the people who sought Chris out didn't understand was why the state legislature didn't know what Chris knew. Chris patiently pointed out that some in the state legislature did know but found it convenient to forget. When asked what could be done about helping them to remember Chris said to show up en masse.

Now Chris stood on the capitol steps to address those who organized en masse.

"Thank you for coming here today. We're here to urge our legislature to action. There's disappointment in the air. Disappointment that this legislature cannot do what previous legislatures were able to do. You see, government based on a constitution is not new. A constitution is a document that limits government and the power of government. A constitution is we the people telling government what we the people are willing to empower government to do. This is not that hard. This has been done many times before. It's been done before in this state. The only thing that makes it hard is greed, corruption, ego, and ignorance."

Chris continued explaining the constitution and what constitutional government meant in practical terms.

Chris closed his exhortation with, "Demand that these people do their jobs, the jobs that the constitution requires them to do and not the job that they pretend to do."

Chris was quite unaware that his speech was recorded by a video camera operated by a soldier from Fort Carson. The video was quickly sent to the Pentagon and was shown to Admiral Denton less than two hours after Chris spoke.

"What do you think, Admiral?" General Martinez asked.

"I think it should be on all of the television stations in the country tonight. It may not be Jefferson, but it's a cogent explanation of the duties of a state legislature. It may spark a few people to demand that their legislatures get their act together," Denton responded.

"Yes sir. Will do," replied Martinez.

"Tomorrow morning, I want you to inform all of the legislatures that we'll be handing over control in two weeks. Emphasize that they need to get their acts together."

37
We are in control here

"What do they mean we have two weeks?" state senator Jeff McCoy stammered. "We are in control here. We'll assume control when we're ready!"

"Umm, Jeff, control is what they're giving you," replied state senate leader Joshua Mills.

"There are so many things that we have to resolve—healthcare, transportation, taxes, education…" state senator Cassie Roseman said to no one in particular.

"This is crazy!" proclaimed McCoy.

"It will take at least a year, maybe two," responded Roseman.

"Well you don't have a year or two, you have two weeks," replied Mills.

"Time to man up," said state senator Brian Barnes.

"You sexist," Roseman chided.

"Yeah, yeah, yeah," Barnes shot back.

"It will take at least a year to stand up a proper government," Roseman said.

"You mean at least a year for your brother-in-law to get his businesses up and running so you can write legislation to give him contracts? You mean that?" Barnes replied.

"Fuck you," Roseman said.

"Classy," Barnes replied.

"We have two weeks to come up with and execute on a system to deliver food, medicine, and fuel to the people of Colorado," Mills interjected, "and work with other states in doing so."

"That's not enough time. What the Committee did was horrible, but their goal of an equitable society was admirable, and we should adopt that goal. They just didn't do it right! We can be smarter," McCoy said.

"We need time to devise a system for a fair and equitable distribution," chimed in Roseman.

"You have two weeks," Mills said.

"We start with what we have: have the military explain to us how they do it, take it over with our own people, and start figuring out how to improve on that. Seems pretty straightforward to me," said Barnes.

"The hard part will be transitioning back to a market," Mills said.

"Well, we have a market. A black market, but a market," Barnes responded.

"That's inherently unfair!" Roseman interjected.

"If you're proposing legalizing the black market, that's just wrong!" stormed McCoy.

"It's okay that we can have markets. We all agree on that. We're not Bolsheviks, you know, but those markets have to be sufficiently regulated so they're fair!" Roseman asserted.

"You all want to force people to do as you think they should do and take their stuff, and have anyone who engages in commerce pay tribute to the state. That's your entire political argument," Barnes chided.

"That's simply not true, Senator Barnes!" Cassie rebutted.

"Oh, it's true. What have you ever proposed that was not a tax, law, regulation, or some other further interference into the lives of people?" Barnes shot back.

"We're here to pass laws, taxes, and regulations. That's the basis of all political ideologies. That's why we have a legislature!" Roseman barked.

"Well, no it's not the basis of all ideologies, and if you would read the state constitution, you'd realize that's not why you're here," Barnes replied calmly.

"Wouldn't hurt you to actually read the state constitution, Cassie," Mills interjected. "Senator Barnes isn't wrong."

"We need to create regulations for markets and we need to hire the people to regulate those markets. That will take time! What if someone sells poison whiskey? Food that makes people sick? What if someone won't sell to a marginalized community? Our primary duty as a state legislature is to make these things safe and fair! What if someone sells raw milk? Those deaths will be on your hands!" McCoy asserted.

"Well, if you were to read the state constitution and if you had listened to the fellow on the capitol steps yesterday, you would know that wasn't your duty, primary or otherwise," Barnes rebuked.

Marcie Bernstein had sat silently listening to the conversation and decided that it was time to weigh in, "These black markets are indeed markets. If we legalize these markets and allow them to expand unhindered, they'll eventually grow to the point that the need for the state to deliver fuel, food, and medicine will no longer be necessary. The television last night announced that the offer by other countries to help stand up a banking system has been accepted. That should lead to a currency that has some value. If someone has apples to sell, why should we interfere? If someone wants to make beer and sell it, why should we interfere?"

"Because they may not do it fairly! Because some people may not be able to afford what they need!" Roseman argued.

"You may want to revisit that 'not Bolsheviks' comment, Cassie," Barnes said pointedly.

"Fuck you," Roseman replied.

"Come on, Cassie, you secretly loved the Committee for the Continuance of Government, didn't you?" Barnes alleged.

"Knock it off!" Mills said firmly. "We have two weeks. Arguing for an additional year or two is pointless. You won't have the personnel to regulate anything. I agree with the obnoxious senator Barnes. Let's go learn how the military is doing this, take it over, and legalize all markets. There're no other options on the table that are workable. Senator Bernstein, draft the legislation today, and it'll be assigned to the Local Government committee. As chair of that committee, you'll also sponsor the bill. We'll have a first reading tomorrow, second reading the day after, third reading on Thursday and we'll vote on Friday. Anyone who votes against it can explain to the people of Colorado why they're no longer receiving food, fuel, and medicine. I'll go inform the Speaker of what we're doing."

38
Watching the Platte flow by

Ray sat on the tailgate of the Wagoneer watching the Platte flow by.

All in all, he thought that everything had gone as well as it could go the last few weeks. The United States had not turned into Bagdad, Mogadishu, or Damascus. There was a path forward to standing up a banking system, a useful currency, and a legitimate Federal government. Some states were openly discussing secession and even talked of forming new unions among them after they seceded. The constitutional convention was still on course.

The one thing that Ray regretted was not finding Katie Davis.

They had found the body of Gary Weiss in the parking lot of the Ludlow Massacre site, along with another man. They had only checked the monument on the advice of Diane Andrews who insightfully observed that it was the type of place that would be difficult for Katie to pass without stopping. They had reasonably assumed that Katie had killed the wounded Gary and killed the other man and taken his vehicle.

A day of investigative work revealed that the identity of the other man was Ramon Vigil and that he had been driving a white Chevrolet pickup.

After that, the Katie trail went cold. They headed south checking in Raton, Cimarron, Las Vegas, and Albuquerque and found no one who recalled seeing Katie. They checked in Roswell with no luck.

Ray, Jerry, and Diana had returned to Denver after visiting Roswell, and nothing of Katie had subsequently been heard. The trail was completely cold.

Ray pondered whether Katie had been captured in Mexico. As much as he desired to wonder if that was true, he dismissed the possibility. If she had been caught, Mexico would have made an announcement. Katie was too big a fish not to be bragged about.

Ray knew that the reality was that Katie could be anywhere.

39
Some god must give It to them

Chris Malone sat down on the bus bench next to state senate leader, Joshua Mills. Unbeknownst to them, it was the same bench on Lincoln Street that John Tribell and Katie Davis had once sat on together.

"Nice to meet you senator," Malone said.

"Nice to meet you. Quite the speech you gave. I'm given to understand that the video was broadcast all over the country. It was something that people needed to hear," Mills said.

"Well, no offense, but politicians in this country forgot what their actual jobs were decades ago. It appeared to these politicians that there would be unlimited credit and endless prosperity and a unipolar world forever. The politicians thought they could do the job that they pretended to have rather than the job the state and Federal constitutions required of them," replied Malone.

"No offense taken, it was especially striking for you to point out that the legislature is not constitutionally empowered to determine what 'fair' is, let alone implement fairness. That the constitution empowers the legislature to protect individual rights rather than implement fairness was an unwelcome shock to a lot of people, including some in the state legislature," observed Mills.

"It has been said that bureaucracy maximizes the distance between a decision-maker and the risk of the decision. Quite a few legislators are discovering that without a bureaucracy, there'll be a direct connection between the decision they make and the quality of life of their constituents. They've never before experienced that. I suspect that the hesitancy we're experiencing is that some of these legislators are scared of making a decision without a bureaucracy to buffer them from the people," Malone replied.

"Without money and a bureaucracy even the most hardcore Progressive has no choice but a free market," Mills said, "but they're not done yet. Trust me. I anticipate they'll move to sabotage all they can, then argue the market failed, then grab as much power as possible."

"Debt and force eradicated what actually creates prosperity and abundance from the consciousness of many people. People believed that abundance and prosperity was an entitlement and that labor and ingenuity and risk-taking by individuals other than themselves, the very things that produced that abundance and prosperity, were somehow not a factor or were even evil activities. They came to believe that government would provide for them when in truth government was simply a parasite reallocating what others had fought to create. The government borrowed and borrowed to fulfill the expectations of entitlement until it could borrow no more – and the whole economy crashed. The ideology was one of government as parent and the entitled as child, or perhaps it was a theology where government was god." Chris said.

Chris continued, "The best a government can do is to protect individual rights and property rights and enforce laws against hurting people and stealing things. Whenever government has viewed their job as making things fair, they've entered a black hole of abuse that always institutionalizes unfairness. At that point it simply becomes a competition between factions fighting over who will profit from the unfairness and who will suffer from the unfairness. The basic problem with government-enforced fairness is that society loses elasticity. It becomes brittle. That's what happened to us, and once government proclaims itself the arbiter of what is fair, it's loath to ever alter its course—no matter how obviously wrong or unfair that course is—for fear of appearing unfair based on its own doctrine of what it's already defined as fair. When a government has proclaimed that it's empowered to determine what fair is, then it's boxed itself in. Government will then heap bad ideas on top of bad ideas in order to comply with its own arbitrary definition of fair, which is actually just the outcome of factionalism, and stacks absurdities on top of absurdities. This is the great trap when you leave it up to politics rather than society to define what is fair. This stroll through the irrational always arrives at the same destination—government using force against the very people they claim to represent in the name of fairness."

"For decades politicians were elected with the intent to use their position to get rich while the country was actually governed by unelected bureaucrats. We mistakenly called that democracy," Malone added as an afterthought.

Mills sat back on the bench.

"What did you do before the hard times?" Mills queried.

"I wrote history, primarily the history of the Soviet Union. When the debt crisis hit, I was working on a dystopian novel, but the country became, you know, dystopian before I could get it published," responded Malone.

"I'd like you to speak everywhere you can. If you come speak on the steps of the capitol every day, I'm good with that. Once we take over food and fuel and such, this is likely to get politically nasty."

"Socialists never admit to defeat. They truly believe in their own supremacy, and they can morally rationalize whatever means are required to gain control and implement their vision because they believe in the end goal of that utopia. Progressivism is an ideology promising to use force to take people's property from them and to use force to require people to do what Progressives believe they should be doing, and their argument is that they're making it fair. That's been the argument they've made since 1848. They believe just a little force here and a little force there, and it'll all be utopia. Of course, they justify it all by personifying anyone who opposes them as evil, racist, sexist, homophobe, whatever term they believe will resonate with the audience. Don't forget that socialists always eventually get around to blaming the Jews, too. What they hate more than anything are people who refuse to knuckle under. The truth is, a little force never makes it fair, so they apply more and more force that inevitably results in ever increasing unfairness. If you could create utopia by force, people would have figured that out thousands of years ago. Unfortunately, we're decades beyond most Americans understanding even rudimentary economics. People hear a promise that Progressives will make their lives easier, that they will seemingly get something for nothing, that someone is being unfair to them, and if we just get the right leaders and give them the right amount of power then we can end the unfairness, that they will get to spend their time in leisure rather than labor, and people eat it up. That the promise inevitably ends in death, misery; and poverty is always excused with 'but they didn't do it right,'" Malone mused.

"I've heard those words already this week from legislators, that the goals of the Committee were admirable, and we should adopt those goals and the Committee was on the righteous path but just didn't do it correctly," replied Mills.

"I'm not surprised. One would assume that after Lenin, Trotsky, Stalin, Hitler, Ho Chi Minh, Pol Pot, Mao, and the Committee for the Continuance of Government that people would figure this out, but they just don't," Chris responded.

"These folks are more likely to point to people like FDR," Mills said.

"You mean the guy who created concentration camps to intern American citizens and invited Mussolini's Fascist from Italy to come to DC and help draft legislation, that guy? That's as close as America came to a dictatorship before the Committee," Chris said mockingly.

Mills replied, "I think they look to FDR as a time that the United States was united in purpose."

"Indeed, Americans were united but they mistakenly attribute that to policy rather than Pearl Harbor. Roosevelt's actual New Deal policies ranged from ineffective to disaster. What united the country was the Japanese attack. At that specific point in time, with those specific Americans, the reaction of the citizens of this country was to crush the Japanese and Germans regardless of what sacrifices were required. The people were united in purpose to win the war unconditionally and that FDR was a Democrat and Eisenhower and MacArthur were Republicans was irrelevant to what they were united to accomplish. That unity carried over for nearly twenty years after the war, but it had nothing to do with FDR's economic and social policies."

"Yeah, they tend not to look at it that way," Mills replied. "They'll say it was progressivism not the Japanese. They want to make the same promises as the Committee made and they intend to fulfill those promises using the same methods. They truly believe that they can do it better, everyone before them just did it wrong. They don't grasp these promises are identical to the promises made by Lenin and Hitler and Mao and so forth."

"Of course not. The thing they're completely naïve about, and perhaps intentionally so, is that the people who supported Hitler and Lenin and Pol Pot and Mao also didn't sign up for what eventually happened. The people that supported the mass murderers didn't sign up for mass murder, they signed up for all the promises of socialism. The promises identical to those made by the Committee and the promises identical to those made by members of our own state legislature. That's the fundamental dishonesty."

"As was once written about the Civil War, 'Different Visions,'" Mills observed. "What was it that Neil Howe wrote? Something like, *each niche will build walls ever higher*? Were those guys ever prescient."

"Indeed. The question is what the proper path may be going forward. Secession is on the table in a number of states. I bet Civil War is brewing in a lot more, most people just don't realize it as of yet. At the end of the day the real question is if what had been the United States has become ungovernable as a national entity, or at least ungovernable outside of violent dictatorship," Chris theorized.

"One might have thought that the lesson from the debt crisis was that there was no free ride. Yet people so badly want to believe that government possesses a magical elixir and they'll buy into whatever political and economic absurdity is presented to them as long as they think they can get something and as long as they can satiate their desire to fault someone other than themselves," Mills said.

"The history of the last hundred years or so of humanity is that people are willing to kill in order to obtain that promised magical government elixir that doesn't exist," Malone replied. "What I said earlier, perhaps it was a theology where government was god. Those who worship at the altar of the state or the government are more than eager to provide their gods a human sacrifice in order to be satiated and blessed. Of course, it's always the lives of other humans, not themselves, that they offer. The nonbelievers if you will. In fact, the people who worship government and the state have no other sacrifice to offer their god aside from the lives of their neighbors. If they had anything else, they were willing to offer they would not be worshipping that god in the first place."

"What you just said, that's what you need to be telling people when you speak. That's the rebuttal of political violence," Mills suggested.

"Thanks, but it's not just violence. It's that the worshippers of the state are willing to sacrifice their neighbors' health, prosperity, and happiness to satiate their worship of the government and state," responded Malone. "If their neighbor's life is diminished, destroyed, or even ended, they care not, so long as the state is exalted. For these people the state is not a tool to enable the success of the citizens but an end unto itself. If they did view it as a tool, then they would've thrown away much of what we've had the past few decades because of the damage it's caused. Instead they excuse the damage and continue to empower their god. I mean, look around. We're sitting here on Broadway with no traffic, no businesses open, no jobs, and people are seriously arguing that we need more of what caused this? To quote James Kunstler, 'Sometimes societies just collectively go insane.'"

"We'll be sending two people from Colorado to the constitutional convention. I'd like to sponsor a bill for you to be one of them. Are you open to that?" Mills asked.

"I would be honored."

40
It's been a difficult few years

State senator Cassie Roseman stood to speak on the north steps of the state capitol.

"Thank you for coming. It's been a difficult few years and unfortunately in the week since the state took over delivery of food, fuel, and medicine, that difficulty has turned into disaster. The people in Aurora didn't get their rations this week. We argued strenuously that this process needed oversight and regulation. We were rebuffed in asking for sufficient regulation by the advocates of the so-called free market! These people argued that the system would just automatically work and that government was not needed. Well, we now know that's not true! Of course, the people who didn't receive rations this week are a community that has historically been underserved and marginalized. Of course."

At precisely the same time that Cassie Roseman began speaking on the capitol steps, state senator Jeff McCoy began speaking to a gathering in Aurora, "Thank you for being here. We've all had a difficult time, and it's become worse the week the state started delivery of food, fuel, and medicine. The people in Capital Hill didn't get their rations this week. We argued that this process needed oversight and regulation. We were rejected in asking for the proper role of government, rejected by the advocates of the so-called free market! These people argued that the system would just work and that our input wasn't needed. Well, we now know that's not the case! Of course, the people who didn't receive rations this week are a community that has historically been underserved and marginalized. We'd expect nothing else from a free market! This is nothing more than vulture capitalism enriching the few!"

State senate leader Joshua Mills stood far to the edge of the portico on which Cassie Roseman was speaking, listening intently and thinking, "What a shameless liar. She's going to get people killed and she doesn't care."

When Roseman was finished speaking, Mills walked to her. Roseman was taken by surprise at Mill's presence and her jaw dropped when he began to address the audience.

"What Senator Roseman just told you is not true; all deliveries were made this week. All of them. What is more, at this time food, fuel, and medicine are being delivered by the state and not a free market. Regrettably some deliveries were late as we work out the kinks in this process, but all deliveries were made..."

Mills was interrupted with a chorus of booing and catcalls aimed specifically at him.

"... believing things that are not true will not..."

Mills paused, his voice drowned by the chorus of boos.

Mills unsuccessfully waited several minutes for the crowd to quiet before finally giving up and walking back inside the capitol building.

"Well, you tried," said state senator Brian Barnes.

"Yeah, this is the start of something," remarked Mills.

"Oh yes, it is. Rumor has it that McCoy is speaking to a rally in Aurora right now. They supposedly have engagements scheduled for the entire week."

"Why can't they help instead of everything being about politics and power? I mean, everything."

"They're betting that everyone will just get sick of fighting and knuckle under to them," Barnes remarked.

"Well, they're going to get innocent people killed," Mills countered. "They believe that all men have a right to prosperity and that the government must give it to them."

"What's that?" Barnes asked.

"Something Malone said to me a couple weeks ago about everyone trying to live off of everybody else."

"Why is that so clear to us and those people will refuse to even acknowledge it, even if they don't entirely agree with it?" Mills asked.

"Because if they acknowledged that it was even somewhat true, they would need a new ideology and a new job, not to mention that they'd owe a lot of people apologies and they're loathe to ever do that," replied Barnes.

"You know, you're almost always an asshole but almost always right. How does that work?" Mills asked laughing.

"I make my living by being right, the asshole part I just throw in for free."

41
Sharing is sharing

"Sharing is sharing. Socialism is not sharing. Socialism is force. Socialism is taking, not giving. Socialism is what the Committee for the Continuance of Government practiced. Government is force..."

Ray stood at the foot of the west steps of the capitol and listened to Chris Malone speak. These speeches had become a daily event, drawing ever more of an audience in a society with precious little entertainment. Chris, Joshua Mills, and liberty-minded speakers on the west steps of the state capitol in Denver, and Cassie Roseman, Jeff McCoy, and other socialist and Progressives speaking daily on the north steps.

Each day the crowds grew and so did the conflict. Fist fights and shoving matches were becoming more common, not less. Inside the capitol building the legislature was paralyzed. The issue wasn't as simple as the legislature not agreeing on what to do. The legislature couldn't agree on what was happening. The legislature couldn't even agree on what they had already done. Paralysis as political strategy, damn the consequences.

As Ray had predicted, John Tribell and Katie Davis and Ted Harris and Mandy Ford had been eclipsed in the public consciousness in a remarkably brief period of time.

Ray glanced about and noticed Joshua Mills off to his right, standing under a tree. This was whom Ray was at the state capitol to meet. As Ray walked toward Mills, Mills turned and walked south. Ray followed him, and Joshua Mills stopped and turned around on the steps of what had been the Colorado Supreme Court Library building.

Ray thought to himself, *These politicians really like standing on steps. Is that a Colorado thing or what*?

"Thank you for meeting me," Mills said.

"Sure, what is up?" Ray responded.

"I understood your cell released the Tribell information and took security headquarters?"

"Maybe. Why do you ask?"

"We may have real problems. Dependable people are informing me that the goal of these afternoon rallies by Roseman and McCoy are not just to paralyze the legislature but building a base for some kind of revolution, or counter-revolution, or counter-counter-revolution or whatever we're up to by now."

"That sounds plausible," Ray responded.

"I need help," Mills responded.

"In what way?"

Mills looked exasperated.

"Umm, stopping it."

"Senator, I don't know that I have a dog in that fight worth dying for."

Joshua Mills paused as he realized exactly what he was asking of this man he had never met before today.

"Yeah, fair enough. Here is what I'm attempting to do: hold the state government together for long enough to get to a constitutional convention and complete a constitutional convention. At that point there'll be new rules, a new paradigm. I don't want the people of Colorado to be ruled, instead of governed, by whomever can assemble the largest, most violent mob. Mob rule is the path this is heading down at frightening speed."

"Didn't you kind of open that mob door yourself by inviting Malone to speak every day?"

"Yeah, I guess I did, but I didn't expect it to go down the path it's going down. I just thought he was a smart guy who understood things that more people should understand."

"He's a smart guy and more people should understand the things he understands, but you had to know the Progressives weren't just going to sit on their hands. You didn't really think this would turn into some kind of salon on the capitol lawn, did you?"

"Okay, I'm an idiot but that doesn't change the problem," Mills responded.

"Well, I appreciate an honest politician," Ray smiled.

"Look, help me out here. You risked your life to get rid of the Committee, and these people are of the same mind as the Committee. They honestly want exactly what the Committee was. They just think they can do it better," Mills said, rolling his eyes. "Rumors are that security agents and infiltrators who worked for the Committee are the people they're counting on to provide the backbone for a coup."

"What about the Governor?" Ray asked.

"Useless."

"The Speaker?"

"Cowardly."

"I see," replied Ray. "So, you're it?"

"The Governor and the Speaker are likely to roll over the first time someone startles them with a dirty word. They'll be in Kansas if they hear a gunshot."

"Will you be in Kansas if you hear a gunshot?" Ray asked.

"I may be an idiot, but I have been shot at before. I didn't run then, I won't run now."

Ray gave Mills a serious look and believed he was telling the truth.

"If I help you out and you run, you know I will hunt you down."

"As you should."

42
The outcomes are remarkably consistent

Admiral Denton looked each of the officers seated around the table in the eyes before he began to speak.

"This is going the wrong way, gentlemen. A few success stories but not enough."

"The outcomes are remarkably consistent. The states with a solid political majority in either direction instituted free markets or something akin to their own Committees for the Continuance of Government depending on the direction of the majority. What used to be known as the swing states are on the verge of civil war," remarked General Helfrich.

"Politicians are actually using the food deliveries as a political weapon and people are okay with that, as long as it's aimed at the other side," Admiral Andersen contributed.

"I recall what President Reagan would say when I was just a child, 'always trust the American people.' I'm thinking that era has passed," said General Nash.

"Where are we with secession?" Denton asked.

"Nearly half of the states have expressed some level of support for secession, a dozen seem hell-bent on seceding," responded General Martinez.

"Who can blame them?" interjected Admiral Andersen.

"What a cluster," said Admiral Ziegler.

"Will states that secede be internationally recognized, Admiral Wright?" Denton asked.

"Yes, almost assuredly."

"The longer we continue in this mode the worst it gets," Denton observed.

"Then we should terminate this mode," suggested General McNeil.

"I agree," General Baumgartner said.

"Let us move the date for the constitutional convention, two weeks from today it will begin," Denton commanded.

"That's a tall order," Admiral Ziegler responded.

"Tall order or not, if we don't do that then we'll almost certainly have shooting. Even moving it up, we may have shooting in some of these states," General Martinez said.

"Some people are very invested in stopping that convention. They feel it will impinge on the fiefdoms they're trying to create," General McNeil asserted.

"How did we become such a petty, self-absorbed people?" Admiral Andersen asked.

"I'll take that as a rhetorical question, Admiral Andersen," Denton said, looking at Andersen firmly.

Denton had little patience for the rhetorical and he made that known often.

"Inform the states that the convention will start two weeks from today."

43
Would you like some more Chardonnay?

"We can't build the critical mass that we need in two weeks, can't be done!" Jeff McCoy complained to Cassie Roseman as they sat in Roseman's living room sipping Chardonnay.

"We can't allow the people that the legislature selected to represent us," Cassie replied.

"Those people were hand-chosen by Mills. Outrageous," agreed McCoy.

"Those people Mills selected actually got a majority vote in the senate! Unacceptable. This is an affront to democracy! The people didn't vote on it and they won't give us time for a vote of the people! We have to stop this. This is worse than the treason Trump committed!"

"How?" asked McCoy.

"Let's get those that are organized to the capitol, a big rally, speeches. Maybe send them into the senate chambers?"

"Send out the message. Whatever it takes we have to stop this," McCoy chimed in.

"Yes, that's good!" Cassie Roseman confirmed.

"Whatever it takes!"

"That's the rally call, cry, 'whatever it takes!'" Cassie blurted.

"Would you like some more Chardonnay?" Cassie asked.

"Oh, yes, please," Jeff replied.

"Can you believe that Barnes? What a jerk. Does he really think we're not in the legislature to pass taxes, regulations, and laws? What does he think we're supposed to be doing?" Cassie vented.

"I know. Him and his 'read the constitution' crap," McCoy said affirmatively.

"Glad that there's only one of him in the senate. Mills takes his side far too often!" Cassie said accusingly.

"That Mills. What's his deal? And Bernstein, too!"

"These people are so blatant in their opposition to a fair and equitable society where we all rise together. It makes me sick. Would you like some more brie?"

"Oh, yes, please. Thank you," McCoy replied.

44
Whatever it takes

"So, the word is that there'll be a big rally on Tuesday at the state capitol. The rally is called 'Whatever It Takes.' They want to stop the two people selected to that constitutional convention," Sheri informed Wesley, Will, and Jay.

"Whatever it takes?" Will asked.

"That's what they're calling it. Looks like a last-ditch effort to stop the convention."

In the two months that the shooters of John Tribell had been in the safe house, Sheri had been their eyes and ears to the outside world. The photographs of the shooters and their names had faded from television, and Sheri had been discretely inquiring as to if there was an active search for them, and it appeared that no one was particularly looking for them. The men had all grown their hair long and now sported beards.

"This could be the opportunity to throw this whole bunch out, or run them out, or shoot them if they won't run," George Wesley remarked.

"Who are these two people they want to stop?" Jay asked.

"You've seen it on TV. Chris Malone and some guy named Paul Bishop," Sheri replied.

"Oh yeah," Jay said though he still didn't recall.

"What do we know about these fascists?" Wesley asked.

"No one knows much about Bishop. He's a retired professor who lives in Ouray, and Mills has known him for a long time. He didn't even come to Denver to be voted on, Mills chose him, and the senate voted for him without ever meeting him. The House confirmed him, though I guess technically they don't have to. They just did it for some unity thing. The other fellow, Malone, he lives in Westminster and he speaks on the capitol steps almost every day other than Sunday."

"Where on the capitol steps?" Will asked.

"West side, usually near or at the top of the steps," Sheri replied.

"There a lot of people come to hear him?" Jay asked.

"Thousands, every day."

"Will Malone be there on Tuesday?" Wesley asked.

"I suppose so. He's there almost every day."
"That sounds like a prime opportunity," Wesley asserted.
"It does," said Jay.
"Let's figure this out."

45
What would you do if you were me?

"What have you found out?" Joshua Mills asked Ray.

"They have this major rally planned for Tuesday, as you know, but it probably won't be much larger than what they draw every day. Billing it as 'Whatever It Takes'. Typical Leftist hyperbole. They plan to have everyone at the rally go into the chambers afterward but just to intimidate with numbers. You could end the session early and let them hit an empty paper bag if that concerns you, but I really don't think it's much. I've looked and looked hard, and these people have no plans for violence or over-throwing the state government or anything like that. Sabotage your choices as much as they can is the plan, but they aren't arming up for a rebellion."

"So, you think the bark is much more threatening that any potential bite?"

"I don't see any intent to bite here at all. I mean, the high-level planning meetings are Chardonnay and brie. They're much more dedicated to their wine and cheese pairing than they are to revolution. By the way, where the hell does Cassie Roseman get brie?"

"I have no idea. No doubt the black market that she claims is so unfair. Go on though," Mills replied.

"They think they can cause a mass disturbance to cause the senate to rethink their choices. That's the gist of it. You don't seem to be of a mind to do that, and I have no idea why they don't grasp that you won't be of a mind to do that, but that's the plan."

"What would you do if you were me?" Mills asked.

"I would end the session early, clear everyone out of the chambers, tell Malone and everyone else not to show up or speak, have no counter-rally, and let them hit the empty paper bag. You can only lose with a confrontation or riot or anything like that," Ray responded. "Avoid the possibility of a confrontation, and you'll demonstrate how weak and shallow these folks are. Time is on your side. Run the clock out without additional drama."

"I'll consider that."

"One other thing," Ray added. "There's always the possibility of the crazies out there. Labeling this rally 'Whatever It Takes' is an invitation for crazies. Someone might show up and assume they really mean that, and anything goes. That includes shooting people they don't agree with. This country now produces crazies the same way it used to produce Buicks—why doing as I suggested is the safest route."

"Thanks again."

Ray walked down the steps of the former Colorado Supreme Court Library building and around the corner to Lincoln Street. Jerry was waiting for him in the Wagoneer.

"How did it go?" Jerry asked as Ray got behind the driver's seat.

"It went well, I recommended he end the session early, clear the chambers, not have Malone or anyone else speak, no counter-rally. What you and I discussed," Ray replied.

"Will he do that?"

"Maybe. He didn't say yes or no. He just thanked me."

"Seems as though he was over-estimating the power of Roseman and McCoy to actually do something meaningful," Jerry observed.

"Yeah, it looks that way. These people are no more capable of planning and executing a coup than planning and executing a trip to Mars."

"Still, the crazies," Jerry said.

"Roseman and McCoy are so consumed with the righteousness of their position that they simply do not think. Where does she get that brie?"

Jerry laughed as they pulled from the parking spot and north onto Lincoln.

46
Reallocate and destroy

"What are your thoughts, now knowing what Ray said to me today," Joshua Mills asked Senators Brian Barnes and Marcie Bernstein.

"I think that Roseman and McCoy have exceeded their level of incompetence. Harris, Ramsey, Ford will be damned by history, but they had a level of competency and social and political guile. Sandrop and Giles certainly don't have that guile, and Cassie has no competency whatsoever. McCoy just follows Cassie around like a puppy anyway. At the end of the day these people can't build, produce, or create anything. All they can do is reallocate and destroy. They believe that the ability to reallocate and destroy is a worthwhile, marketable skill to possess."

"Ultimately our path to success is by demonstrating that their only skill is to reallocate and destroy. There's no other outcome to what they propose," Bernstein responded.

"One might assume that after the last two years people would be fed up with what Cassie and Jeff want to do," Mills replied.

"Cassie has to continue to portray anyone with a different view as evil. The reason she has to portray anyone who doesn't agree with her as racist, sexist, homophobic, and evil is to distract from the reality that all they can do is reallocate and destroy. It's an ideology predicated on whataboutism. It's morally vapid, but it allows people who buy into it to feel superior. One might think that after the last handful of years that the majority would conclude that virtue signaling makes for disaster as public policy, but decades of lies have impaired our critical thinking faculties," Barnes observed.

"Yep," Mills agreed.

"Remember Monty Python? They nailed it when they said that strange women lying in ponds distributing swords is no basis for a system of government. These folks have nothing more to offer than using Critical Theory to create a false moral paradigm premised on a blend of race, gender, and Marxist ideology and then proclaim that false moral paradigm as the basis for a system of government. Their moral and intellectual underpinnings are no more solid than ladies in lakes handing out swords.

Creating a mythology that entitles you to rule is as old as mankind, and Cassie has embraced that mythology. There's no quantitative difference between these people and an aristocracy," Marcie interjected.

"On top of that, they adamantly deny they're Marxist while spewing Marxist dogma as an eternal truth. It's still almost impossible to differentiate between the obtuse and the dishonest," Mills added.

Barnes and Bernstein slowly shook their heads in disbelief.

"I ask Cassie once if she actually believed that people in government were superior to everyone else and she actually said, 'yes'. I ask how that could possibly be, and she told me they are just better," Marcie said.

"Asking them to explain monetary policy is always a fun way to respond to their belief in their own superiority and inherent right to rule. No different than that old movie where Doc Holliday asked Ike Clanton to spell cat. They want an omnipotent government while pretending the few things that government actually does to make things work don't exist because their Marxist professors didn't tell them about those things and didn't tell them because it demonstrates the absurdity of the entire ideology," Barnes laughed.

"Be that as it may, I have things I need your input on," Mills said as he attempted to steer the conversation back to the meeting agenda.

"At the end of the day it's not much more than the belief that I should get stuff because I'm a better human than you are. That lady in the lake, i.e., Critical Theory, told me so, it must be true. That's an attractive argument on many levels to quite a few people. Convince people that the other guy is racist, sexist, and homophobic, and that they themselves are not, hence making them morally superior humans and that they're then entitled to make the decisions and get the other people's stuff by virtue of that moral superiority. That it's predicated on bullshit doesn't seem to bother them or even enter into their consideration. They view equitable as ideological and not premised on if what you do is constructive or not. Their solution to every problem is to send men with guns to enforce a government law, tax, or regulation," Barnes replied, ignoring Mills attempt to reorient the conversation.

"People like Cassie long ago made the decision that tribalism was morally acceptable. Tribalism and racism are just two sides of the same coin in the context of Progressivism. Progressives mandate tribalism and claim to abhor racism. They then demand the allocation of public funds and laws by tribe. It's remarkable how, in retrospect, we had confused how much money was spent on a given item with how effective that spending was. This was such an elementary error that it's startling that we propagated it so mindlessly. The only people who profited from that error are the corrupt—but that this error was so ubiquitous should have given us a good clue to the level of our own corruption. Not enough of us paid attention to that clue, and eventually that corruption destroyed us. The Committee was the outcome of corruption. Cassie and McCoy want a return to a system that's less corrupt than the Committee but still corrupt. They've normalized corruption as the purpose of government and rationalized that all government is corrupt; hence, it's only fair that they be corrupt as well, with the self-assurance that their corruption is more beneficial to the masses than other corruption is. Of course, they would never apply the word corrupt to themselves," Barnes propounded.

Marcie added, "When the main motivation for voting becomes what can I get government to force someone else to give to me, the only possible outcome is corruption. People like Cassie sincerely believe that they have the solution to all of the ills of the world, and she has drawn the conclusion that anyone who doesn't agree with her solution is in favor of the continuation of the ills of the world. People like Cassie can't make the connection that they torment people with their mandatory solutions in order to satiate their own conscience and greed. Just as Frederick Douglass said, 'The limits of tyrants are prescribed by the endurance of those whom they oppose.' We long ago lost the endurance to oppose petty tyranny, and consequently, major league tyrants like Harris showed up, and most people still did nothing. In fact, people chose to describe the petty tyranny as 'services' rather than tyranny. Now the question is if enough people will stand up to allow us to have honest government once again rather than be forced by men with guns to observe the imagined morality of a handful of people. These folks like Cassie simply can't see that forcing their morality and vision of what life should be on others results in the grossest immorality imaginable. They lie with impunity because they believe someone else some other place lied so it's only fair that they do so for political advantage as well. It doesn't take long in that moral model for everything to be based on lies."

"Indeed, Mussolini would be so proud. Cassie and Jeff simply pretend that removing your volition and compelling you to comply with their version of corruption is the same as making you moral. It's egoism as ideology or perhaps even theology. They're repeating all of the errors of their socialist and fascist predecessors in proclaiming that only they can do it correctly, only they're enlightened enough to decide for everyone," chuckled Barnes.

"Of course, they think that we're just as obtuse as we think that they are," Mills observed.

"Maybe we are?" Barnes responded.

"There's certainly an argument for that. Decades ago conservatism went from conserving the constitution to diametrically opposing whatever the Progressives said, and the Progressives pretty quickly figured out that when the opposition was so predictable that also made them incredibly easy to manipulate. Conservatives forgot why they existed in the first place and assumed it was just to be one hundred and eighty degrees opposite of Progressives. If Progressives said the sky was blue, conservatives would say it was green out of spite. Progressives were able to use this predictability to confine the political debate to the trite rather than the meaningful. Progressives would have lost badly on the meaningful, but conservatives didn't stop and think about that. They just kept arguing on the trite terms the Progressives relished. A single serious question, to your point about something like monetary policy, and Progressives would have been relegated to the cartoon character quality of governance that they embrace. Instead conservatives kept arguing with them on a cartoon level and made themselves cartoonish in the process. That's about as obtuse as it gets," Marcie observed.

"These Marxist professors taught their students all about the concept of privilege but taught them nothing about how wealth transfers to the one percent occur due to monetary policy. These silly Leftists then argued for policies that were nothing more than wealth transfers to the one percent while arguing how much they detest wealth transfers to the one percent, and the more bad ideas that they made into reality in the name of progress, the more wealth transfers to the one percent there were; and they were never provided the educational tools to make that connection. They taught students all about intersectionality and nothing about rehypothecation. Every time you would try to explain this to them, that their socialist policies merely benefited the wealthy, they would call you a racist homophobe who should check his privilege. They never grasped what they were actually doing; they simply repeated the myth of what they thought they were doing. When the hard times hit, those one percenters all took off to Europe and New Zealand and wherever, and these poor miseducated people were left holding the bag. In the end we got what we deserved," Barnes noted.

"Well, enough bitching about Cassie and philosophizing and competing for who can remember the most quotes, as enjoyable as it is. At the moment we have no bureaucracy to speak of and no state funds in Colorado, so what Cassie wants to do is purely academic. If she got her way, she still couldn't get her way under the current circumstances. The best Cassie can do is delay events until there are funds and bureaucrats to execute her will. What do you think we should do about Tuesday?" Mills asked.

"I would agree with Ray, run the clock out on them. Cassie and her ilk are getting an education in that alleviating poverty requires construction not deconstruction," Barnes said emphatically.

"Ditto," said Marcie.

47
Be practical and just choose from what works

"We have to be practical in how we reach the goals of equality and inclusion," Cassie remarked.

"It's like the last real President, Obama, said, 'be practical and just choose from what works,'" McCoy added.

"We know that free markets don't work. Only the privileged favor free markets. Our job as state legislators is to stand in the stead of those who are not privileged," Cassie interjected.

"We have to delay this until we can stand up a real government that can appropriately regulate these markets and ensure inclusion and equality. Hunger, healthcare, equality—we can solve these problems, but we can't do that without a strong government to solve them. Why do these people hate so much that they don't want to solve these problems? Deeply embedded racism and sexism and xenophobia, that's why!"

"Mills and Barnes and that gender traitor Bernstein are what privilege is. That we're not yet in a position to have a minimum wage or unionize indicates that government is not mature enough to move away from rationing. True patriotism is ensuring an equitable society. Only government can ensure that society is equitable. It will be anarchy if Mills moves forward with his plan!" Roseman bemoaned.

"Without public institutions, we can't have a society worth calling itself such. Society is defined by what government provides. Otherwise, it's simply the exploitation of the masses by the privileged," McCoy commented, oblivious to the reality that no public institutions available to the masses had existed under the reign of the Committee.

"You're so right, Jeff. You know what Barnes actually told me once? That if there were no government assistance that people would take care of each other! Do you believe he actually said that? How demeaning and belittling it would be to have to ask other people for charity. It makes my skin crawl that poor people would have to lower themselves to that level. You know people like Barnes get off on having that power over other people, the power to help them or not. Who knows what terrible things would be extorted out of poor people in exchange for food or medicine or a place to live in a system like that. It takes people like us to stand up and say, 'NO!' to people like Barnes, otherwise people would have to bow to others and who knows what else," Roseman ranted.

"Those Barnes diatribes over natural rights! As though we were all living in the wilderness hunting for food and not in the twenty-first century. Life has changed; people have changed. These people are just Neanderthals who refuse to move forward. Without government, there can be no civilization. There can be no progress without government leading that progress. That's just plain fact. What they want is the opposite of progress; they oppose any changes where they're not on top," Jeff McCoy sputtered.

"I know! It's all about privilege. We have to take that privilege away from them in order to have an equitable society. I think I'll use that in my speech on Tuesday," Cassie said.

"Oh, I like that!" McCoy concurred.

"They're so obtuse not to recognize that free markets are inherently unfair. Why can't they see that? Standing up to bullies is the hallmark of a civilized society, and we'll stand up to Barnes and Mills and Bernstein. Barnes and Bernstein talk about freedom but ignore the imbalance of power in society. The Committee was at least committed to ending the imbalance of power in society. Barnes and Mills and Bernstein just don't care. We do care; that's why we need to stop this with whatever means are necessary. We don't have to sit back and watch our meritocracy be replaced by an aristocracy. People need government to give them a fresh start and a free market will not do that. Mills doesn't understand how people fear a free market. Mills and Barnes will destroy community when people pursue having one more dollar than their neighbor has," Cassie said defiantly.

"The people are so lucky that we're here to stop this." McCoy triumphantly asserted.

"Yes, it is, and we're not powerless. The people are with us!"

"We're the voice of the people, the voice of those without privilege!" McCoy chimed in.

"Tuesday, we stop this!" Cassie declared.

"It's an outrageous abuse of power that the senate approved those two men that Mills nominated for the convention. Neither of them will fight for guaranteed basic income, healthcare as a right, the rights and reparations of marginalized communities, a guarantee of gender equality, non-binary gender identity, the constitutional rights of the environment, free college, affordable housing, and making corporations pay their fair share. This is a unique opportunity to finally bring this nation into the twenty-first century, and we'll lose this opportunity if Malone and Bishop represent us," McCoy decried.

"We can't allow Democracy to lose simply because we don't have enough votes," Cassie said.

48
Always an establishment hack

"Mills was always an establishment hack. He's going to sell us out! He always took advantage of the built-in advantages of incumbency and establishment entrenchment in party offices as well as corrupt money flung about by sleazebag political operatives. He'll make a deal with McCoy and Roseman, just watch. Barnes is the guy we need in charge," Leland Johnston screeched.

The small gathering in Leland's living room nodded in agreement.

"These losers in the state house won't represent our interest. They'll sell out. We all know it!" Dennis Busse said.

"Two years of the Committee, lost the war to China, debt crisis destroyed the economy—I am done with these politicians and politics. Done," Tony Newkirk stammered.

"I think we all go down to the capitol Tuesday and see it's done right. Not going to let these commies run us anymore," Johnston said.

"I don't see any difference in any of them anymore," Busse said.

"I feel confident that a heavily intoxicated one-eyed man on a galloping horse couldn't tell the difference," Newkirk said.

Everyone in the room looked at Newkirk until Busse asked, "What does that mean?"

"I don't know, just heard it somewhere," Newkirk responded, shrugging his shoulders.

"These bastards have nearly starved me, won't let me have any gas, put my company out of business, tried to take my guns, and we can't even get on the internet anymore! I'm done. I have had it with these pussies. We're going to go down there Tuesday and set things right!" Johnston stormed.

"Yeah!" Busse added.

"Let's do it!" Newkirk yelled.

"What do you propose going down there to do, Hoss?" Jim Kearns asked.

"I say we get our rifles and go make a statement," Johnston responded.

"Just go stand around with guns then go home?" Kearns replied.

"Yeah," Johnston stated.

"Not sure what that does," Kearns said dismissively.

"You have a better idea, smartass?" Johnston roared back.

"Doing nothing is better than that," Kearns replied.

"Horseshit!" Johnston blurted.

"You can go if you want, but I got better things to do," Kearns said.

"Chickenshit," Busse said looking at Kearns.

"No, but if you're just going to go stand on the grass and listen to politicians talk, I got better things to do," Kearns shot back at Busse.

"Somebody has to let these politicians know that real people are out here and that we're fed up with them," Johnston said.

"Yeah, somebody has to tell them," Newkirk echoed.

"You're appointing you to be that someone?" Kearns asked.

"Yeah, what if I am?" Johnston asserted.

"Take a whole lot more than just three or four of you to get them to listen," Kearns said.

"Maybe we can get more," Johnston replied.

49
It's going to hell quickly

Admiral Denton looked each of the officers seated around the table in the eyes before he began to speak.

"Where are we at, gentlemen?"

"It's going to hell quickly, Admiral," General Martinez replied.

"We destroyed the global economy, lost a war, had a Stalinist dictatorship for two years, and these people still won't stop arguing over the same things they were arguing about before that all happened!" General Baumgartner exclaimed.

"Unfortunately, that arguing has escalated to shooting in more than a dozen states," added General Helfrich.

"Twelve states are at peace and working to improve things, ten states set up something akin to their own Committee for the Continuance of Government and those states wish to perpetuate something like a communist model while twenty-eight states are in or nearing civil war," Admiral Anderson informed the meeting.

"I think there's a serious question as to whether what was once the United States is now governable as a national entity," General Nash postulated.

"We moved the date for the convention up to hopefully curtail violence and division, but there's grave doubt that we'll make it to a convention with a useful team of players. Half of these states are horribly, violently divided over the representatives being sent to the convention. Whatever may be agreed to at the convention is likely to spark further division in those states and further violence. People are not in a mood to compromise or hear the other side out or even acquiesce to reality," said General McNeil.

"These legislatures are arguing over the same things they argued over way back when Trump was President. That there is no Federal government, no real banking system yet, the currency is worthless, the states have no money and no personnel to speak of, and that the citizens are starving are irrelevancies to them. No joke, people are holding up unity over things like

Gay Rights and immigration. What world do they think they're living in?" Admiral Ziegler observed.

"Most of the countries in the world are emphatic in their preference for a united United States. They much prefer that we not break into pieces, but they understand that's a possibility," said Admiral Wright.

"What can we do within the bounds of propriety and fairness to alleviate the division and decrease the nonsense?" Denton asked.

"Admiral, can you define propriety and fairness in this context?" Martinez asked.

"Short of lining politicians up against a wall and shooting them." Denton barked.

"Admiral allow me to interject; I think the time has come that we develop a plan for the military if the country does indeed break up into constituent pieces," General McNeil said.

"Yes, General McNeil, the time has come to prepare for the possibility of that outcome. If that disassociation does in fact occur, we'll want that to be an orderly process," Denton responded. "I am tasking you and Admiral Wright to develop that plan ASAP. I will remind you to be cognizant that most soldiers will return to their home states. Fixed assets are easy to allocate, but shall we distribute the navy by homeport or some other method? The nuclear weapons are of critical importance.

"You're also tasked with discovering a path to avoid that.

"I want to remind you all of Robert E. Lee's resignation letter from the United States Army addressed to General Winfield Scott: 'Save in the defense of my native State, I never desire again to draw my sword.' If this event comes about, we will swear all departing personnel to an oath not to make war on their fellow states. I do not want a B-2 to drop its payload on Connecticut next year."

The room had become very somber.

"I foresee no more dismal or heartbreaking outcome than the dissolution of the union, but if that's what this will be then we will do it with honor. Someone in this country must carry on with some honor."

"Admiral, I ran some numbers in preparation for the possibility of this conversation," General McNeil remarked.

"Go on, General," Denton replied.

"62% of the military personnel originate from the thirteen Confederate states. Most of the remainder of the troops originated from the mid-west states and the inter-mountain west. This will probably be far from a proportional allocation of military resources. For example, there are fewer than five hundred military personnel from Vermont, Rhode Island about eight hundred, and Connecticut about a thousand."

"They have the National Guard, or they did," Denton commented.

"Yes, Admiral, but for example, when Connecticut gets New London and the submarines that call that their home port, they're unlikely to have the personnel to operate those submarines."

"I see your point, General," Denton replied. "I should have thought of that myself."

Admiral Denton was embarrassed that an Army general had pointed out a submarine dilemma to him.

"If we can't match men to equipment to states then the equipment becomes inoperable, and if enough strategic assets become inoperable, then the territory that was previously known as the United States can't be defended. Our grandchildren then grow up speaking Chinese or something," General Helfrich remarked.

"Exactly," responded McNeil.

"A foreign power could devour the real estate piecemeal," Ziegler said.

"States in dire economic condition could potentially be colonized, a foreign power would not necessarily even have to wage war or even threaten war to gain the territory," Martinez contributed.

"Let us help you out..." General Baumgartner interjected sarcastically.

"China remembers well how they were colonized, and they would recognize that the United States could be ripe for colonization. As you said, 'let us help you out' would be the pitch to engage in colonization," said General Nash said.

"This is the price that nations pay for partisanship run amuck," Admiral Ziegler said.

"Most people want to eat and prosper and raise their children how they see fit and live in peace, and they inevitably come to some arrangement between themselves to do so if left alone," General McNeil observed.

"When did we become such a stupid people?" Admiral Andersen said.

"Rhetoric," Denton warned.

"Sorry, Admiral."

"General McNeil, I am charging you and Admiral Wright with devising a plan for dissolution with an eye to the issues brought up in this conversation and the future strategic paradigm, and a strategy to avoid that if possible," Denton commanded.

"Yes, Admiral."

"Remarkably enough, gentlemen, our most trying times may yet be in front of us," Denton remarked.

"May I ask a question, sir?" Admiral Wright interjected, sensing that they were about to be dismissed.

"Yes, Admiral Wright."

"We have in custody the former members of the Committee for the Continuance of Government as well as a few others accused of atrocities. The plan had been to transfer their custody to a new Federal government. If a new Federal government fails to materialize what shall we do with those in custody?"

"Good question, Admiral. Since they are held at Fort Eustis, we could turn them over to Virginia if no Federal government materializes. Any other thoughts?"

The room was silent.

Denton returned to his original question, "What can we do within the bounds of propriety and fairness to alleviate the division and decrease the nonsense?"

After waiting a few minutes in silence for a response, Denton said, "That's not encouraging."

50
Deciding against sharing a tent with a corpse

George Wesley walked silently through the sea of tents in Civic Center Park in the dark. Wesley stepped around small mountains of trash between the tents, causing rats to scurry with each step. The tents had formerly been home to the multitudes of people that had patronized the virtual reality centers in downtown Denver. The tent village was now mostly abandoned as the majority of the addicts had finally given up on the virtual reality feed being restored. Some tents were flattened by the weather, many were sagging, and a few were upright.

Wesley kept his eyes in the west steps of the capitol across the street, keeping in mind that he required a clear line of sight in order to complete his mission. He carried an M4 carbine in his hands and a 1911 in the holster on his belt and a Ruger EC9 on his ankle. In front of him, with a clear line of sight to the capitol steps, was a mostly upright dome tent. He knelt behind the tent and drew his knife. He cut a slit in the tent that he intended to crawl through but was startled by two bare feet exposed by his cut. He could tell by the color and texture of the skin that the occupant of this tent had been dead for some time. Rats peered out at him through the slit he had cut in the tent.

Deciding against sharing a tent with a corpse and the rats feeding off of it, Wesley looked about and spotted a tube tent in front of and to the right of the dome tent. He approached the tent with caution, thinking to himself that a cheaply made tent that was still standing was likely to be occupied. Crawling along the side of the tent to the zipper, he worked it gently until it gave and opened the flap. Peering inside he was happy to see that it was unoccupied.

He crawled inside the tent and cut a horizontal slit in the rear that he would use if he needed a quick escape. He then cut vertically on the front of the tent and peered through. He had a line of sight through the trees to the southern two-thirds of the capitol steps; however, the northern third of the portico was blocked by the statue of the Union soldier that stood in front of the west portico of the capitol.

Wesley settled down for a long wait in the tent with the nagging thought of possible bed bugs occupying his mind. He thought Will should have worked his way onto the upper floor of a building that had once been the headquarters of a Denver newspaper directly to the north of him and Jay should be ensconced in the back of an old pickup truck with a camper shell on it half a block down the street on 14th between Broadway and Lincoln by now. Will and Jay's task was to provide suppressing fire in order to support Wesley's escape.

Wesley had many hours to wait for the rally to start and for Malone to appear.

Joshua Mills started his day at the capitol early. He had taken Ray's advice and cancelled the senate session for the day. The House chamber had also decided to cancel. Cassie Roseman and Jeff McCoy had been angry, but it wasn't their decision. Mills had also informed Chris Malone that he would not be speaking that day on the capitol steps. In fact, with the convention just days away, he had decided against having Malone speak on the steps any more at all before the convention.

Mills decided he would just run the clock out on Roseman and McCoy.

Mills had invited Ray and Jerry Sandoval to spend the afternoon with him, and they arrived at noon. If things broke in an unexpected way, he desired to have their advice at the ready.

"I would offer you some coffee, but we haven't seen that in two years," Mills remarked glancing at the dust covered coffee maker.

"Maybe Cassie can spare some brie?" Ray replied sarcastically.

"I'm glad you cancelled the session and told Malone to stay home," Jerry remarked.

"Yeah, we'll let them have their rally and go home without any drama," Mills said sardonically.

"People are already gathering out there, less than an hour to show time," Ray said.

"We may wander out for a peek after they get good and worked up," Mills replied.

From his prone position inside the tent George Wesley watched through the vertical slit. He caught glimpses of a crowd on the north side of the capitol and he could hear cheering and applauding, but the west side was empty other than three men standing under a tree, two with AR-15's and one with a Mini-14. Wesley had the dispiriting realization that the Malone rally had been cancelled.

The only Plan B at hand was to wait for dark and leave the tent camp as quietly and unseen as he had entered it. Wesley contemplated how many more hours he would have to worry about bedbugs and shoo away rats until he noticed that three men had walked onto the west portico and stopped to chat. He peered through the EOTech 512 on his M4 at the three men. One man he didn't recognize, but of the other two, one was a security captain who had defected named Sandoval and the other was state senate leader Joshua Mills.

George Wesley thought that if he was going to start a counter-revolution this might work.

"They're getting all riled up to go home and do nothing," Ray observed of the *Whatever It Takes* rally.

"Hitting an empty..." before Joshua Mills could complete his sentence a bullet slammed into his chest instantaneous with the sound of a gunshot. A second gunshot rang out two seconds later with another bullet entering Mills chest.

Mills collapsed, bleeding from his chest and with blood coming from his mouth as his punctured lungs tried unsuccessfully to contain his breath. Ray and Jerry grabbed him by each arm and dragged him along the portico attempting to get to safety of the south side of the portico. More gunshots rang out from the north and south of them.

At the sound of gunfire, the crowd that had been listening to Cassie Roseman speak fled in panic. Most ran safely to the east, but a few ran west and into the spray of bullets coming from Will and Jay. Gathered under a tree on the west lawn Leland Johnston, Dennis Busse, and Tony Newkirk instantly dropped to the grass. Johnston and Newkirk began locating the shooters while Busse lie with his head down quivering. Seeing a man in Civic Center Park exiting violently out of the back of a tent with a rifle in hand, Johnston and Newkirk both sighted on the man through their ACOG equipped AR-15's and repeatedly fired until the man dropped.

Seconds after George Wesley went down in a bullet riddled heap, Will and Jay ceased firing and executed their exfiltration.

51
Like Yugoslavia

Admiral Denton looked each of the officers seated around the table in the eyes before he began to speak.

"The convention starts tomorrow gentlemen. What are your updates?" Admiral Denton asked.

"Increasing chaos, Admiral. Many states are getting worse. All hell has broken loose in Colorado since the leader of the state senate was assassinated. By the way, we have confirmed that the assassin was one of the Committee's killers who executed Tribell. Two Progressive leaders were assassinated in revenge this morning, Roseman and McCoy. Armed gangs are roaming the Denver area with running gunfights and taking out anyone they think is sympathetic to the other side," General Martinez informed.

"We're looking more and more like Yugoslavia in the 1990's," Ziegler observed. "Neighbor against neighbor."

"What are our risks with the convention?" asked Denton.

"The convention will be secure. The risk is that we've decided to televise it and re-run the day's events until the next day begins, and that what America and the world will see is simply a continuation of the intractable bickering," replied Admiral Wright.

"One of the delegates from New York is vocally calling for a Union of Socialist States, and when people in Wyoming and Texas see that on television, well, it's unlikely to go over well," interjected General Baumgartner.

"Meetings began yesterday with five delegates selected by lottery to draft the rules and format of the convention," General Nash said. "If they can't agree on rules and format, then it's all downhill from here."

"The lottery delegates range from professors of constitutional law and historians to communist community organizers. Madison versus Alinsky. Or maybe Trotsky. Who knows?" Admiral Andersen added.

"It would seem to me that the key here is engaging the American people in a manner that they understand that they have a stake in this and then giving the American people the tools to aim that stake at the heart of these delegates. For decades, people believed that the purpose of any position of responsibility was in being able to make a decision and then transfer the risk that decision incurred to other people who had not made that decision, along with any negative consequences of that decision. Government did it, banks did it, corporations did it, scientists did it, and schools did it. All these people cared about were that the negative consequences were not realized until after they left the scene with their pile of cash. In the last two years we have realized all of those risks seemingly all at once. This is exactly what killed honor and virtue in this country. We have far too many people who are perfectly happy to continue to operate under that model, and it must stop. The people who make the decision must incur the risk of that decision and the consequences of that decision. How do we make that happen, gentlemen?" Denton queried.

Denton scanned the room as the officers stared silently at the table.

"Rubber hits the road right here, right now. For more than two years it's been one unthinkable disaster after another, and our resilience is at an end. If we fail at this, we will be done forever and slip into the history books as yet another failed republic. No one at this table wanted this, none of you signed up for this, but this is what we have. What is it going to be, gentlemen?" Denton asked again.

"Admiral, I think you should explain this to the American people as well as the delegates to open the convention tomorrow," General Helfrich suggested.

"I agree. I think you should lay out in simple terms what's at stake," Admiral Anderson concurred.

"Yes. Cut it to the bone, Admiral," General Martinez asserted.

"I am not of the mind to give political speeches or to be engaged in politics whatsoever, gentlemen," Denton replied.

"Admiral allow me to be so bold as to echo your own words. 'No one at this table wanted this, none of you signed up for this, but this is what we have.' What is it going to be, Admiral? You currently possess the most honest view of where this country is at, where it's been and what has to occur in order to have a viable future. You didn't ask for this and you didn't want this, but this is where you are. We all appreciate and honor your virtue in separating the military from the civil, but your duty here is not as an Admiral but as a patriot. What most Americans believe about the last two years is as much rumor as it is fact, and they know virtually nothing about the true state of the nation. Admiral, you know more about what's transpired the last two years and the current state of the nation than any man alive. For decades we've all had to attempt to sort out the fact from the contrived, the politically convenient from the truth, reality from fantasy with varying levels of success. Lies became the currency of the nation and, to your point, those who told the lies rarely incurred the risk of those lies or the consequences of those lies. You, and only you, have the ability and opportunity to stand up and dispel the delusions, relegate the fantasy to the ashbin, and tell the American people the truth," General McNeil pleaded.

"Only when they know the truth will they understand what's at stake with this convention," added Admiral Ziegler.

"We've waited weeks now for politicians to stand up and tell the truth, and a few have but far too few. What's more, these politicians in the states don't understand the entirety of the situation or how dire it is. You do, Admiral," General Martinez joined.

"Do you think they would receive the truth? Honestly, gentlemen?" Denton replied.

"Admiral, we destroyed the economy, defaulted on our debt, lost a war to a major power, and suffered two years of a communistic dictatorship starving people on purpose. Despite all of that, many or even most still prefer a fantasy to a reality. The American people have suffered through all of the consequences of the truth without anyone bothering to actually inform them of the truth," interjected Admiral Wright.

"I would think, since the American people already paid the price for that truth, they're entitled to hear what they paid for, Admiral," General Nash observed.

Denton looked down at the table in deep introspective thought.

52
The air-conditioned Clark Auditorium

Chris Malone sat in the air-conditioned Clark Auditorium at Fort Bragg listening to the delegate from New York drone on about all the advantages of socialism. He felt fortunate that he had been one of the lottery choices selected to arrive early and develop the rules for the convention if for no other reason than he was allowed to bring his wife and children. In the twenty-four hours since they had arrived at Fort Bragg, he had visibly observed the stress and tension leaving his wife, Jennifer, and their daughters. They stayed in air-conditioned quarters with their own bath, regular meals, and no plausible possibility of violence. Jennifer and his daughters viewed it as heaven. There was even a playground that they could safely indulge.

"We have a unique opportunity to ensure a fair society. We can never go back to a society dominated by capitalism who had no interest in anyone but themselves. We can't cater to the frauds who proclaim that they desire freedom when they really desire racism. They want to exploit the people; for the rich and the powerful to grow richer and more powerful.

"These people that are advocating for free markets and so-called liberty are driven by greed and privilege. They want to destroy government and prevent government from helping those who need help the most. They want a government that will pledge allegiance to the wealthy and privileged.

"These people are about nothing but greed. They want government to serve the powerful," Jeffrey Holmes of New York ranted.

Chris pondered how Holmes had famously been worth over a hundred million dollars before the debt crisis and how he had allegedly lost all of it on the infamous Crédit Agricole trade that had brought down Wall Street overnight and cascaded through the global financial system. Holmes had acquired his now lost fortune by exploiting the distortions in the credit markets created by government policy that he had helped formulate, an exploitation premised on who you knew rather than what you knew.

"The Committee for the Continuance of Government overstepped their bounds, but an equitable society is a worthy endeavor," Holmes continued "To me, democratic socialism means equality. It means fairness for trade unions, civil rights, the women's movement, gay rights movement, and the environment!"

Chris wondered what decade Holmes thought he was living in.

"What we want for this country is what the American people want. We are not radicals. We want an economy that works for everyone and an end to privilege and supremacists.

"We have to control the privileged, the privileged on Wall Street and in the pharmaceutical industry, the fossil fuel industry, and everywhere the privileged elitist dominate. We end the private possession of weapons. Climate change must be aggressively fought with a constitutional tax on carbon. We must ban fracking. Colleges and universities must be tuition-free. We must guarantee health care to all people as a human right. We must fight for justice!

"Many of the delegates selected want to eviscerate government when the proper role of government is to protect all of us, especially from the privileged. What is more..."

"Mr. Holmes, we're not here to govern a country or develop policy. We're here to develop rules for a convention," interrupted Ken Wilkerson, delegate from Wyoming. "Can we please get on with that task?"

Chris Malone sat back in his seat thinking, "This will be a long process."

53
How colossally stupid do you have to be to screw that up?

Brian Vann leaned against the pecan tree listening.

"So, the way I figure this, there'll be enough fertilizer for each of us to farm thirty acres if we go light but only enough diesel for about twenty acres," Joe Meigs was explaining.

"Better than none but not enough," Pete Ross remarked.

"I have a walking plow and mules. We can tractor twenty acres and farm the rest with mules is what we can do," Andy Vann suggested. "And this time when we farm with mules, the Committee people won't take it away from us!"

"We could do that," Brian affirmed.

"Let's figure what everyone is going to plant," Meigs said.

The farmers had gathered in the pecan grove next to highway 64 in order to figure out the best way to apportion the fuel and fertilizer that the state had provided them. The Oklahoma state legislature had quickly figured out that fuel and fertilizer to farmers was the quickest path to alleviating hunger.

"It's already so late to plant. I think we go with carrots, spinach, peas, turnips," Meigs replied.

"Arkansas potatoes for everyone," Ross chided as they all chuckled at the colloquial term for turnips.

"We should have eighty days even after we plow," Vann observed.

"The state says we'll have more fuel and fertilizer but not until after it's too late to plant," Vann remarked.

"They got us what they could as quickly as they could, so we could get some crop in this year," Ross reminded them.

"Yep," Vann said.

"I wonder how that convention will go?" Meigs wondered.

"We'll get a good idea starting tomorrow," Vann replied.

"Some of those states sent flat out communist," Ross observed.

"I have had quite enough of that for a lifetime," Vann said.

"I'm not living under that again, sons of bitches tricked us into that once. They want us to be ruled by red bastards. They can go to hell. My father fought them in Viet Nam, and my uncle fought them in Korea, and if I have to fight them in Sequoyah County I will. I know y'all will, too," Meigs asserted.

"If they come up with some socialist bullshit, Texas will leave, and Oklahoma and Arkansas will leave right along with them, along with a whole bunch of other states," Ross said.

"What are those assholes in New York and California gonna do without food and oil?" Vann threatened.

"People want to eat, we want to grow food and sell it to them so they can eat, other people want to sell us diesel and fertilizer and tractors and seeds. How colossally stupid do you have to be to screw that up?" Meigs observed.

"The government kept trying to screw that up for decades until they finally broke it," Ross responded.

"All the while telling us that we were the ones that were too stupid to understand," Vann added.

"We can get together in a pecan grove and figure out what we need to figure out between us. We don't need sons of bitches in Washington figuring anything out for us!" Meigs nearly shouted.

"These DC people all want to be Andrew Jackson on steroids. They all think they know what we should be doing and how we should do it while they starve us out," Ross complained.

"Let's farm," Vann replied.

54
There have been a great many lies told

Admiral Denton stood at the podium at the front of the Clark Auditorium looking into the eyes of the one hundred state delegates assembled for the constitutional convention.

"I would like to welcome all of the delegates to the constitutional convention and welcome all of you watching on television and listening on the radio. Most importantly I want to encourage you to continue to watch on television and listen on the radio for it is you, the American people, who have the stake in what goes on here. When the convention adjourns for the day, television and radio will replay the events of the day until the convention is gaveled to order the next day. Everyone in the United States needs to watch and listen and understand what happens here.

"I had great reluctance agreeing to speak at this convention. The civil and the military should not be confused. I am here speaking to you as a citizen and not as an Admiral. I am speaking to you as a patriot and not as a sailor. The last several years I have been in a position to observe first-hand a great many things that occurred in this country, and many of those things were terrible for us all. I want to share with you how we reached this point and why this is the most critical moment in the country's history.

"There have been a great many lies told and a great deal of myth-making going on.

"As was pointed out to me, you, the American people, have paid the price for these lies and myths, and it is only fair that someone tell you the truth and allow you to know exactly what you paid for.

"For decades we, all of us, allowed a culture to develop and grow. This culture was premised on the belief that people empowered to make decisions would not incur the risk of those decisions, and they would not suffer the consequences of those decisions. This was true of elected officials, bureaucrats, the military, academia and education, corporations, and banks. They could transfer the risk and consequences from themselves to others, such as the taxpayers and everyday citizens, while enriching themselves and collecting paychecks and pensions along the way.

"Some people rationalized this culture by claiming that it has always been this way and that there was no other way. That is a lie.

"The constitution of the United States had been created in such a manner as to prevent this sort of thing from happening. The constitution set up a system for us to be warned; and to change course; you may liken this to dogs barking when danger approaches. The White House, the Senate, the House of Representatives, the states, and the media, and ultimately the voters, were all dogs that were empowered to bark in order to warn of danger.

"Our dogs did not bark. Laziness, complacency, greed—whatever it was, the danger approached, and the dogs did not bark. Instead of doing their jobs and barking to warn of danger, they were all ensconced comfortably in the myths and lies that no danger could ever approach us. We were the United States of America, and the idea that we could not manage debt or that we could ever lose a war were myths and lies that we bought into in order to justify no one having to do their job and bark.

"In short, we own what has happened to us.

"Our dogs did not bark. Not one of them. They didn't bark because the dogs themselves became part-and-parcel of the danger that they were designed to warn us of.

"That's a bitter pill, but it is true.

"We created debt that we could never pay back; in fact, paying that debt back was the farthest thing from our minds, and we believed that accumulating debt that could never be repaid would not ever be an issue. We assumed that it would always be a unipolar world that the United States would lead and that no country could challenge our leadership let alone defeat us in a naval war.

"These lies and myths were a direct result of the culture that was premised on the belief that people empowered to make decisions would not incur the risk of those decisions and that they would not suffer the consequences of those decisions. We broke that connection between decision and consequence, and we collapsed. In retrospect it is rather obvious. Every society that breaks this connection inevitably collapses.

"All of that risk that was, for decades, moved off onto other people, even moved off onto the next generation, and even the generation after that; we have now realized all of that risk all at once, and we're living the consequences.

"That we could court risk in terms of debt and court risk in geopolitics without ever having to suffer the consequences of that risk was a foolish belief. The probability of eventually realizing these risks was one hundred percent. We simply convinced ourselves that because we had not yet realized the risk that we never would. We behaved as churlish children for decades and rationalized our childish behavior with shallow substitutes of token responsibility while flouting the abuses that would eventually do us in.

"We elected politicians who told us how interested they were in justice, politicians who tweeted about fighting the oligarchy from their third home at the lake. We had an education system that no longer provided people the tools to understand that these charlatans were simply enriching their friends. We elected politicians who promised to increase freedom but could never show a single tangible action that contributed toward increasing freedom for anyone. We elected politicians who promised to reduce the debt but only increased it.

"Then we re-elected them because otherwise you would be stuck with the other guy.

"Both parties used issues such as immigration, education, and healthcare as wedge issues to keep people at each other's throats without any intention of ever resolving anything but just to create emotion and hate that they could turn into votes and power and campaign donations.

"The Committee for the Continuance of Government gained power via an executive order signed by the late President. They were empowered under an emergency decree to assure that the essentials of life would continue to be provided and that order would be restored and maintained. The Committee took this as permission to reconstruct society, culture, and government in the image that they desired. Anyone who opposed their vision was to face elimination, in fact people that they identified as even having the possibility of questioning their power and vision were executed. This included, as you all now know, the President, First Lady, Vice President, Speaker of the House, and even fellow members of the Committee. State Senator John Tribell of Colorado and many others. In fact, just a few days ago assassins for the Committee killed the leader of the Colorado state senate on the capitol steps in Denver. We are not yet clear of the menace that the Committee represented.

"There are delegates at this convention that will tell you that the Committee was on the right path, that they just did it wrong. They will tell you that they can do it better. What these people are arguing in favor of is the continued disconnect between decisions, risks, and consequences. They wish to be empowered to make the decisions and they wish for you, the people, to incur the risk and suffer the consequences of their decisions.

"People usually only see a future that they want to see and ignore the facts. After all that we have been through, one might think that we have learned the lesson of ignoring the most grossly obvious facts, but current events indicate a meaningful number of people continue to ignore the most grossly obvious facts in pursuit of their own wishes.

"That is vanity.

"They are all about ideology and want nothing to do with accountability. They want your skin in the game, not their own."

Denton paused and then said, "I implore you all to cease the violence."

The delegates stood and applauded.

"Our future, all of us, everyone in this country, depends on this convention and what happens afterward. This nation has absorbed disasters that just a short while ago we would have thought unimaginable. We are at the end of our resilience. We cannot absorb another disaster. Everyone in the country needs to understand that. This convention must be a success, and we must make a success of the government this convention creates going forward. Much more important than that, society and culture must find success for this country to succeed. We cannot continue to bicker and be divided over the lies and myths created for political advantage. People are arguing, committing violence, over things that simply have no relevance to the issues at hand. Things that are not even true, let alone relevant.

"Some states have talked of secession. Allow me to address that. After experiencing the Committee for the Continuance of Government first-hand, I understand the urge to leave. I don't condemn you for the desire to find your own way after the abuses and catastrophes of the last few years and the malfeasance of the last few decades. However, without going into details, if this country breaks up, we'll be unable to defend the pieces. Any states that leave are likely to be devoured piecemeal by foreign powers. Your children or grandchildren will likely live under the control of another nation and have little to no say in their own lives. I would ask you to remain in the union, and I would ask the convention to find a path forward to keep the union together.

"Thank you."

As Denton finished all but two-dozen of the delegates rose in applause. The two-dozen that remained seated sat with their arms folded, scowling.

Chris Malone sat in the second row of Clark Auditorium and thought, *Perfect*, as he applauded vigorously.

As Admiral Denton exited the auditorium, General McNeil remarked to him, "Excellent speech, Admiral. Most everyone got it. You said what needed to be heard."

"General, recall what Cromwell said about not to trust the cheering because those cheering would cheer as much if you or I were going to be hanged.'"

55
The cemetery south of Colfax

Ray sat on the knoll next to the cemetery south of Colfax, near where the cities of Lakewood and Golden met, scanning south and east with his binoculars. Ray excelled at human intelligence, and the intel he had collected in the days after the Mills shooting indicated that the surviving committee assassins were based on the west side of Simms between Colfax and 6th. For two days Ray had surveilled the neighborhood. South and east of Ray's vantage point, Jerry was doing the same thing. Ray had reactivated his resistance cell, and twenty men with rifles were assembled in the Applewood neighborhood north of Colfax awaiting Ray's direction.

Ray pondered how in the days since the Mills shooting, the whole thing had gone to hell. The Governor and Speaker had indeed fled. Cassie Roseman and Jeff McCoy had been hunted down and assassinated by Leland Johnston and his crew after which Ray had apprehended Johnston and friends and placed them in the custody of Air Force officers for future trial. Senator Barnes had escaped an attack that began with Molotov cocktails being thrown through his windows. Barnes was in hiding, and no one knew where Marcie Bernstein was.

It got worse. Citizens had already started working together to improve their situation, and this was anathema to the Committee loyalist. Two fellows who had pooled their gasoline to go to the mountains and catch fish were gunned down trying to trade those fish in Golden. The day before, three neighbors were shot while repairing the roof of a house in Morrison. *The logical outcome of an ideology of forced equality of outcome premised on mythology—death, misery, and poverty*, Ray thought.

"I see a man with an M4," Ray heard Jerry say on the radio sets they had liberated during the takeover of security headquarters.

"On 13th, half a block off Simms." Jerry continued, "He's loading a car. Second man now also loading a car. Looks like bottles in cardboard boxes."

"Team, you have that?" Ray asked.

"Roger," was the response.

"Half of you go south on Union, the other half south on Simms. Halt before 13th and stay out of sight," Ray commanded.

Jerry cautiously approached the intersection of Pleasant and Simms while Ray rose to his feet and worked his way southwest through the cemetery and neighborhood to 13th and Union. Jerry and Ray waited patiently for the rest of the team to arrive at their designated positions.

"George would never have let you go outside with those guns so visible," Sheri lamented to Jay as he prepared to carry another box of Molotov cocktails out of the living room to the car.

"Yeah, yeah, yeah. This is revolution. The time for caution is gone," Jay retorted.

"OPSEC matters, you fool," Sheri replied.

"We won't be returning," Will informed Sheri.

"Where will you be going?" Sheri asked.

"The less you know the better. That's OPSEC," Jay replied dismissively.

The relationship between Sheri and the assassins had grown ever more strained after the death of George Wesley.

"So, you're just going to leave me here?" Sheri asked with tears in her eyes.

"You can go where you want, but you can't come with us," Jay responded.

Sheri did an about face and stormed into the kitchen crying as Jay and Will exited through the front door with the last of the boxes in their hands. Sheri tried to dry her eyes with a dishrag as she peered out the kitchen window. Looking across the neighbors' backyard Sheri detected motion behind the lilacs. Sheri dried her eyes once more and squinted at the shape behind the lilac bush. She was sure it was a man with a rifle. Sheri rushed to warn Will and Jay. She got as far as the living room before she heard a volley of shots that stopped her in mid-stride.

"Sweep the house," Ray yelled to his team as he stood over the body of a man with a single attachment point M4 slung on his back and a cardboard box of shattered bottles lying next to him. A second man with an M4 still in his grasp lie next to the open trunk of the car in the driveway.

As the team scrambled into position to sweep the house, a solitary gunshot was heard from inside the home.

"Definitely the two who killed Tribble," Ray observed.

"Jay Smith and Will Sanders. Hopefully this breaks the back of committee loyalist," Jerry said hopefully.

"We just need people to stop shooting each other, and as long as these two were running around loose, they were going to keep shooting people just to keep it going," Ray lamented.

"House is clear. One suicide in there. Female," a team member yelled out to Ray and Jerry from the porch.

Ray and Jerry looked at each other, and at the same moment uttered, "Pointless."

"Johnston and his morons are in custody. These two are dead. Hopefully, now people can figure out how to make their lives better without risk of getting shot for doing so," Jerry remarked.

"You would think that would be a simple thing, wouldn't you?" Ray replied.

"Roseman and McCoy had no idea how big a bite they were taking. Words mean things, and they didn't figure that out until it was too late for them," Jerry said.

"A lot of that going around."

56
The only modern choice

Chris Malone sat in the Clark auditorium listening to the delegate from California attempt to explain why the warnings of Admiral Denton didn't apply to him.

"In conclusion, a strong central government that can provide for the people is the only modern choice. We have a moral obligation to provide for people, to alleviate poverty, and to assure healthcare."

As the California delegate left the podium, Chris stood and strode forward to address the convention. It had been agreed that each state should have one delegate address the convention for five minutes. Chris had noted that all but one had conspicuously exceeded the time limit.

"Thank you. I'm Chris Malone from Colorado. There have been points made in regard to limited government, strong central government, socialism, democratic, and otherwise, so on and so forth. I think we may be missing a few of the fundamental points in regard to the current situation and the catastrophe of the last two years.

"One that Admiral Denton alluded to: the people who made decisions didn't have to incur the risk of those decisions or the consequences of those decisions. In fact, the Admiral more than alluded to that, he flat out stated it. Another is the very enticing mistake of confusing money with wealth. The government made promises, promises that the delegate from California wishes to return to, to provide for people, to alleviate poverty, and to assure healthcare."

Chris paused for effect before continuing.

"The government did what governments always do: they promised far more than there was wealth to pay for, and they promised these things in exchange for votes. Because the government didn't have the wealth to pay for these things, they created money out of thin air in order to fund them. The problem with this age-old temptation is that for the masses, each dollar created makes them poorer. The only people who prosper from this model are those in a position to invest in the creation of the money, and these few grow ever wealthier with each additional dollar created, while everyone else grows poorer. The poorer people grew, the more money they demanded to be created to alleviate the poverty, and government was eager to satiate that desire, and the people grew ever poorer still. Eventually, as inevitably happens, this entire system imploded. Decades of government market distortions that were required in order to perpetuate this system created enormous tail risk. When those risk were realized, the economy was destroyed.

"The basic misconception or deception, depending on your viewpoint, of socialism is confusing wealth and money. They're not synonyms, as socialist would wish people to believe, and once you grasp the difference between money and wealth, you grasp why socialism can only produce misery, poverty, and death.

"I think that what we need to focus on is affirming that all laws apply equally to everyone in a given civil jurisdiction to include elected officials and agents of the government. All laws. The other issue we must focus on is sound money and fiscal responsibility, not just a balanced budget but accounting for all future obligations to be paid for.

"Again, to echo Admiral Denton, 'our constitutional dogs did not bark to warn us. We must have dogs that bark at danger.'

"Thank you for your time."

Chris returned to his seat as the next speaker, the delegate from Connecticut, addressed the convention, "First let me offer a rebuttal to the delegate from Colorado. Modern Monetary Theory was not the source of our..."

Chris had his focus broken as his fellow Colorado delegate, Paul Bishop, whispered to him, "Word is the other two Mills shooters were killed this morning. They were apparently involved in the killing of Tribell as well."

Chris enjoyed a moment of relief. Both he and Bishop knew full well that they were marked for death in Colorado as long as those two remained on the loose. After the assassinations of Mills, Roseman, and McCoy it, was still unclear how safe Colorado was. It certainly had to be safer with those two no longer roaming the city.

"Maybe we can have some peace," Malone whispered.

"Would it be too much to hope for?" Bishop replied.

"Monday they'll launch the new currency. When people get something with some value in their pockets and are no longer required to rely on barter for everything, the economy can take the next step up. Some hope for people," Chris whispered.

"Real money, real banking system, then people will start real businesses as long as government doesn't get in their way," Bishop replied.

"Get the delivery of food and fuel out of the hands of government," Chris whispered.

"To think there are delegates at this convention that want to return to what we just came from," Paul whispered in response, "It's as though they've learned nothing."

"Like a dog to its own vomit," Chris said a little too loudly.

57
Can't go wrong selling mutton and beer

Cindy Tribell knew that once the constitutional convention was announced that her fifteen minutes of fame was up. Cindy had returned to her trailer in Tombstone where Len and Lori had greeted her as though she had only been gone for an afternoon.

"You probably knew more than we did while you were out of the country," Lori remarked.

"What's the latest on Mandy Ford?" Len queried.

"Canada has detained her until there's a Federal government to hand her over to," Cindy responded.

"What are other countries saying?" Lori asked.

"It varies, but mostly they're hopeful for the convention. It seems that no one other than China supported the Committee," Cindy replied. "Most people want American leadership, at least economically. They need us to be functional, so the world economy can again become fully functional."

"What was your favorite place?" Lori quizzed.

"I liked London and Paris, but the best was Barcelona."

"Wow."

"Hey, the new currency comes out next week," Len interjected.

"We plan to turn the Crystal Palace into a restaurant and serve beer at the Oriental," Lori added.

"Tourist won't be back anytime soon, but at least people around here will have a place to go," Len said enthusiastically.

"Where will you get the food to serve? Things haven't changed that much," Cindy asked.

"Some of those folks over on the San Carlos Reservation have been raising vegetables and have sheep. Lots of sheep. They came to see me last week. They're willing to send us sheep and a few vegetables once a week on sort of a profit-sharing model. They provide them, we cook and serve them," Len blurted out.

"If they get more gas more than once a week," Lori added.

"That sounds great," Cindy said.

"Mel, you remember him, he lives over on Sixth Street. He has all the beer making equipment, and I know a fellow in Tucson, Andy, who used to deal in the ingredients. Barley and such. Mel and I pooled our gas and went to see Andy last Tuesday. He still has barley in a warehouse. He says it's past its shelf life, but, hey, it can make beer. People will be happy to have any beer no matter how bad it is. Mel and Andy and I will do profit-sharing on the beer too. Andy thinks he can get a good line on a consistent source of barley and such" Len explained.

"We'll start out opening just the Crystal; then as we get more product and customers, we'll open the Oriental too," Lori said.

"Can't go wrong selling mutton and beer," Len said.

"Working on where to get enough flour to make fry bread," Lori said.

"That sounds wonderful," Cindy replied.

"Billy Pruitt, you know him, just a teenager, told me he'll go out and get rattlesnakes, so we can serve snake, too. At least once in a while. He has visions of having his own rattlesnake farm. You know how that goes with teenagers. I don't know how reliable he'll be," Len said.

"You never know with teenagers," Lori observed.

"This is all so wonderful," Cindy said.

"You know you always have a job with us," Len promised.

"You're family, Cindy. Since we don't have any children, we think of you as part of us. If you want to be part of this, part of us, the offer is always open," Lori said.

"You're a national hero now, but I'm not sure what they pay for that kind of a gig, so you always have a place with us," Len asserted.

Cindy blushed.

"Someday the tourists will come back," Lori said confidently.

"The town's too tough to die," Len added.

58
We obliterated it

"We should talk," Jeffrey Holmes, the delegate from New York, suggested to Chris Malone as Chris stood after having finished dinner with his wife and children in the Fort Bragg cafeteria.

"Certainly," Chris responded as Holmes motioned for Chris to sit.

"I'll see you back in the room," Jennifer told Chris as she exited with the children, and Chris sat back down.

"You and I seem to be at polar opposites. Perhaps we can find some common ground?" Holmes asked.

"Perhaps," Chris responded with doubt.

"This country is a wreck. You certainly recognize that it'll take an extremely strong and active central government to rebuild it?" Holmes queried.

"It seems to me it was the strong and active central government that wrecked it," Chris responded.

"We can do better with a strong and active central government than they have in the past. You know that's so. We have to put stringent guidelines around that government," Holmes suggested.

"We did have stringent rules, it was called the constitution, and we obliterated it."

"The constitution didn't keep up with the times or what people wanted," Holmes responded.

"How much of what people wanted was from government propaganda and what their lap dogs in the media were responsible for in the first place? Manufacture a crisis or injustice with a premade solution that robbed people of their wealth and power."

"People wanted justice," Holmes replied with a hint of anger.

"We had not had a world war or a nuclear device delivered in anger since 1945, we ended the Cold War peacefully, and the world was more prosperous that it had ever before been. It's not that there were no major problems, there are, er, were, but let's not forget how good things were on an historical perspective. Yet people, and especially people in the government, contrived ever more grievances that were used as an excuse to provide the same government people that were proclaiming the grievances with ever more power, power that they by and large used to enrich themselves and impoverish the masses in the name of justice," Chris responded curtly, leaving unsaid that Holmes had built a vast fortune exploiting government policies.

"I did what anyone in my position would have done," Homes replied defensively.

"No, you did what you did, and you own that. False moral equivalencies don't suffice in justifying your individual actions or desires," Chris succinctly replied.

"Well, at the end of the day, that's all in the past. Let's look to the future. People require certain guarantees. Guarantees that they'll have food and housing and healthcare. You understand that, right?"

"I understand why you're saying that, but no, I don't agree with that," Malone asserted.

"This is the proper role of modern government," Holmes shot back.

"Let us be frank, shall we? What you're proposing is that the particular moral and intellectual limits of a bureaucrat or elected officials should be the limits of society, and that the moral and intellectual limits of government should be enforced via violence. In the model that you propose, government, culture, society, and personal action have no distinction and are driven and defined by an empowered elite few. Your basic political argument boils down to your having superior morals and intellect than the Committee for the Continuance of Government possessed; hence, we should empower you to inflict your intellect and morals on all of society. Is that not the essence of your proposal?" Chris asked.

Holmes stared back blankly.

"Yes?" Chris asked.

"So basically, you support no laws," Holmes accused.

"No, I support laws that protect people and property. Don't hurt people, and don't steal things, and don't harm their property. I do not support laws that compel people to action, laws that take peoples' stuff, and laws that force people to do what some politician or bureaucrat thinks they ought to be doing," Chris replied emphatically.

"That is anarchy," Holmes replied.

"No, what anarchist desire is very different," Chris retorted.

Malone and Holmes became consciously aware that all other conversation in the cafeteria had ceased and that all eyes were focused on them.

"People have an inherent right to food, housing, and healthcare," Holmes suggested.

"No, people have an inherent right to follow their conscience. People have an inherent right to defend themselves. People have an inherent right to dispose of their property as they see fit. People have an inherent right to associate with whom they desire to and not to have to associate with whom they don't desire to," Chris explained.

"That is racist," Jeffrey Holmes accused.

"Interesting point. You're premising that observation on it being the role of government to abolish racism and not the role of society to do so. Of course, that premise goes even deeper, doesn't it? In order to arrive at the conclusion that you've arrived at, one must believe that it's the government's obligation to make things fair and equal, rather than the obligation of society. What's more, you must believe that government is chartered to make things fair and that government actually has the capability to make things fair. There is no substantiating example, in all of history, that you can point to where government made something fair. In fact, each attempt to do so has simply resulted in what Mencken once called 'an advance auction sale of stolen goods'. Every example in history of government attempting to make things fair ended up in factions fighting for the spoils. I seem to recall that you were rather effective at fighting for your share of the spoils," Chris said, wondering if he had dug the knife in a little too deep.

"You have zero respect for me, don't you?" Holmes replied.

"I find the moral and intellectual underpinnings of your argument vacuous and self-serving," Chris replied honestly.

"That's not how they view me in New York."

"Well, you have that going for you," Chris replied sarcastically.

"You have no desire to find common ground. It wasn't easy to come over here and ask you to talk, you know," Holmes said.

"Where would you propose that we find common ground?" Chris asked.

"Healthcare. We can certainly agree that government should provide healthcare, right? At least for some people," Holmes responded.

"A little leaven leaveneth the whole lump," Chris replied.

"You're impossible," Holmes stormed.

"No, I'm improbable, but you probably didn't watch that TV show. Here is why there's no compromising with you: because you believe that healthcare is a right. I know full well that any compromise with you is pointless because anything I concede for the sake of comity, you would then come back and demand more and more and more. Not right away, but over years. It's what Progressives do. The truth is that the only thing that government can create is money, and the great temptation throughout history is to create so much money that the government destroys itself—because that's the only thing that government can create. If your only tool is a hammer, then every problem looks like a nail. Anything else that government wishes to do, it must use force against its own citizens to accomplish. That includes healthcare. At the end of your argument is nothing more than the rationalization of using force against people for their own good. But that alleged good is tempered by the reality that it's limited by the morals and intellect of the people that comprise government, so the good you achieve by the use of force is less than the good a free people can voluntarily achieve without the government limiting and forcing them."

"Some people will not be able to afford healthcare," Holmes retorted.

"That's undoubtedly true. In that case, you will provide it for them out of the goodness of your heart that you keep reminding people you have, or they can form voluntary collectives to share the cost, any number of possible solutions to that problem other than government," Chris replied.

"Those solutions are unworkable, and you know it. Government is neutral and will not turn people away, private charity can turn people away," Holmes asserted.

"That's a fascinating assertion and on the surface makes my position seem entirely heartless and inhumane," Chris responded. "However, at a second glance, that's not so. What you propose removes the connection between people, between neighbors helping neighbors. It creates sterility and consequently removes compassion from the equation. You believe you're helping the unfortunate but in reality, you're not helping them but robbing them—robbing them of part of their humanity. You profess a desire to create community while erasing all that it means to be part of a community, to have to rely on each other. Of course, when people know they must rely on each other, they treat each other better. They behave better. The ties to the community are real and not faux government creations. Government 'helping' has done much to foster the inhumanity we have seen over the last decades."

"You and I see the world very differently," Holmes observed.

"The difference is that you wish to inflict your vision on me and everyone else. What I propose leaves you free to participate in the system that you prefer. If you wish to form a voluntary, socialist, collective, you would be free to do so. However, you and I know that will not happen because socialism is a bad idea. Voluntary socialism is a non-sequitur. Socialism only works via force. Socialism is taking, not sharing. Taking and sharing are one hundred and eighty degrees opposite of each other. I propose a system premised on voluntary sharing. You propose a system premised on taking by force."

"Government has a moral obligation," Holmes replied sternly.

"No, Mr. Holmes, people have a moral obligation, not government," Malone responded. "Government merely has the power to force people to do as it wishes. There's nothing moral about that."

"Good night," Holmes said as he stood and quickly departed the cafeteria.

Chris Malone looked about the silent cafeteria that had been absorbing every word.

A delegate from Delaware, Mary Rodier, said from the next table, "So what type of existence for humans do you see as ideal? Because I can't think of a time in our known history of 10,000 years that the many don't enrich a few?"

Malone responded, "Freedom, liberty. The enriching of the few by the many is done by force—resist that force. That means resist the laws, policies, and regulations which transfer wealth, which force people to buy a product or deny them the right to buy a product, which set the price for a transaction or terms for a transaction or that tax a transaction. That's how you fix it."

Rodier countered, "Right but everything is attached to a profit. How are you avoiding it in your life? All that you're saying is a great theory, but implementing for millions of people seems rather challenging."

"I don't avoid or oppose profit whatsoever. I oppose people using force to make a profit," Chris explained.

"Let me put what you just said into application. Walk everywhere, make all your own clothes, growing your own food not sure where the seeds would come from, disconnect from all things like water and gas. Don't use modern sewers, well you get the idea," Rider retorted.

"No, I don't get the idea. I have no clue how you would possibly draw that conclusion from what I've said," Malone responded, mystified.

"Without government, that's what you would have," Mary Rodier attempted to clarify.

Chris Malone blinked like an owl.

"First off, no one has advocated for no government. In fact, our very presence at this convention contradicts that conclusion. Are you arguing in favor of force to make people buy a product or deny them the right to buy a product, for government to set the price for a transaction or terms for a transaction or to tax a transaction?" Chris asked.

"It's necessary for an equitable society. If government doesn't make things fair, then the strong take advantage of the weak," Rodier elucidated.

"Where was government ever chartered to make things fair? What example do you have in all of history, your ten thousand years, where government ever succeeded in making things fair rather than government itself taking advantage of the weak?"

"It's the natural role and right of government to do so. This is why government exist," Rodier replied, wondering why this was not obvious to everyone.

"I'm just making a point, Mr. Malone," Mary Rodier continued.

"I don't think that the point you made is the point that you think you made," Chris responded.

"I think I'll go to tell my family good night now," Malone informed the delegates. "It's been a pleasure."

59
We may soon be able to go home

Katie Davis lounged on the sofa, contemplating her next move, while listening to Blaine chat on the ham radio with someone in Rhode Island.

The voice on the radio squawked, "And you should have heard Malone yesterday at the convention. He said, 'For the gazillionth time, socialism is not sharing—socialism is taking by force. Sharing is sharing; socialism is stealing. Sharing is ennobling and enhances the humanity of both the one who gives and the one who receives. Socialism is taking by force, and it's dehumanizing to all those involved.' It was gold. First time we're having a real debate on this stuff."

Katie and Blaine had received periodic second-hand updates on the convention for a month. Katie knew that the general trend of the convention was against her, and she hid her distress from Blaine along with her true identity.

Blaine signed off from the radio, looked at Katie on the sofa, and said, "Isn't it great Katherine? We may soon be able to go home!"

After having shot Gary, Katie had wondered aimlessly west on county roads and eventually found herself in Fort Garland, where she had encountered Blaine. Katie had instinctively resorted to her primary life-skill, the ability to beguile men, and Blaine had taken her in at his cabin in Copper Gulch near the tiny community of Bonanza. The cabin had no television reception, and the ability to receive radio broadcasts from Denver was spotty. Blaine had been a prepper. The cabin had solar and wind power and a generator. Blaine had pre-stored abundant fuel and food prior to the hard times, and it was a comfortable existence. Elk and deer filled the freezer.

Blaine treated Katie as though she was just another prepper accessory.

"That's wonderful!" Katie responded in an attempt to be as convincing as possible.

"If they get a government that's not just a bunch of commies, then I can head back to Pueblo. Return to normal life. What about you?" Blaine asked.

"I don't know where I'll go," Katie responded. Katie was always taken aback that Blaine was so obvious in considering her a temporary part of his life. The men that Katie had beguiled as part of her undercover work had always thought of her as permanent. Blaine never hid that he was only interested in a food-and-shelter for sex arrangement. Katie was humiliated that Blaine so openly used her.

"It's a big world out there," Blaine remarked. "I can set you up with some fuel and food. I'm willing to do that."

Katie sarcastically thought, *How noble of you*, but instead mumbled, "Thank you."

"Really, it's not a problem," Blaine replied proudly.

"Maybe we should make plans for that?" Katie suggested.

"Ok, we can do that. What are your thoughts?"

Katie pondered how to disguise her desire to go to Mexico.

"How much do I need to go to L.A.?"

"Is that where you want to go? Become a movie star?" Blame chuckled.

Katie secretly seethed at Blaine's willingness to openly mock her on a daily basis.

"Maybe," Katie replied submissively.

"That old truck you have'll probably require a hundred gallons or more to go to California. When I made the offer, I figured you wanted to go to Denver or something."

"Please give me a hundred gallons?"

"I don't know, that's a lot. I have maybe a hundred and thirty gallons left," Blaine responded dismissively.

"Please?"

"Nothing you can do for me is worth a hundred gallons of gas."

"Oh really?" Katie responded in her best seductive voice.

"I'll give you maybe fifty. You can figure it out from there."

"How far would that get me?"

"Western Utah, I would think. Maybe St. George. Maybe even Las Vegas if you drive slow."

"Only Utah?" Katie said disappointingly.

"I'm sure that you're able and willing to convince someone to give you some more gasoline when you run out," Blaine said a little too insightfully for Katie to be comfortable with.

Katie thought, *What a bastard*, while saying, "I don't want to have to convince anyone but you."

"Yeah right," Blaine replied.

"Please?"

"Fifty."

"What can I do for you for a hundred gallons?"

"Nothing you can do for me now that you haven't already done for oatmeal," Blaine responded honestly.

The truth in Blaine's response cut Katie to the core.

"Is that all I am to you?" Katie blurted, her anger compelling her to slip out of character.

"That's all you are to anyone. Why are you pretending otherwise?"

Katie stood up from the couch and stormed out the front door of the cabin while Blaine thought, *Well this is over.*

Waiting a few minutes, Blaine followed Katie outside where he found her rummaging through the cab of her truck.

"Katherine, I'm sorry, I shouldn't have..."

Blaine froze mid-sentence as Katie spun about to face him holding the Glock G43.

"Don't..." was all Blaine was able to verbalize before the bullet entered his chest.

Katie walked to where Blaine lie and muttered, "Bastard."

She spent the rest of the afternoon filling the gas tank of the F150 that Blaine had been so proud of, filling jerry cans for her journey south, and deciding what food items to take with her. Katie also, for the first time, contemplated her life trajectory.

Once Blaine's truck was packed, Katie sat on the steps of the porch pondering closure. After thinking for a while, she used a pail to gather gasoline, bucket by bucket, and spread it through the cabin. The final two pails she poured onto Blaine.

Katie lit a match and threw it into the cabin instantly igniting the gasoline. It took her half a dozen matches to get the gasoline she had poured on Blaine to ignite, but when it did, Katie left for Villa Grove and 285 south in Blaine's F150.

60
Some are recalcitrant

Admiral Denton looked each of the officers seated around the table in the eyes before he began to speak.

"What are your updates, gentlemen?"

General Helfrich responded first, "The briefing of the convention went well. They now all understand the price to be paid for secession in practical terms of defending the territory."

"Some are recalcitrant in that they continue to use the threat of secession as leverage in order to attempt to inflict their will on the other states," Admiral Andersen added.

"Yes, but half of those states demanding 'my way or the highway,' have dropped that demand after the briefing," General Baumgartner reminded the officers.

"We still have half a dozen states claiming that they won't remain if they don't get a constitutional amendment guaranteeing healthcare as a right, free college, and a minimum guaranteed income. Those are the points they're sticking to," General Nash asserted.

"The compromise is so obvious in that they would be free to do those things without requiring it of other states, but that's not acceptable to them. They don't think that way," General Martinez observed.

"The assertions made in support of those amendments are blatantly false. The issue here is how many people no longer particularly care if something is true or false but rather if something false advances their own agenda or if something true damages their agenda. They take full advantage of the people watching on television living in an information desert," General McNeil commented.

"That's how we arrived at this point in history in the first place," Admiral Ziegler remarked.

"Despite our personal observations, our role is not to interfere in the political process," Denton reminded them.

The officers seated around the table nodded their heads in agreement.

"Where are we internationally?" Denton asked Admiral Wright.

"China and Russia sense that it's a real possibility that we'll succeed at the convention and are starting to make noise. Beijing's blue water fleet will depart soon for exercises."

"Saber rattling or something more, Admiral Wright?" Denton quizzed already knowing the answer.

"China seems intent to remind us of our recent experiences and that getting the band back together, so to speak, is something that they wish to put a cap on," Admiral Wright replied.

"Cap in what manner?" General Nash asked.

"China doesn't desire a militarily resurgent United States, and they associate our potential military power to our economic power. A coherent national government that will restore economic vitality will eventually lead to military vitality in their mind. They were content with the Committee for the Continuance of Government for just that reason," Admiral Wright replied.

"Admiral Webb?" Denton asked looking at the monitor on the wall.

"Admiral, as long as we're out of range of China's land-based missiles, we can hold our own in a naval battle. The issue is a longer war of attrition. China can replace their losses, and we can't do so for the foreseeable future."

"Increased Russian air incursions over Alaska, Washington, Oregon, and northern California as well, Admiral. Usually between twenty and thirty events a day, often with multiple aircraft," Admiral Wright added.

"What are our options here?"

"Admiral Denton, the Chinese blue-water navy is not of sufficient strength to immediately overpower us throughout the Pacific but, as Admiral Webb mentioned, they could wage a war of attrition. That would most likely be accomplished with a submarine fleet that's formidable," Wright replied. "It'll be many years until we'll be able to replace capital ships, so China could take their time about it and adopt a low risk strategy that bleeds out our naval power slowly. In that case they would control the entire Pacific, not because of their increased strength but due to our inability to replace losses."

"What does China look like without a blue water fleet?" Denton asked to the visible surprise of everyone in the room except McNeil and Wright.

"Define without, Admiral?" Admiral Ziegler asked.

"Their capital ships are lying at the bottom of the Pacific," Denton replied.

"Do you think that's a possibility, Admiral?" General Martinez asked, trying to hide the doubt in his voice.

"Focus on the question that I asked, gentlemen. What does China look like without a blue water fleet?"

"Weak in terms of projecting power in the Pacific, Admiral. I might add, internationally humiliated as well," Admiral Wright replied.

"How does it change the current dynamic?" Denton responded looking at Admiral Wright.

Admiral Wright mentally prepared his response knowing that Denton already knew the answer, "That dynamic would change considerably, Admiral. China and the rest of the world perceive that Beijing has come out on top and is working diligently to create a new unipolar world. The United States is viewed as the sick man of the world, on our deathbed. If, and I'm emphasizing the if, the United States were to counter-strike in such a manner, it would not restore the balance of power, but the United States would be considered too formidable to press even in our weakened state."

"Recall Rommel; mass and surprise. I can think of no greater possibility for surprise than at this moment," General McNeil interjected.

"Go on, Admiral," Denton prodded.

"After the credit crisis, the Chinese economy was in nearly as bad a condition as our economy. Of major importance to the Chinese government is quelling domestic unrest, and unrest was growing due to the rapid economic decline that ensued. Hence China made war on the United States to distract from their economic duress and to demonstrate a government success. There's a long history of animosity between the Central Committee and the PLA though. Two years ago, the PLA was unhappy that the Central Committee took the lion's share of the credit for defeating us."

"What is the Chinese economic situation today, Admiral Wright?"

"The Chinese economy has not meaningfully improved in the last two years."

"What effect would a military reversal have on their domestic situation?" Denton asked, again knowing the answer beforehand.

"It's reasonable to assume that domestic unrest would increase and that the government would of necessity have to reallocate resources from their efforts to complete the long-term subjugation of the United States and create a new unipolar geopolitical model in order to counter that unrest. The issues between the Central Committee and the PLA would increase significantly."

"Would China have a nuclear response?" Denton asked.

"No, Admiral. That's off the table for them both due to their long-term goals and the self-defeating nature of nuclear war. They don't want to trade nukes with us."

"Do we have the means to accomplish this?" General Nash asked.

"We were behind the curve in developing hypersonic weapons compared to Russia and China; we were in the test and evaluation phase when the war started. The Navy has thirty-two missiles that were built for test purposes in inventory in Hawaii. Unfortunately, the only method of launch for these particular missiles is a land-based launch system of which we have twelve launchers," Admiral Denton replied. "Test results on these missiles had indicated excellent accuracy out to six hundred miles. We would also engage submarines and cruise missiles, but the attack on the capital ships would be hypersonic. Where will the Chinese fleet exercises take place, Admiral Wright?"

"The exercises are believed to take place in the vicinity of Midway Island, Admiral. They're kind of obnoxious in that way, sir."

"Can we pull them in eight-hundred miles closer?" Denton asked.

"We can try," Wright responded.

"How would we do that?" General Martinez asked.

"Up the ante," McNeil answered.

"Precisely. They have a tendency to jab us in the eye with a stick, and if we protest too loudly, they just jab harder. If we protest loudly enough, they may decide to jab us much harder in terms of these exercises. I would think an international protest, raise as much of a stink as we can, perhaps we can get some friendly folks to give a speech or two about the Chinese menace at the convention, that sort of thing. Please note that China is now attempting to solidify their position as the top dog in a unipolar world. Their goal is in demonstrating to the rest of the world that they're in charge and no longer will they respect the United States in any way, shape, or form—because they're now top dog. We may be able to use that to our advantage," Admiral Wright added.

"Casus belli, Admiral Denton?" General Helfrich asked.

All of the officers looked to Denton with anticipation.

"Gentlemen, not one of the internationally accepted lawful justifications for waging war will fit this proposal. We all have based our careers on those lawful justifications. By international law, this is not justified. It's justified by significantly enhancing the prospects of the future survival of the United States as a sovereign entity. The geopolitical goal is quite clear, level the playing field that was tilted in the favor of China when they attacked us and in doing so buy time for this country to recover. As I see it, the other alternative is to allow China to squeeze us into submission at their leisure. Does anyone wish to be excused?"

Denton scanned the face of each of the officers for a hint of hesitancy.

"Very well. I intend to snatch victory right out of their jaws."

61
Is this south?

Katie was now completely lost.

The most recent road sign she had seen said 40 West, Arizona, but she was quite unsure how she had reached this point. She had driven south on 285 and then become completely confused in Santa Fe, and it seemed the next thing she knew, she was in Arizona with the sun rising to her back. Katie wished that someone had taught her how to read a paper map.

She also wished that she was not so tired from having driven all night, but she was determined not to stop until she reached Mexico.

Katie worried if she had allowed enough of a fuel margin to accommodate getting lost. She thought, *Arizona is not even on the way to Mexico. It's the way to California*. "I need to go south," Katie whispered while silently berating herself, a habit that she had compulsively developed living with Blane.

She saw a road sign proclaiming "Winslow" and seemed to recall that was a song or something.

She took the Winslow exit.

She turned left at the bottom of the off ramp and drove until she saw a sign for 87 South. In Katie's mind south was south and she took it.

She had never seen terrain such as she now travelled through. Endless miles of desert broken by mountain ranges. The occasional house and small town. Strawberry. Pine. Payson. Rye. Tonto Basin. Globe. Oracle. She had never heard of these places before.

She had no idea where she was going, but when faced with a choice, she turned in the direction that her instincts told her was the direction of Mexico. She had no idea if her instincts were correct, but she hoped they were because she had poured the last of her jerry cans filled with gasoline into the F150 at Oro Valley.

Katie drove into Tucson and once again became hopelessly confused and lost. With no conscious understanding of how it occurred, she found herself driving east on Interstate 10.

"South," Katie repeated out loud to herself over and over.

She exited I-10 at Benson where she found an elderly man sitting with a dog by the side of the road. Katie rolled the driver's side window down and asked the man, "Is this south?" The man merely nodded his head up and down.

With the sun now starting to go down in the west, she passed a tattered billboard that indicated Tombstone was ahead. She seemed to recall that she once knew someone from Tombstone, or maybe someone she knew had known someone from Tombstone? She had now been awake for more than thirty hours and driving for more than twenty-four hours and her brain and body were now barely functioning. She attempted unsuccessfully to recall the Tombstone connection before discarding the thought as unimportant.

Katie entered Tombstone to find it quiet and dark. She drove slowly on Fremont Street as her exhaustion became overwhelming and she fought to stay awake. Her mind argued with itself in slow motion. Should she try to trade for gas or steal gas or was she close enough to Mexico that she didn't need more gasoline?

Off to her right, a block down, she saw a building with lights on and a few cars parked. She circled the block to see a sign on the building, Crystal Palace. Her exhaustion decided the argument for her. She would stop and trade for gas and maybe take a nap.

She parked and exited the F150 and slowly approached the Crystal Palace, peering in the window. Katie noticed through the window two-dozen people who appeared to be eating and laughing and having fun. She hadn't seen anything like this in more than two years. It appeared that people were even drinking beer.

Katie gently opened the door and entered the Crystal Palace. Her fatigue was apparent, and her gait bordered on feebleness as she approached the bar where a girl in her twenties was chatting with a dark-skinned man in a cowboy hat.

"I was hoping I could trade for some gasoline? I have some of the new money."

Cindy turned to look at the woman making the request and her jaw visibly dropped.

"Katie Davis? You're Katie Davis! You killed my brother!"

As Cindy screamed the words, Katie reached to pull the Glock from the holster on her belt. In her exhaustion she was too slow and fumbled her grip, allowing the dark-skinned man in the cowboy hat to forcefully deliver a chop to her forearm that knocked the Glock from her grip as she was sliding the gun from the holster and sent the weapon spinning across the floor. The pain to her forearm momentarily took the breath away from the exhausted Katie, and before she could recover, other patrons had pinned her arms behind her back. Len was frisking her for weapons before Katie's weary mind coherently understood what had just happened.

"Are you sure this is her?" Len asked Cindy.

"Absolutely, the photograph of her is burnt into my mind," Cindy replied, trying to slow her heart.

"What do we do now?" Lori asked.

"I don't know," Len replied.

62
These people are living in the past

"We have to stick to our guns here," Jeffrey Holmes pleaded to eight of his fellow delegates gathered in the twilight outside of the Clark Auditorium. "These people are living in the past. The world has changed. China will control the future. That's so obvious. We need to work with them, and the Chinese government will reward those of us who work with them. China has single-payer, free, higher education, guaranteed housing; they're the future, and their model won out. Let's just deal with reality. At the same time, China allows really smart people to make lots of money. They have the perfect balance."

"I get it. These constitution people want to resurrect some idea from hundreds of years ago that already failed rather than moving forward like the rest of the world has," remarked Duane Manning of California.

"We make a deal with China, it's all good. No more wars. The whole world can be one," Holmes asserted. "I've talked to these Chinese officials. They'll reward those who work with them. They see the value in that."

"We'll demand a Progressive constitution. Those other states will leave but be so weak that they won't be a threat to anyone. We can dominate this when they leave and steer it toward merging with China. Then those states that secede will have no choice. It's the future," Barbara Brewer of New Jersey added.

"Why can't those people like Malone grasp how beautiful this can be with no more wars, everyone with a home and food and healthcare?" asked Mary Rodier.

"Reactionaries without vision can't be allowed to determine our future," Manning replied.

"I don't know why the Committee didn't just work a deal with China," Jeff Hodgkins of Vermont wondered.

"The Committee had too many egoists," Holmes argued.

"We're realist. It's the only way to be," Brewer said.

"Realism requires that we work a deal with China and abandon this antiquated idea of nationalism," Holmes affirmed.

"A world without borders. China would go for that," Hodgkins said.

"Indeed, they would. It's what communism is all about, and China has figured out how to do communism," Holmes rejoined.

"We can't screw this up like the Committee did though," Hodgkins warned.

"We have the opportunity to bring the whole world into a single system of government. Justice. Fairness. Never has this opportunity been so near to fruition," Barbara Brewer observed.

"Let's all agree; we'll stick to our position," Holmes said.

"Agreed," the eight delegates from six states said in unison.

63
We have arrived at that time

Sherry Black stood at the podium and cleared her throat, "When I was elected Chairperson of this convention, I understood that there would inevitably be a make or break time in this process. We have arrived at that time. We have made tremendous progress in so many ways. We're at the point where a few constitutional changes that a few states are demanding is holding up the completion of what we have been task with accomplishing. These states are threatening to leave the union if these changes are not adopted. Furthermore, if these changes are adopted, yet other states are promising to secede in response to those changes being adopted.

"This is madness. When the great state of Ohio sent me to this convention, it was to produce a functional government and not to spend my time babysitting the unreasonable. The delegates to this convention have worked hard to restore trust between viewpoints and a productive working relationship and compromise, and now a handful of holdouts want to destroy all of that productive work.

"I cede the floor to delegate Holmes of New York."

"Ms. Chairperson, I'm taken aback by your description of delegates abiding by the principles of those who nominated them to this convention as unreasonable or unproductive. We have the same rights to our views and principles as every other delegate. We only want what's best for the American people. Healthcare, education, assurance that every American will have a guaranteed income—these are the principles that we stand for. Who would not want these things for the American people? These are human rights and standing for these rights is far from unreasonable. The desire for these rights is mainstream; Americans want this. We'll stand firm in demanding this.

"I cede the floor to delegate Slater from Arkansas."

"Thank you, Mr. Holmes. I'm presenting a resolution to be voted on today condemning Chinese military exercises around Midway Island. This is an affront to every American, and this convention must produce a means of standing up to China. It's mandatory that we do so. We must form a government to push back on Chinese aggression and imperialism. May we take a voice vote on the matter at this time, Ms. Chairperson?"

"Yes, all in favor? All opposed?

"The, 'ayes,' have it. Approved at this time, a condemnation of Chinese military exercises in the vicinity of Midway Island.

"Thank you. I cede the floor to delegate Malone of Colorado."

"Thank you, Mr. Slater. My patience is running thin these days. There are some at this convention specifically here to prevent a government of the union from being formed. People have brought their own agenda to this convention for what the future of the world should be and with the specific intent of depriving the American people of a voice in what the future may be. Let me remind you of what von Mises said, 'The worship of the state is the worship of force.' We have vile and corrupt men and women among us, fellow delegates. Delegates that will worship the state and wish to see the state empowered to use force to compel their fellow citizens to do what these few delegates wish for the American people to do. After the credit crisis caused by corrupt incompetent government followed by the Committee for the Continuance of Government, we have had quite enough of those who worship the state.

"I cede the floor to delegate Brewer."

"How incredibly offensive it is to be called unreasonable, and then, for Mr. Malone to call us vile, corrupt, and whatever other words he used, oh, incompetent. Every American deserves healthcare, every single one. Every American deserves an education. Every American deserves a guaranteed income. Every single American. How can someone be so horrible as to oppose healthcare or education? Most Americans have received no healthcare for two years or more and people such as Mr. Malone wish to continue to deny them healthcare! He wants the universities to continue to be closed? Who is paying him to be here? We must acquiesce to the new reality and work with China and not condemn them while working toward social justice at home.

"I cede the floor to delegate Wilkerson of Wyoming."

"Thank you. I wish Bastiat was here. He would have a field day. That we oppose these people's healthcare plans means that we oppose healthcare? That's the daily absurdity that this convention has become. I could not resist that observation though what I intended to remind the nation of was the menace that China represents to us all. I want to thank delegate Slater for introducing the resolution condemning China, and I want to thank

Chairperson Black for the immediate vote on the resolution. China must be opposed. No question about it.

"I will cede the floor to Chairperson Black."

"It's now time to join your committees. Committee reports are due to the secretary by three o'clock with debate and possible votes to follow."

Colorado state senator Barnes turned the television off and looked at Ray, "What do you think?"

"I think the bitter-enders will try to torpedo the whole thing."

"Only half a dozen states that are still being jackasses," Barnes replied. "How are you doing by the way?"

"I'm doing good, and you? How is your house?"

"I need a new one. Moved in with my sister for now."

"Brave woman."

"Yeah, one word for it. Anyways, I asked you to come down to the capitol because I have a request."

"Go on."

"You certainly heard that Katie Davis was caught in Arizona."

"Oh yeah, unreal. Walked into the place Tribell's sister was working at," Ray laughed.

"That whole lucky than good thing," Barnes replied.

"No kidding."

"Well, the governor has asked for extradition and there being no courts working at the moment, the governor of Arizona said to come and get her. Quickly. You want the job? Go down there, get her, bring her back. Alive."

Ray drew a deep breath.

"What will happen when she gets here?"

"Put her on trial. Motivation to set up a real court. We had to do it sooner or later. People have been functioning off of something akin to Miner's Courts, but it's time we formalized that; and she's the perfect excuse for it. Then we have Johnston and Hunley and others to put on trial after Katie Davis."

"What happens after you convict her?"

"We've been debating that a great deal around here as of late, and I think we'll just leave it up to the jury to decide what happens to her."

"Hmmm."

"You in?"

"Yeah."

64
Let us be measured about this

Admiral Denton looked each of the officers seated around the table in the eyes before he began to speak.

"What is the latest, Admiral Wright?"

"We appear to be succeeding. The speeches from the convention and our international protestations were useful, but Japan put it over the top. The Japanese have raised an international ruckus and threatened to bring on other sea-going nations in protest, and, due to the particular history between Tokyo and Beijing, China views this as a direct challenge to their new-found supremacy, and they appear to be moving the exercises much closer to Hawaii as a result. It would appear that the farthest thing from their minds is that anyone may strike at them."

"Let us be measured about this. We want them off the coast of Honolulu not Santa Barbara," Denton cautioned.

"What does the blue water fleet consist of?" General Martinez queried.

"Three carriers accompanied by twelve type 052D destroyers and nine type 055 destroyers along with an unknown number of submarines. We would guess six submarines, but we will not definitively know. The PLAN identifies this as Fleet 167."

"Three carriers is all that they have," Admiral Ziegler added.

"Correct, a fourth under construction," Wright agreed.

"It's believed that the post-exercise plan is for the carriers to be established in faraway waters, one in the Indian Ocean, one in the Pacific, and one in the Atlantic in order to demonstrate Chinese naval prowess and power," Wright added.

"Supplant the role the United States played until two years ago," General Helfrich observed.

"Indeed, they don't actually have the wherewithal to do that, but they'll produce the illusion of that in the absence of competition," said Admiral Wright. "The PLA and the PLAN appear quite giddy at the moment."

"Please give us a report, Admiral Webb?" Denton commanded.

"We're good to go Admiral. Twelve launchers, thirty-two missiles. The first barrage will be four missiles at each carrier. The second barrage will be a single missile at each type 055. The final barrage of eight missiles will only be fired if any carriers or type 055's are still afloat. We anticipate three hours. We'll task submarines to hunt down the type 052D's. We also have air-launched cruise missiles available as a final option."

"Are we sure about the effectiveness of these hypersonic missiles?" General Nash asked.

"As sure as we can be, General. They tested well, but they were only in the test and evaluation phase when war broke out two years ago. Consequently, they were not far enough advanced in their development to have air or sea launch systems in place. However, land-based launch systems were built for test purposes, and we still have those. As long as they come in range, I'm quite confident of success," Admiral Webb replied.

"Why were the missiles in Hawaii in the first place, if I may ask?" General Baumgartner asked.

"They were in transit to Kwajalein when the war started," Denton replied.

"We'll know soon," Admiral Andersen commented.

"Meeting adjourned."

65
We will have rules to address that

Jeffrey Holmes looked Chris Malone in the eyes and said, "You know the world has changed. You know that sooner or later we'll have to make an accommodation with China, and the sooner we do that the less pain we'll suffer. You know that accommodation will be a societal arrangement along the lines of how China has organized their society. It's inevitable."

"I'm not much interested in living in a society where the government decides if I have the appropriate social credit to buy a train ticket," Chris Malone responded.

"After all we've been through, how can you argue against government making people get along, providing incentive for not being anti-social?" Holmes asked.

"How many ways and times must I explain this? Government consist of people, itself, your model is simply the people in government imposing the limits of their morals and intellect onto society. After all your cries to fight against supremacist, at the end of the day you're arguing for nothing more than a system of supremacy premised on position rather than skin color," Malone replied sternly.

"Meritocracy. The best and brightest will end up in government and direct society," Holmes explained. "That's not supremacy but meritocracy."

"Here is where you and I differ. You want the government to be the oligarchy. You think that's a good thing. The United States was founded as the first system of government in which the oligarchy and the government were not the same people. You want to return to the state and the oligarchy being one. Same people as the state and oligarchy, and you believe that in this model the state will limit the oligarchy rather than the oligarchy taking full advantage of the power to force people to do as they wish. That's insane. That's the formula for every disaster that has befallen mankind. The flaw in your paradigm is in believing that enabling what you refer to as the *best and brightest* to control the lives of others is not another form of supremacy and oligarchy and that these best and brightest are not just as flawed as every other human on the planet. You're merely providing them a platform to amplify their flaws throughout all of society at the point of a gun."

"We will have rules to address that," Holmes countered.

"We had rules. It was called the constitution, and we destroyed it. If people like you refused to follow the constitution that was agreed upon, then we know you won't follow a new set of rules either. Be it the constitution or any other agreed upon set of rules, it only works if people follow the rules and respect the agreement. That's why John Adams remarked that the constitution was only useful for a virtuous people. If you keep finding excuses to break the agreement then it does not work for anyone. The virtue is in voluntarily abiding by what was agreed upon," Malone returned. "What you propose is the oligarchy as executive, legislature, judge, jury, and executioner; those are the rules and agreement you're fighting for. We get it. That's what the Committee was and what every tyranny inevitably becomes."

"You just want anarchy," Holmes rebutted.

"No, anarchist disown me in a heartbeat. What I want is constitutional government and the powers of government limited to protecting the rights inherent to you along with providing the basic functions of government such as defense and a patent office and court system and such. Once government requires you to do something, such as violate your conscience or compelling you to engage in commerce against your will, then it's exceeded the bounds of protecting your natural rights," Malone replied.

"How can you oppose education and people having healthcare?"

"I'm a big fan of education and healthcare. In fact, had we not allowed the education system to devolve so significantly due to it being run by the government, then people like you would have been laughed out of town decades ago."

"You're an ass," Holmes asserted.

"Well, at least I'm not a commie."

"Neither am I. I'm a capitalist, and I had the fortune to prove it. I'm also a realist. Your time has passed. You're part of history. We're the future. I know it. You know it. Only your pride prevents you from admitting it," Holmes shot back.

"You made your fortune from government policy that you helped create. That's not capitalism and not a free market. However, that you must insist on that as evidence that you're a capitalist is indicative of either how obtuse or dishonest you are. I know it. You know it. Only your pride prevents you from admitting it," Malone chided. "Your argument consists of your presenting your previous success as a thief as evidence that you should be allowed to continue to steal. I get it. Rationalizing that a new system should be adopted that would allow you to steal because that's in the best interest of the people is not a compelling argument. In fact, I think I will point that out this morning. Thank you for leading me to that insight."

"Let's talk about China. You know they hold all of the cards now. You're a smart man even if you are an ass. You know we'll have to come to some accommodation with them, and the sooner that we do that, the better it will be for everyone. That we voluntarily make concessions now in order to reach an agreement will be much better than resisting only to have to concede at some future point when we're even weaker. The best deal on the table with China is the deal we make today, every day our position will weaken, and their position will strengthen. You know that's true in your heart," Holmes insisted.

"Again, I'm not much interested in living in a society where the government decides if I have the appropriate social credit to buy a train ticket," Chris replied while silently acknowledging the logic in Homes assertion.

"Indonesia is offering to mediate a long-term arrangement. China is willing to help us rebuild, and the concessions they require are reasonable," Holmes said.

"That requirement is that China would be suzerain. I'm not much interested in playing the Transylvania and Ottoman's game again."

"It's either a long-term peace now on terms more favorable to us or long-term misery after which we'll have to acquiesce on terms much less favorable to us," Holmes argued.

"I'm glad that you know what will happen tomorrow. I do not," Malone rebutted.

"Come on, you know what I'm saying is true," Jeffrey Holmes replied.

Chris Malone had to internally concede the logic of Holmes position, and he didn't like having to make that concession even if he would never verbally concede to Holmes. Instead Malone replied, "What was that Churchill said about nations that go down fighting, rise up again and those that surrender tamely are finished?"

"So, you would rather that the American people suffer endless misery and deprivation as China squeezes us into submission than make a deal today to alleviate the pain? And you would rather do that in the forlorn hope that someday in some way the United States would rise again? That is your argument?"

Chris Malone didn't much like feeling like he was on the losing end of a debate.

"Pragmatism should override principle when those principles create misery and poverty," Holmes asserted.

"I believe that you think China is a much more benevolent regime than I think they are. That China is intrinsically imperialist and would subsequently bleed the United States of wealth and resources with little or no regard for the welfare of the people, I don't find a debatable point. You ascribe to China all of the characteristics of a John Lennon song. I see China as a ravenous entity with the goal of strip-mining the rest of the world in order to provide an ever-improving quality of life to the billion and a half people who live there in order that those people never get the notion of rebellion in their mind. Realpolitik."

"I think China understands that they have a unique opportunity to bring about a peaceful and equitable world," Homes replied.

"Occam's Razor would indicate otherwise, Mr. Holmes."

"No evidence that what you say about China is true," Holmes replied.

"Tibet."

"Well those people rebelled," Holmes explained.

"You think millions of Americans won't? Is that your premise? Look at what China did to the Uighurs, they put over a million of them into concentration camps!"

Chris was quite pleased with himself in having recovered his debate position.

"They don't have to if people like you will get on board. The outcome is inevitable; it's just a matter of how much pain we'll have to suffer to reach that outcome. The completely unnecessary resistance will be the source of that pain," Holmes replied.

"For someone who not so long ago completely bought into the mantra of, 'RESIST,' that's quite a bold statement you're making. I recall you advocating for people to resist during an appearance on cable news channels. In fact, you proclaimed the need to resist when you were on your buddy Giles' show. Famous photo of you in the newspapers holding that banner in fact."

"You know I was resisting the oligarchy," Holmes shot back furiously.

"You were resisting a new President putting tens of millions of dollars of your illicit profits in jeopardy by abandoning the policies that you grew rich from," Malone retorted.

"Fuck you."

"Oh look. It's time for the session to start again," Malone observed.

66
Dirty Katie

The Wagoneer rolled down Fremont Street in Tombstone with Ray at the wheel and Jerry in the passenger seat. They'd been driving for thirteen hours and were ready to be done.

"Gosh, I was here when I was a kid. Family vacation. Where's Val Kilmer?" Jerry laughed.

"I just want to know where the Crystal Palace is," Ray replied.

"Off to the right somewhere," Jerry answered.

Ray steered the Wagoneer to the right onto Fourth Street.

"Make a left now," Jerry advised.

"Backseat driver," Ray responded.

"There it is," Jerry exclaimed.

Ray and Jerry parked and entered the Crystal Palace.

"Are you Cindy Tribell?" Ray asked.

"I am," Cindy responded as the customers at the bar reached for their side arms and stared at Ray and Jerry.

"We're from Colorado. We're here to extradite Katie Davis. Here is a letter from the governor. I don't know what process you want to follow here, but I should let you know that I am the one who took the photos of your brother after he was assassinated and both of us were witnesses," Ray explained in an attempt to establish his credibility.

"How do you want to do this?" Jerry asked.

"Len!" Cindy called over her shoulder.

Len walked from the back of the saloon to the bar where Cindy stood.

"These men are here to extradite Katie Davis," Cindy informed him.

Ray handed the letter to Len who read it quickly.

"I imagine you want to stay the night and leave in the morning?"

"That would be a good idea," Ray replied.

"We can put you up at our place. Want a beer, on the house?"

"How about we go see Katie Davis then have a beer?" Jerry responded.

"This way," Len said walking toward the door.

Before following Len out the door, Ray turned to Cindy and told her, "Nice to meet you," while nodding in respect.

Ray and Jerry followed Len down Allen Street to what had previously been a public rest room converted to an impromptu jail. Two men with shotguns guarded Katie with revolvers in the holsters on their belts.

Len opened the door to reveal Katie sitting on the floor, hands tied behind her back.

Katie looked up and shouted, "Pigs!"

"That's her," Jerry remarked.

"She's filthy," Ray said.

"Well, yeah," Len agreed.

"Let's see if we can't find some clean clothes for her before we leave, and hose her off, too," Ray said. "I don't want her in my Jeep like that."

Len closed the door, and the three walked back down Allen Street.

"Doc Holliday she isn't," Len laughed as they progressed down the boardwalk to the Crystal Palace.

"Cold-blooded killer is what she is," Jerry observed somberly.

The three men re-entered the Crystal Palace where Lori was now talking with Cindy.

Len asked Lori, "Can we find Ms. Davis some clean clothes?"

"Sure," was the response as Lori exited the saloon.

"How about that beer now?" Ray asked as they took seats at a table.

Cindy brought four beers to the table and took a seat next to Len along with keeping one of the beers for herself.

"I want to hear all about what happened to my brother, everything," Cindy demanded.

Jerry took a sip of beer and made a sour face to which Len responded, "Beggars can't be choosers."

"I don't recall beer tasting like this."

"Nobody does," Len responded.

Ray and Jerry spent the rest of the evening recounting John Tribell's murder to Cindy to include their unsuccessful hunt for Katie and Gary and the killing of George, Will, and Jay. Cindy asked many questions, and Ray and Jerry answered them all in a forthright manner before retiring to Len and Lori's home. Unfortunately, they could not tell Cindy where the other shooters were or what happened to them.

After arising the next morning and eating a rattlesnake and mutton breakfast, Ray, Jerry, and Len took the Wagoneer to the makeshift jail.

"Take her out," Len directed the guards.

The guards opened the door and, each grasping one of Katie's arms, dragged her out into the sand in front of the public rest room building as Katie screamed "No! Noooo! You bastards noooo!"

Ray walked behind Katie as the guards held her arms and, drawing the knife from the sheath on his belt, cut the restraints holding Katie's hands behind her back.

As Jerry dragged a garden hose from a nearby building and Katie rubbed her wrists, Ray commanded her, "Strip."

"No, you perverts!"

"Either you do it or we do it. Either way it is getting done," Ray said. "You are not getting into my car like this. You don't want to go down in history known as the Bed Bug Killer, do you? Dirty Katie maybe?"

"I like that, Dirty Katie," Jerry chortled as he held the garden hose at the ready.

"You Marines laugh at the weirdest stuff," Ray advised Jerry.

"Come on, strip!" Ray barked at Katie.

Katie gave Ray her dirtiest look and complied.

Jerry sprayed her down with the hose before Len threw an Arizona Diamondbacks tee shirt and a pair of athletic shorts in the wet sand at Katie's feet.

"Put those on," Ray barked.

Ray and Jerry restrained Katie's hands and ankles and placed her in the back seat of the Wagoneer. Jerry sat beside her while Ray drove.

They left Tombstone in silence.

All three were silent until they approached Deming, New Mexico, when Katie asked, "Where are we going?"

"Colorado," Ray replied.

"Why?"

"So, you can have a trial."

"You know I'll do whatever you want, just let me go. Anything you want. You can just tell them I escaped."

"You're far too famous for that to work anymore," Jerry replied.

"I have to pee."

"Okay," Ray replied, pulling the Wagoneer to a stop on the side of I-10.

Jerry and Ray got out of the Wagoneer and walked to the passenger side rear door which they opened and lifted Katie out of the Wagoneer.

Jerry pulled her athletic shorts down while Ray held her shoulders and bent her back at the knees.

"Go ahead, pee."

"Not like this, not on the side of the road. You're animals!"

"This is how it will be done, you are not getting untied or going into a building."

"Idiots!"

After that, Katie was silent until Los Lunas when she decided a diatribe was in order.

"You know you're all doomed. Your world is dead; you just don't know it yet. You sexist, racist pigs! You'll all die! I'm an example for all the others to kill you all! Others will follow me! You kill me, and you'll never sleep soundly again! You Klansman! Death to the oligarchy! Death to the patriarchy! Death to—"

Katie had failed to notice that Jerry had turned sideways in his seat and reached into the cargo area of the Wagoneer where he found a roll of duct tape, of which he tore off a strip and placed it over Katie's mouth.

"You just compulsively make everything worse, don't you?" Jerry pointed out to Katie.

"We're going to need gas here," Ray mentioned to Jerry as he exited I-25 at Los Lunas.

Ray pulled into a gas station as the attendant approached.

"How much can I buy?"

"Did you hear the news?" the attendant interrupted.

"Probably not," Ray responded hoping the news the attendant intended to share was not that Katie Davis was being extradited to Colorado.

"We sank the Chinese fleet. The carriers. Everything!"

"When?" Ray asked dubiously.

"Just this morning. It's all over the radio and TV. Man, payback feels good!"

Ray considered that the man seemed sincere, but he still was not convinced.

Ray stepped back to the Wagoneer and re-inserted the key in the ignition and turned the radio on while telling Jerry, "Let me know what you hear," he then stepped back away from the Wagoneer and turned to the attendant.

"Well, be that as it may, I still need gas. How much can you sell me?"

67
This changes things

Chris Malone and Paul Bishop sat next to each other in the Fort Bragg cafeteria watching the television with all of the other convention delegates.

"Unreal," Malone whispered.

"This changes things," Bishop replied.

"Be right back," Chris whispered to Bishop.

Chris Malone had spied Jeffrey Holmes across the room and approached Holmes in a deliberate manner as Holmes observed Malone's approach with dread.

Malone got as close as he could to Holmes' face and said, "Huh," in the most self-righteous, loud voice that he could muster.

As Chris walked back to his seat next to Bishop, he criticized himself for his pettiness while also relishing how satisfying that was.

"This is completely illegal!" Barbara Brewer asserted, loud enough for everyone in the cafeteria to hear, "It won't end well. They'll strike back at us even worse!"

"Denton just changed the entire dynamic, internationally and domestically," Bishop whispered to Malone. "People may debate the legality and morality but no debating how effective it is and, plainly, brilliant."

"Those six states just had their legs chopped out from under them," Chris replied.

"The Chinese hopes for a unipolar world just got a lot dimmer. Again, the morality is debatable, but it is the most politically astute move in at least eighty years," Bishop added.

"We better figure this out for the future, because Jennifer told me last night that she thinks she's pregnant," Malone replied.

"Congratulations. It's a brave new world," Wilkerson whispered from the far side of Paul Bishop.

"Whatever terms Holmes thought he could get from China, that notion is dead," Bishop whispered back to Wilkerson.

"And congratulations, I think," Bishop whispered to Chris.

Admiral Denton sat in his office awaiting further reports. Admiral Wright, General Helfrich, and General McNeil sat with him.

McNeil studied a report and commented, "No response from China, militarily or otherwise, as of yet."

"China is at this moment full of doubts. Everything they thought they knew to be true has been demonstrated false in the last six hours," Denton surmised. "They'll now have no idea what else they believed to be true that's false, and that's exactly what we want them to be confused about. They'll be paralyzed by doubt for some time. If they do respond, it's likely to be rash."

"They'll have great hesitancy in responding militarily. The military no longer has confidence in their own knowledge and judgment, and the political leaders now have zero confidence in the military leadership. I see firing squads in the future of quite a few senior officers," Admiral Wright added.

"Attempting to avoid those firing squads will be the motivation behind the rashness if they do respond," Denton said.

"General Helfrich, any further Russian incursions are to be aggressively deterred," Denton ordered.

"We want the Russians to have the same doubt as the Chinese, or at least to adopt a position of extreme caution," Wright contributed.

"Yes, sir," Helfrich responded.

"Japan is pretty happy. Philippines, too," Wright reported.

An Army major entered the office and reported to Denton, "Admiral Webb on the monitor from Hawaii."

Denton swiveled his chair to face the monitor and with the remote in his hand engaged the system.

"What do you have for us?"

"The latest is that all three carriers are destroyed, we continue to receive confirmation that the first reports were accurate. Ten of the twelve type 052D's splashed, and all nine type 055 destroyers are splashed or burning. Fleet 167 no longer exists."

"Any indication of a response?" Denton asked.

"No. No indication of a response."

68
Idigai

Brian Vann stood in the Gore cemetery with his hat in his hand.

He was grappling with emotions. He intellectually understood that he should feel for the parents of Chinese sailors who were now suffering the same way he had suffered two years ago. This intellectual knowledge was overwhelmed by the visceral pleasure of vengeance.

As much as Brian Vann knew he should feel for the Chinese sailors now at the bottom of the Pacific and their families, what he actually felt was redemption and justification, and he did now know what to think of that.

Brian was grappling with the base emotion that the death of his son had been avenged, and he felt guilty for experiencing that emotion.

Joe Meigs crossed the bridge over the Arkansas and turned the curve on highway 64 when he saw Brian's truck in the cemetery. Joe slowed and turned left into the cemetery.

"How are you doing?" Joe asked after parking his truck behind Brian's.

"Struggling."

"I bet."

"I'm feeling good about this, and I think I shouldn't."

"It's okay. It's okay to feel those things."

"War is not good. None of this is good. So why do I feel good that the Chinese navy was destroyed?"

"Human nature. They killed your son and were then destroyed in turn. Who would not feel good about that? Consider where we were before all that happened and then everything that happened afterward. That story and this feeling is as old as man. Solomon had it when he said there was nothing new under the sun," Meigs replied.

"I guess so."

"We have spent decades trying to make people not behave like people. That the people who killed your son were killed in turn is a perfectly okay thing to be happy about. You think Americans were not happy with every Japanese killed after Pearl Harbor? Of course they were. We try to pretend we're better than that, but we really aren't, and we shouldn't be. I guarantee you, the Chinese were thrilled when they sank our two carriers. Balance. Idigai."

"True."

"For years people tried to convince us that we were better and smarter than all those who came before us and that we had moved past all of the hard things in life. The last couple of years have shown that that was never the case. Just let yourself be human, Brian. You don't have to live up to some false standard someone else created. For thousands of years people felt exactly what you're feeling and never questioned it. It's okay to feel it and not question it," Joe Meigs continued.

Brian looked at Meigs, cocked his head sideways a bit and pondered the words.

"Somehow virtue signaling replaced being a real person," Joe Meigs observed sadly. "It got ingrained in all of us to some extent. Same way having the government create program after program after program replaced actually caring about your neighbor. Actually, caring about our neighbors would have been more useful than all of the government programs ever created."

"Gadugi," Brian replied.

"Gadugi."

69
I have to play nice now

"Well, here she is," Ray said as senator Barnes peered into the backseat of the Wagoneer at Katie Davis.

"What now?" Jerry asked.

"Those gentlemen over there will take custody of her," Barnes replied.

"Congratulations on your new role of senate leader by the way. I know it's been a while but better late than never," Jerry said.

"Thanks. Hopefully it works out better for me than my predecessor."

"How did you end up being in charge of Katie getting returned? Not a task the leader of the state senate is usually given," Ray queried.

"The governor told me that leadership was a character trait and not a job title. I think he read too many business books back in the day."

"Not a character trait that he apparently possesses," Jerry laughed.

"I have to play nice now," Barnes responded. "Part of the job."

"Things certainly changed since we left for Arizona," Ray observed.

"Indeed," Barnes replied. "Domestically and internationally there's now no premise or assumed paradigm from forty-eight hours ago that's still sacrosanct."

"Spoken like a true politician," Jerry laughed.

"Any news on Chinese retaliation?" Ray asked.

"No, but some reports, unconfirmed mind you, that some PLA officers had their careers cut short with, what was that line from *Apocalypse Now*, 'extreme prejudice,'" Barnes said.

"I imagine there's complete disarray in the military-political relationship in Beijing," Ray added. "The military-political relationship in China has not always been a happy one."

"Again, unconfirmed rumors of a military coup attempt. Makes sense, if you think they're going to line you up on a wall and shoot you. Then you have nothing to lose in a coup," Barnes informed Ray and Jerry.

"Interesting," Jerry remarked.

"Short story is that no one, outside of maybe Denton and his crew, knows what exactly is happening, but China seems to have gone internal with the response rather than external," Barnes said.

"They keep taking out the military leadership, they won't be in a position to respond to us for quite a while," Ray said.

"If China ends up in a civil war, then they won't respond at all," Barnes speculated.

"Is Denton really that smart or is he just lucky?" Jerry asked.

"Does it matter?" Ray answered.

"No, it really doesn't," Barnes responded.

"I suppose not," Jerry surmised.

"Those people at the convention arguing for a deal with China and claiming it was inevitable that we would have to knuckle under now have all the credibility of Benedict Arnold though, so we have that going for us," Barnes said.

"Hoping they get that convention done quickly," Ray said.

"Malone sent me a note just a bit ago, we actually have digital communications between the legislature and convention delegates now, saying that the sense was that they could wrap it up in a week now," Barnes informed Ray and Jerry.

"Holmes and his bunch have no standing to obstruct," Jerry added.

"None," Ray added.

"I know you didn't like this question, but seriously, is Denton really that smart?" Jerry asked again.

"Three hundred and fifty million people in this country, or there used to be, so we had the right guy in the right position at the right time to make the right decision was sort of a statistical inevitability if you want to look at it that way. Lord knows we had a long stretch with all the wrong people in the wrong positions making the wrong decisions at the wrong time, so the Law of Large Numbers would have to work in our favor eventually," Barnes replied.

"Could have just told me, 'yeah, he's that smart,'" Jerry laughed.

"Denton took realpolitik to a whole new level," Ray said.

"Oh, he took it back to a medieval level," Barnes asserted. "Ruthless. Fall upon your enemy when they feel most secure and leave no survivors."

"Wonder if he's drinking wine from skulls of the vanquished? Rurik had nothing on this guy," Jerry added.

"Since when did Marines ever learn about Rurik?" Ray chided.

"Who do you think we patterned ourselves after?" Jerry joked back.

"The mood of people has changed. It's palpable. Walk down Grant or East Colfax and you can feel it. See it on the faces of people, in their body language, in how they walk. I think it's quite simply that the United States actually accomplished something successfully after so many disasters. We're not necessarily doomed to failure," Barnes interjected.

"That the success had a ring of retribution to it didn't hurt either," Ray said.

"Losing a war, no longer being top dog, probably was more devastating to the psyche of the people than anything else. We grew so accustomed to things and took so much for granted that it was so unexpected when we lost to China. Now people will just view the last two years as half time. China won the first half, and we won the second half. People will be okay if it ends in a tie, emotionally okay. They were not emotionally okay with being subjugated," Barnes theorized.

70
Find some Commies that didn't blame the PLA?

Admiral Denton looked each of the officers seated around the table in the eyes before he began to speak.

"What do we know, gentlemen?"

"We know that the situation in Beijing is very confusing. That's the only thing that we can claim to actually know, Admiral," Admiral Wright replied.

"What do we think we might know?" Denton responded.

"Reports are that two Generals of the PLA and three Admirals of the PLAN were arrested and shot last night. The Central Committee of the Communist Party has been in continuous session since shortly after we executed our mission. It might appear that the PLA believes that the Central Committee acted, shall we say, rashly in having these officers arrested? Unconfirmed reports of tanks and armored personnel carriers moving into Beijing. Unclear that if this is so, as to whether it's a move toward a coup or the Central Committee has ordered them moved into Beijing to quell a potential coup or to be on hand to address civilian unrest. If these troops are moving on Beijing, we don't know which side they may be on or if there necessarily are sides at the moment," Wright commented.

"Japan seems convinced that there's a PLA revolt underway," Admiral Ziegler added.

"That may be wishful thinking by the Japanese," Denton replied.

"Germany has indicated that it may be a real possibility as well. The rumor in the diplomacy mill is that the German embassy has allegedly received Chinese government officials requesting asylum," Wright interjected.

"That's interesting," General Helfrich observed.

"It gets a bit more interesting. The son and daughter-in-law of the General Secretary of the Central Committee arrived in Ho Chi Minh City an hour ago, quite unexpectedly. One might rationally surmise that they had fled China rather than decided on a spur-of-the-moment shopping trip. These events don't lead to a conclusion, but they're certainly indicative that something is afoot. It's not a stretch to construct a scenario along the lines of the Central Committee rashly executing PLA officers, the PLA deciding they're unwilling to accept this outcome and moving on the Central Committee. Of course, that's all conjecture, but it's certainly a plausible turn of events," Wright said.

"Who will win if it comes down to the PLA against the Central Committee, Admiral?" General Nash asked Admiral Wright.

"The PLA. A battle between the Central Committee and the PLA has been brewing for decades," Wright answered.

"What might the PLA course be after they have won?" General Baumgartner asked.

"They would have to govern a country. I do not know that the PLA has the competency to do that anymore than we have had the competency to do that ourselves the last few months," Denton interrupted.

"The major difference in the two situations is that we have tried to hand it off to a representative government. The PLA really has no one to hand it off to other than the people that they took it from. There's been no other tradition other than communist dictatorship for so long," Wright added.

"Find some commies that didn't blame the PLA?" Admiral Andersen wondered.

"Something along those lines in all probability," Wright replied.

"The wild card here is civil unrest," Denton observed.

"That and the long-held presumption that the PLA would prefer to see Chinese society return to something akin to the Cultural Revolution," Wright added.

"If either the Central Committee or the PLA wins a potential showdown, will either one turn on us?" General Martinez asked.

"Probably not for a long time, but then again, they never expected our strike yesterday, so they may attempt to make surprise their ally as we did," Wright responded.

"Whoever would win that battle will have to spend some time consolidating power and soothing hurt feelings and attempting to mollify the civilian population," Denton said.

"Which is why we need to keep our guard up. For what you just said is what we'd expect from them, and knowing this, they might view it as an advantageous opportunity to strike," General McNeil warned.

"Noted," Denton replied.

As Admiral Denton completed his sentence, an Air Force Colonel entered the conference room and handed a note to Admiral Wright.

"For what it's worth, the BBC is now reporting that a PLA coup is underway in Beijing. Airports are closed, trains are stopped, ships not being allowed to leave port."

71
Think we have the appetite for that?

Chris Malone sat back in his seat in the Clarke Auditorium satisfied.

"We did it," Paul Bishop said as Chairperson Black gaveled the convention to a close.

Chris was extremely satisfied with the end result and how quickly the convention had progressed after the strike on the Chinese fleet. They had readopted the old constitution with three new amendments. The new amendments were to protect individual conscience from government compulsion, an amendment to make it hopefully impossible for the Federal government to interfere in state matters and to require a balanced budget and sound money and included funding all future obligations. They had also repealed the 16th and 17th Amendments.

The product of the convention would now go out to the states for ratification, but no one believed that would be an issue. The majority of states had already scheduled a quick vote. No one wished to prolong the current state of affairs.

Elections were scheduled for congress, the senate, and the White House. Barnes had declared his intention to run for the senate and had urged Chris to do the same. Chris had been noncommittal in his reply to Barnes, but he was leaning toward returning to his preferred vocation. Chris felt called to write a history of recent events rather than running for office. His experience at the convention had convinced him that he didn't have the patience for a deliberative body and that when his patience ran out, he became very petty. He didn't much care for that quality in himself.

"Nice to honor Denton on the day he announced his retirement," Chris mentioned to Paul Bishop.

"Yeah it was. I understand that Wright will take his place and McNeil is the Vice," Bishop responded.

"Think Denton will run for President?" Chris asked.

"I don't know, but if he does, he'll win," Paul replied.

"Back to Colorado tomorrow," Chris remarked.

"Q&A with the state legislature the day after that, then that Q&A on TV the day after that, and we're done," Bishop said ruefully.

"Sounds like you'll miss it?" Chris asked.

"In some ways it's been a nightmare, but it's not something any of us will ever get to do again," Bishop replied.

"What do you think the new government will do when they're handed custody of the former members of the Committee for the Continuance of Government?" Chris queried.

"A trial, but I don't know what that looks like. I kind of hope it's a Nuremberg trial kind of set up. People should know what these people did and, just as importantly, why they did it. In my opinion a major difference in post-war Germany and post-Cold War Russia was that Russia never put those responsible on trial; hence they continued a certain romanticism of those who committed mass murder, a romanticism that was exploited by people like Putin," Paul Bishop opined.

Chris Malone pondered that response.

"Think we have the appetite for that?" Chris asked.

"I hope we do," replied Paul.

72
An ideologue

Judge Sizemore: This is the case of the People versus Katie Davis. Let the record show the defendant is present with counsel and the jury is in the jury box along with the alternates. Okay. We'll start out for the day, Mr. Smith. Go ahead.

Defense Attorney Smith: Yes, Judge Sizemore. Good morning. The opening statement is a road map. It is not supposed to be an argument. What we will do, and what we will show you in this case, is what we believe is true. And we will show you what is not true as presented yesterday to you by the prosecution. I think this will show that Katie Davis is not only not guilty, but actually acted lawfully.

One of the first things that I think that we have to address is that Katie is charged with six counts of murder. She is not charged with anything else.

Clearly you want to call Katie an ideologue. You want to say her behavior is inappropriate, and her views of the world are extreme. We're not going to dispute that. But the fact of the matter is, did she murder John Tribell and his colleagues? And I'm going to run through, if I could, with you what the prosecution's claim is, and then I'm going to also show you that Katie was acting under the lawful orders of the existing government at the time, so it could not be murder.

Their first item, as you saw yesterday, they showed you the pictures of John Tribell, then they showed you the picture of Katie, her picture from the security agency, and contrasted the fact that Katie was employed by the government as though that was an evil thing and Tribell was an innocent bystander—

Prosecutor Williamson: Objection, your Honor. This is out of bounds.

Judge Sizemore: Here we go. Overruled.

Smith: Thank you.

So, the fact of the matter is, is that what their theory is, their motive for this crime is that Katie is an evil monster. What they haven't told you is that at the time that Katie supposedly meets Tribell and allegedly makes the decision to have Tribell killed, she was employed to do so. That was not the decision of Ms. Davis but the decision of her superiors. And the evidence is going to clearly show you that Katie was just following orders. She was doing what the government had employed her to lawfully do. And she ends up being put in an untenable position by merely abiding by the directions of the lawful government.

Their theory would be that Katie was behaving wholly of her own volition and wanted to kill. The evidence is going to show that she didn't want to kill, that she didn't want to have a phony relationship, and that she was, therefore, just following orders.

The next thing that they keep focusing on is that Ms. Davis went on the run. But what you have to understand about that, understand what the evidence is actually going to show, when her photos and name were broadcast on television and radio, she justifiably feared for her life. The prosecution alleged that Ms. Davis committed murder while she was on the run. She is not on trial for anything she did during that time and for the prosecution to alleged that is quite discriminatory. One might say it's underhanded for the prosecution to even allude to matters that Ms. Davis is not on trial for.

Mr. Williamson went through this whole painting the picture of what happened: seduce Tribell, discover the names of his friends, and lure them into an ambush.

The fact of the matter is, the security agency had arranged all of that. She was trying to prove to them that she was simply an obedient employee and avoid punishment herself. Don't buy the prosecution's allegations. As early as the previous month, you will see from the records, Katie had regrets about the entire undercover way of doing things. She was the one who was trying to change how this was done.

The interesting thing is that, you have heard this so many times, that it was all her idea.

It was not her idea. She didn't want to sleep with John Tribell. Let's make that perfectly clear. She despised him. He had plans, and everybody will tell you this, to resist the lawful government. You will see the copies of the Executive Order signed by the President making the Committee for the Continuance of Government the de facto lawful government, and Katie Davis was operating under the lawful direction of the legitimate government in regard to John Tribell.

The government had plans, and Katie was simply an employee carrying out those lawful plans. Every government has the right to oppose those that would overthrow that government. That has been true since George Washington sent troops to suppress the Whiskey Rebellion. If you would not convict the soldiers that George Washington sent to put down the Whiskey Rebellion, then you cannot convict Katie Davis. If you would not convict the Union Army under Abraham Lincoln, then you cannot convict Katie Davis.

Now, yesterday, there were some statements that were made about Katie that were not true. Well, these statements are just flat-out going to be contradicted by the evidence. In fact, does anybody remember yesterday, I don't have the transcript in hand, but they mentioned that Katie had told Diane Andrews how much she enjoyed killing? Do you know what the context of that conversation was? Of course not, because the prosecution didn't tell you that. The context of that conversation was in not displeasing Diane Andrews. Put that all together. Katie was afraid, truly afraid, of Diane Andrews and would not dare tell her how much she detested the undercover assignments. Diane Andrews is the one who should be on trial here, not Katie Davis—

Prosecutor Williamson: Objection, your Honor. This is outrageous.

Judge Sizemore: Sustained.

Smith: It was a total misrepresentation of the conversation. This woman, Katie Davis, has been an opponent of racism, sexism, and homophobia since childhood.

Now, this is incredible to me, Diane Davis didn't tell Katie not to kill. Something else they didn't tell you about. That it's clearly a fact. In fact, at one point, Diane Davis assisted Katie in planning her next undercover assignment. But the idea that Diane Davis was not an avid supporter of the Committee for the Continuance of Government and the security agency is just belied by what the evidence is going to show you.

The other thing that they don't tell you about, is clear, is the security agency trained Katie. They make it seem, the idea was all Katie's in what Mr. Williamson was telling you yesterday, but the evidence shows that it all originated with the security agency. That the very witnesses the prosecution intends to call were fully complicit in the undercover operations that they employed Katie Davis in and that they planned the outcome of those undercover operations, not Katie, is quite clear.

Now, they also brought up the fact that Katie had a long history of activism. That's not a crime. And the import is, and I think Mr. Williamson told you that Katie often advocated for and carried signs in support of violence, that she is not on trial for that. What they don't tell you is that, in the records, actually, they didn't even have to get the records, that Katie was recruited by the security agency. When she was recruited by the agency, she was then trained by the agency. After she was trained, she was then assigned duties. They have got this in the records. They're in evidence, and you will see them here. This was not the first undercover agent that the very witnesses brought to testify against Katie trained themselves. Katie is completely a product of those who trained her and assigned her to complete tasks. The very same people who trained her and assigned her these tasks, for which she is on trial, will be witnesses against her. They knew about it. They knew what she was doing, and they're responsible, not Katie. They know it's true, and it's in evidence.

The witnesses are responsible, not Katie.

Prosecutor Williamson: Objection, your Honor. This is, again, outrageous.

Judge Sizemore: Sustained.

Smith: Now, they also made much yesterday about this idea that Andrews and Sandoval were not active in undercover operations. I don't know where that comes from, because clearly what the evidence is going to show, they have got reports, and they knew about the tasks. She was in a weekly phone meeting with Andrews and Sandoval, every week right up until the time that Sandoval disappears.

Now, you're going to hear testified, and I think Mr. Prosecutor referred to it yesterday, how she had gone to intentionally meet Tribell to seduce him. Remember, there was that timeline, and that Sandoval had talked to her in the phone meeting. And then some time shortly after Sandoval talked to her, she went up to Tribell? When she went up to Tribell, you will hear that she was trying to meet him, the state senator, who still wears a suit, has had a long history of political agitation. We have evidence that this whole affair originated with the security agency and not Katie, and she was merely following orders. Tribell always intended to overthrow the lawful government. Remember that simply because you don't like the Committee for the Continuance of Government does not mean that it was not the lawful government. It was. And that within the week to ten days prior to Tribell's death, Katie was demonstrating hesitancy in completing her assigned task, the task that the security agency had given her.

Now, you're also going to hear today probably—as long as I don't take the whole day talking—from Diane Andrews. She is the security agent who was working closely with Katie. She would meet every other week. She would meet in the morning, I think it was on Mondays. She'll tell you today that Katie was an animal, but that's not what Diane Andrews said then. We have the reports. Remember, this is when they're saying that she's apparently not active in undercover operations. Andrews left and went to Arvada because she claims she was having issues of conscience over the undercover activities. Not what the reports say. She was doing the planning. She had gone to Arvada because she was not very good at her job. She got six, five or six reprimands. Diane Andrews will tell you when she comes and testifies today, I'll ask her. Diane Andrews didn't help Katie when Katie wanted out. Diane Andrews insisted that Katie do her job.

The other reason, just parenthetically, that that's interesting is, remember yesterday you heard from the prosecutor, that Diane Andrews was transferred due to moral objections? If you listened, this is one of many lies—

Prosecutor Williamson: Objection, your Honor. This is completely out of bounds.

Judge Sizemore: Overruled.

Smith: So, you have these accusations by those actually responsible that it was all Katie—

Prosecutor Williamson: Objection, your Honor.

Judge Sizemore: Overruled.

Smith: Now, let me tell you what else you've got. You've got many witnesses to her with Tribell. And I'll get into that before we're done. But you're going to have a succession of witnesses who saw her with Tribell, and saw her walking with Tribell, affectionate with Tribell. And she would tell people that she was in a relationship with Tribell. And that's what she did for employment. Katie was very concerned with the morality of her assignment right up to the end of the affair, and, by the way, she voiced that concern.

The day that she went with Tribell to the Rampart Range, the records show that was not her idea. That's exactly what she was assigned to do. She wasn't doing this of her own volition. She was roughly made to understand that if she didn't successfully complete her assignment, things would go very badly for her. So, not her choice, not her volition.

And she was sad about it. She was concerned about her conscience. She was concerned about the morality of what she was doing. And she would talk about that to her superiors.

Now, there is also this idea that Katie wanted to kill as many members of the resistance as she could. And that's something that seems to be, the prosecution is fixing on. The fact of the matter is, is that Diane Davis and others arranged this work for Katie in order to improve the chances of the Committee for the Continuance of Government to succeed. Katie had a very difficult time with her conscience doing this work. She had her own moral issues. And it was such that she had to do, she had to vent. She was taking every opportunity to protest her assignments. And when she was struggling with her conscience, she would call up Diane Andrews, have her listen to her protests about the work.

There are numerous prosecution witnesses, it's replete through the argument, who will tell you that Katie was excited about killing members of the resistance. In fact, the prosecution will admit to you, and they're going to have witnesses up here, that one of the things they did is, they went to find everyone who Katie ever said a positive word about the security agency to, and they, every single person there, will testify to that. They asked everyone, they asked, "Was Katie happy to do this work? Did she say it was okay? Was, did she look excited?" Nobody said a word about Katie's moral doubts. The fact of the matter is, the evidence will show you, the prosecution went to every single person who ever knew Katie; and, as I indicated before, the prosecution was seeking people excited about seeing her convicted and that the prosecutor was the one who personally built a case premised on people who hate Katie.

Prosecutor Williamson: Objection, your Honor.

Judge Sizemore: Overruled.

Smith: Now, the former security agents accuse Katie of cold-blooded murder. Kind of disingenuous of them, as I indicated before. They're here to convince the jury that she is guilty instead of themselves. It's a mantra that they chant. Katie is the one who simply did what they told her to do. Remember that the prosecutor was claiming yesterday and showing you what Diane Davis and Jerry Sandoval had to say? They didn't go into what they themselves did. That was to lead you to the conclusion that it was all Katie. The prosecutor is the one who said here, here is all you need to know. He provided that testimony.

And he also hired an investigator to go and search for witnesses that would say horrible things about Katie, because, as you saw yesterday from the prosecutor's opening argument, as you're putting those thoughts into your head, it's the entire argument, Katie is a horrible person who did all of this.

In fact, those witnesses don't know the whole story. And witnesses who were there, who saw and heard things that Katie said, didn't see and hear other things that Katie said and did. In fact, they know only part of the story.

Now, this other idea of the prosecution, that Katie intentionally sought out victims. Remember that. When you see the actual security agency records, when you see what people like Jerry Sandoval told Katie to do, the last thing you will remember is that she was just following the orders of those who now accuse her in order to escape their own culpability. Indeed, these security agents recruited an impressionable young lady and trained her to be a killer, then required her to kill or suffer dire consequences at the hands of those who accuse her today. She had no choice.

That's the truth to the matter.

Judge Sizemore: Are you finished, Mr. Smith?

Smith: Yes, your Honor.

Judge Sizemore: The court will break for one hour. When we return be prepared to call your first witness, Mr. Williamson.

As Ray exited the gallery of the courtroom he thought, *Some things never change*.

73
Like I want anything to do with politics

"Did you vote already?" Brian Vann asked Joe Meigs.

"I did. You should have listened to me and run for the House seat. You would have won," Meigs replied.

"Like I want anything to do with politics," Brian responded. "I just want to farm."

"I hear you."

"Well, one thing we know for sure—Denton will be President! No one would run against him!" Brian Vann laughed.

"The hard part was just convincing him to run. Once he decided that it was all over," Joe replied.

"It can only get better, right? I mean it can't get any worse than the last three years," Brian Vann said hopefully.

"Nope. It truly can't."

"You better be telling the truth," Vann replied.

"Once the new government is sworn in, Ford and Sandrop and Giles and that whole bunch from the Committee will be handed over to them. Word is they'll have a big public trial, like Nuremberg."

"I heard last night that Canada said they'll send Ford back here tomorrow. As soon as the election is over," Vann added.

"I think we'll find out a bunch that we didn't know if that's really what they're going to do," Meigs said.

"Turn on the TV and let's see the returns."

Chris and Jennifer Malone walked out of the elementary school after having cast their ballots.

"You did this, you know!" Jennifer told Chris.

"A lot of people did this," Chris replied.

"Without you, it wouldn't have happened this way."

"I don't know about that," Chris responded.

"Our children will tell their children who will tell their children who will tell their children that you did this," Jennifer retorted.

"You don't have to flatter me, I already decided to keep you," Chris replied.

"Seriously, you made history."

"Hopefully, now I can write about that history."

Ray sat on the tailgate of the Wagoneer and contemplated the meaning of the vote that he had just cast. Ray reflected on his years of service to the old government and the lesson that he had learned around the world: that tyranny was always fragile. The trick was never in overthrowing tyranny but in not replacing tyranny with yet more tyranny.

That tyranny was not replaced with yet another tyranny was what his vote represented to him.

Marcie Bernstein and Brian Barnes sat next to each other in the diner on West Colfax awaiting election returns at what they anticipated to be a victory celebration for Barnes' election to the new United States Senate.

For months they had kept their affinity for each other a secret. The election returns didn't just represent an advancement of Barnes' political career. They had agreed it would be the point when they publicly announced their engagement.

Admiral Wright looked each of the officers seated around the table in the eyes before he began to speak.

"Gentlemen, have you completed the appraisal and the request to share with the new congress?"

"Indeed, we have, Admiral," General McNeil replied.

"Very good. General Martinez are you prepared to present the appraisal?"

"Yes, Admiral."

"It's critical that we get off on the right foot with this congress. China won't be in disarray forever, and it's vital that we take advantage of this time to rebuild a posture that would deter the PLA from having any thoughts of seeking revenge in the future. Recall what Eugene of Savoy long-ago advised, 'Rearmament is worth more than a piece of paper,'" Admiral Wright asserted.

Cindy, Len, and Lori gathered behind the bar of the Crystal Palace.

"Can't believe they hanged her!" Len remarked.

"On election day!" Lori added.

"I don't know what I was expecting, but I'm not too comfortable with the brutality of it. Who would think a modern jury would arrive at that as punishment?" Cindy observed with unease.

"If anyone ever deserved, it she did," Len said in an attempt to comfort Cindy.

"I don't feel about it the way I thought I would," Cindy added.

"Good afternoon, Mr. Sandrop. My name is Derrick Quinn, and I've been assigned to be your defense counsel. As soon as the new government is sworn in, you will be charged with crimes against humanity along with the other incarcerated former members of the Committee for the Continuance of Government."

74
I answered that question yesterday

Chris Malone sat in his favorite chair in the living room looking at the ragged carpet and holding his newborn daughter. He thought he really should work on his book, but he was tired from having attended the Barnes-Bernstein wedding and reception that evening, so he turned the television on to watch the replay of the trial.

Prosecutor: You're aware that you are uniquely positioned to expound to us the true purposes of the Committee for the Continuance of Government and the inner workings of its leadership?

Sandrop: I answered that question yesterday.

Prosecutor: You, from the very beginning, together with those who were associated with you, intended to overthrow and later did overthrow, the republic?

Sandrop: That was, as far as I'm concerned, my firm intention. Progress and a republic are mutually exclusive.

Prosecutor: And, upon coming to power, you abolished republican government?

Sandrop: We found it to be no longer necessary. It was archaic, an anachronism.

Prosecutor: You established the Committee for the Continuance of Government, which you have described as a system under which authority existed to enact equality in all ways as the Committee saw fit, is that correct?

Sandrop: In order to avoid any misunderstanding, I should like once more to explain the idea briefly. The United States had failed; it was a failed state. The Committee for the Continuance of Government was the legal heir, and our goal was an equitable society. We were legally bound by no previous documents, agreements, or arrangements.

Prosecutor: In other words, you did not believe in and did not permit government, as we call it, by consent of the governed, in which the people, through their representatives, were the source of power and authority?

Sandrop: That's not entirely correct. We repeatedly called on the people to express unequivocally and clearly what they thought of our system. We also took the point of view that even a government founded on the catastrophe that had occurred could maintain itself only if it was based in some way on the confidence of the people.

Prosecutor: But you did not permit the election of those who should act with authority by the people, but edicts were designated from the top downward, were they not?

Sandrop: Quite right. We didn't advance to the point of an election, but we intended to.

Prosecutor: You say that you repeatedly called on the people to express unequivocally and clearly what they thought of your system. When and how did that occur?

Sandrop: Giles collected that and reported to us the results.

Prosecutor: Allow me to go on. The principles of the authoritarian government which you set up required, as I understand you, that there be tolerated no opposition which might defeat or obstruct the policy of the Committee for the Continuance of Government?

Sandrop: You have understood this correctly. By the time the Committee came to power, we had lived long enough with political opposition, and we had had enough of it. Through opposition, this country had been completely ruined. It was now time to be done with it and to start building up.

Prosecutor: After you came to power, you regarded it necessary, in order to maintain power, to suppress all opposition? Even to the point of murdering anyone who might present opposition?

Sandrop: We found it necessary not to permit any more opposition, yes. As for murder, well that was Mandy Ford, not the Committee.

Prosecutor: Did you not, yourself, vote in the Committee to liquidate all malcontents? In fact, did you, yourself, not second that motion when presented?

Sandrop: I do not recall that.

Prosecutor: The Committee's own records show that you seconded the motion to liquidate malcontents and voted in favor of doing so. And you also held it necessary that you should suppress all individual opposition by violence lest it should develop into organized opposition?

Sandrop: Insofar as opposition seriously hampered our work of equality, this opposition of individual persons or organized resistance was, of course, not tolerated. Insofar as it was simply a matter of harmless talk, it was considered to be of no consequence. Racist and supremacist and capitalist should never be tolerated.

Prosecutor: Now, in order to make sure that you suppressed individuals, you found it necessary to have a security agency to detect opposition?

Sandrop: I have already stated that was Mandy Ford.

Prosecutor: And upon coming to power, you also considered it immediately necessary to establish clandestine operations to take care of your incorrigible political opponents?

Sandrop: I have already stated that the reason for suppressing the opposition was that the opposition was opposed to equality. Mandy Ford was in charge of how that occurred, I knew nothing about it. But it was necessary, as I said, to develop a system to fight the oligarchy.

Prosecutor: But you're explaining, as the authority of this system, to men who don't understand it very well, and I want to know what was necessary to run the kind of system that you set up. The clandestine operation was one of the things you found immediately necessary upon coming into power, was it not? And you set it up as a matter of necessity, as you saw it?

Sandrop: You asked me if I considered it necessary to establish clandestine operations immediately in order to eliminate opposition. Is that correct?

Prosecutor: Your answer is yes, I take it?

Sandrop: Yes. That's no different than what previous American governments had done. Hoover spied on Martin Luther King for example.

Prosecutor: Was it also necessary, in operating this system, that you must not have persons entitled to public trials in independent courts? And you immediately issued an order that your clandestine operations would be empowered to apply the death penalty as the agents saw fit?

Sandrop: You must differentiate between the two categories; those who had committed some act of treason against the new state or those who might be believed to be able to commit such an act in the future. The suspected, however, of whom one might expect such acts, but who had not yet committed them, were taken into temporary custody for the sake of creating a state of equality.

Prosecutor: You did prohibit all court review?

Sandrop: That I answered very clearly, but I should like to make an explanation in connection with my answer.

Prosecutor: Please, explain.

Sandrop: In connection with your question that these cases could not be reviewed by the court, I want to say that a decree was issued through the Committee to the effect that those who were turned over to custody were to be informed after 24 hours of the reason for their being turned over. These people were given an opportunity of making a protest to the security agents as to why they should not be in custody. Anyone unfairly held in custody was due to the security agents, not the Committee.

Prosecutor: This meant that you were taking people into custody who had not committed any crimes but who, you thought, might possibly commit a crime?

Sandrop: Yes. People who opposed equality. That's a moral crime.

Prosecutor: Now, it is also a necessity, in the kind of state that you had, that you have some kind of organization to carry propaganda down to the people and to get their reaction and inform the leadership of it, is it not?

Sandrop: The last part of that question is unintelligible.

Prosecutor: Well, you had to have organizations to carry out orders and to carry your propaganda, didn't you?

Sandrop: Of course, we carried on propaganda, and for this we had a propaganda organization under the responsibility of Matthew Giles for content and Geoffrey Snider for the technology.

Prosecutor: And you carried that to the virtual reality centers through the leadership of the Committee for the Continuance of Government, did you not?

Sandrop: The leadership was there, of course, to advise on how to spread our ideas among the people.

Prosecutor: Through your system the commands and information went down from the authority, and information as to the people's reactions came back to the leadership, did it not?

Sandrop: That is correct. The orders and commands that were to be given for propaganda or other purposes were passed down the grades as far as necessary. On the other hand, it was a matter of course that the reactions of the broad masses of the people were again transmitted upwards, through Giles, in order to keep us informed of the mood of the people.

Giles consistently informed us as to the popularity of our program, that what we were doing was quite successful.

Prosecutor: And you also had to have certain organizations to carry out orders—executive organizations, organizations to fight for you if necessary, did you not?

Sandrop: Yes, administrative organizations were, of course, necessary. I don't quite understand—organizations to fight what?

Prosecutor: Well, if you wanted certain people killed, you had to have some organization that would kill them, didn't you? The President and First Lady and the rest of them were not killed by Harris' own hands nor by yours, were they?

Sandrop: The President—that whole affair I explained already clearly—that was a matter of necessity—

Prosecutor: I did not ask you—

Sandrop: —and was carried out by Mandy Ford.

Prosecutor: But when it was perceived to be a State necessity to kill somebody, you had to have somebody to do it, didn't you?

Sandrop: Yes, just as in other countries.

Prosecutor: And the security agency was the organization that carried out the orders and dealt with people on a physical level, were they not?

Sandrop: The security agency never received an order to kill anybody, not in my time. Anyhow, I had no influence on it. I know that orders were given for executions, and these were carried out by the security agency, that is, by Ford.

Prosecutor: At what time did the security agency perform this function of acting as the executor of the Committee for the Continuance of Government?

Sandrop: After the seizure of power, when the security agency came to be more and more in the hands of Mandy Ford. It's difficult for me to explain where they were active. I have already said that Harris and Ford worked very closely together. It's known that the security agency carried out police functions.

Prosecutor: And carried out other functions?

Sandrop: To what functions do you refer?

Prosecutor: They carried out all of the executions and assassinations, didn't they?

Sandrop: I knew nothing about that.

Prosecutor: Now, this system was not a secret system. This entire system was openly avowed, its merits were publicly advocated by yourself and others, and every person entering into the Committee for the Continuance of Government was enabled to know the kind of system of government you set up, didn't they?

Sandrop: Every person who joined the Committee knew that we embraced equality and knew the fundamental measures we wanted to carry out, so far as they were stated in the program. But not everyone who joined the Committee knew down to the last detail what was going to happen.

Prosecutor: But this system was set up openly and was well known, was it not, in every one of its details? As to organization, everybody knew what the security agency was, did they not?

Sandrop: Yes, everyone knew what the security agency was.

Prosecutor: And what its program was in general, not in detail?

Sandrop: I explained that program clearly. At the very beginning of my testimony three days ago, I described that, and I often spoke in the Committee meetings of the tasks of the security agency, and I even wrote about it for Giles' broadcasts, why it was necessary for equality.

Prosecutor: And there was nothing secret about the establishment of a security agency as a political police, about the fact that people were taken into custody for holding to beliefs and opinions that were not approved of by the Committee? Nothing secret about those things, was there?

Sandrop: There was nothing secret about it.

Prosecutor: As a matter of fact, part of the effectiveness of a secret police and part of the effectiveness of the penalties is that the people do know that there are such agencies, isn't it?

Sandrop: It's true that we intended for everyone to know that if they acted against the Committee, they'll end up dealing with the security agency. But the original reason for creating the security committee was to keep such people whom we rightfully considered enemies of the State from opposing us. No different than what any other country does. Every government has the inherent right to fight for continued existence.

Prosecutor: Now, that's the type of government, the Committee, which we have just been describing—the only type of government that you think can create an equitable society?

Sandrop: I wouldn't say that it's the only type of government that can create an equitable society, but that over and over it's clear that only a progressive government can create a progressive society that is equitable.

Prosecutor: But all of these things were necessary as I understood you, for purposes of being equitable?

Sandrop: Yes, these things were necessary because of the opponents that existed to our creating an equitable society.

Prosecutor: And I assume that that is the only kind of government that you think can function in an equitable society?

Sandrop: Under the conditions existing at that time, it was, in my opinion, the only possible form, and it also demonstrated that the country could be raised in a short time from the depths of racism, sexism, and oligarchy to relative equality.

Prosecutor: Mr. Sandrop, you have related to us the manner in which you and others co-operated in concentrating all authority in the Committee for the Continuance of Government, is that right?

Sandrop: I was speaking about myself and to what extent I had a part in it.

Prosecutor: Is there any defendant in the box you know of who did not co-operate toward that end as far as was possible?

Sandrop: That none of the defendants here opposed or obstructed the Committee is clear, but I should like to point out that those on the Committee who did oppose the majority of the Committee were taken into custody by Ford.

Prosecutor: Now, I want to call your attention to the fruits of this system. You, as I understand it, were informed by Mandy Ford on several occasions that hunger was a dire problem? That hunger motivated the resistance?

Sandrop: I have explained just how far I was informed of these matters.

Prosecutor: You believed an increase in rations not only to be unnecessary, but also to be to the advantage of those who opposed you?

Sandrop: At that particular time, I was of the opinion that this increase in rations should be postponed in order to carry through other tasks which I considered more important.

Prosecutor: You did not see any necessity in increasing the rations at that time, even from the point of view of quelling opposition? Certainly not to stave off starvation?

Sandrop: Naturally, I was fully aware of the efforts of the opposition, but I hoped first to put into effect the other measures, described by me, to improve the people's position.

Prosecutor: I can only repeat my question, which I submit you have not answered. Did you, at that time, see any necessity to increase the rations?

Sandrop: I personally believed that at that time the danger was due to those who had lost their privilege, and therefore the increase in rations might not yet be necessary. But that was my personal view.

Prosecutor: You were the second most powerful person on the Committee at that time, were you not?

Sandrop: It has nothing to do with my being second in importance There were conflicting points of view in regard to strategy.

Prosecutor: I have understood from your testimony, and I think you can answer this yes or no, and I would greatly appreciate it if you would; I have understood from your testimony that you were opposed, and told Harris that you were opposed, to an increase in rations. Am I right or wrong?

Sandrop: That is correct.

Prosecutor: Now, you were opposed to it because you thought that it was useful to the opposition to increase rations; is that correct?

Sandrop: Yes, I was of the opinion that the moment—and I repeat this again—that increasing rations would only improve the abilities of the opposition.

Prosecutor: And yet, as I understand you, you found food to be an important weapon in battling the opposition? Even as innocent people went hungry? You found the hunger of the many to be morally acceptable in an attempt to fight off the opposition?

Sandrop: These are several questions at once. I should like to answer the first one.

Prosecutor: Separate them, if you wish.

Sandrop: The first question was, I believe, whether I took the opportunity to tell the Committee about this danger of the supremacist acquiring more food. I had occasion to do this. We were rebuilding society from the ground up, and such differences of opinion, as far as strategy was concerned, could not be more important than the goal of an equitable society. Secondly, as far as innocent people are concerned, I do not wish even to discuss that. I believe that people received sufficient calories. That's what the experts told us. If that was inaccurate, that was their fault. Thirdly, I was not the man to forsake the people, to whom I had given my life to make their lives better, every time something was not of my way of thinking. If that had been the case, there would have been no need to limit food at all. It was in the best interest of everyone that we eliminate the opposition.

Prosecutor: Insofar as you know, the people were content with the volume of food they received?

Sandrop: The people did not know how much food was available. The people, therefore, had nothing to do with this. The people were not asked; they were told what would happen and the necessity for it.

Prosecutor: At what time did you know that limiting the food, as regards achieving the objectives that you had in mind, was causing innocent people to suffer?

Sandrop: It's extremely difficult to say. At any rate, according to my conviction, rooting out the opposition was a necessary requirement before improving the economic condition of the people. This is where previous progressive states had failed.

Prosecutor: Well, it broke down didn't it? You failed as well?

Sandrop: That's not at all correct. We had reverses, or rather, the goals which we had set were not all reached. The push for equality proved well enough that there was no question of a core American desire for a society premised on equality. Some ideas, which we had pushed forward, were merely bad ideas, and some were withdrawn. The totally unexpected nature of the Tribell matter doomed us, not our actions or policies or the American desire for progress.

Prosecutor: You said, "There was no question of a core American desire for a society premised on equality." The expression that you used does not tell me anything, because I don't know what you regard as equality. Will you tell the world in fixed terms what equality means in terms of the Committee for the Continuance of Government?

Sandrop: When, after the pension crisis, debt crisis, and war with China, the United States essentially was a failed state and at the same time the government could no longer provide for the sick, the disabled, the poor, and the elderly. It was then that I was forced to realize that equality could not be attained in a republican form of government. Up to that time, I had always hoped that, on the one side, the people would vote in a progressive government, on the other side, the lure of capitalism would recede.

Prosecutor: Now, that did not answer my question. Will you tell the world in fixed terms what equality means in terms of the Committee for the Continuance of Government?

Sandrop: I just said after the pension crisis, debt crisis, and war with China, the United States essentially was a failed state. After that there was no more hope. Equality in the context of the Committee meant that everyone would be materially equal, except previously marginalized communities in which reparations would be made via enhanced equality.

Prosecutor: And you believed that starving innocent people and murdering your political opponents was key to attaining an equitable society? What definition of equitable are you using where that might be the case?

Sandrop: There were people intractably opposed to an equitable society, and those people influenced others to oppose our efforts.

Prosecutor: Is this akin to what Lenin allegedly referred to as terror as social hygiene?

Sandrop: I will not dignify that with a response.

Prosecutor: Do you want it understood that, as a career politician and political appointee, you did not realize until the old government reached collapse that progressivism could not be successful in a republic?

Sandrop: As I have already said, we must draw a sharp distinction between two possibilities: First, the successful democratic installation of a progressive government, and second, the collapse of the United States. As regards a successful outcome, the moment when it was realized that that was no longer possible, to democratically install a progressive government was the collapse, whereas the realization of the fact that the collapse could set in motion a progressive government, became apparent.

Prosecutor: For some period before the collapse, you knew that a successful democratic installation of a progressive government was not possible and could only be accomplished if you could come to some kind of emergency situation and install a progressive government as a result of that emergency; was that not true?

Sandrop: No that's not true, a successful democratic installation of a progressive government was always the primary goal. That's what I call a successful outcome. I call it a necessity, when the government came to power as result of the collapse. This doesn't bring the success which electoral victory would have brought but, on the other hand, it still produced a progressive government.

Prosecutor: But you knew beforehand that it was Harris' intent to use the executive order from the President to abolish the republican form of government and you knew that as long as Harris was the head of the Committee, the republican form of government would be opposed with violence, did you not?

Sandrop: I knew that there was an opposition that emphasized that under no circumstances would there be a progressive government. That Harris didn't want to negotiate away the advantage that the Executive Order provided him, I also knew, but not in the way that you imply. Harris wanted to negotiate if there were some prospect of results; but he was absolutely opposed to hopeless and futile negotiations that prohibited a progressive government. Because of the declaration of the opposition in the congress after the Executive Order, as far as I remember, that under no circumstances would they negotiate with Harris but would force on him their will, Harris's resistance was stiffened to the utmost, and measures had to be taken accordingly. If I have no chance of creating a progressive government through negotiations, then it's useless to negotiate, and I must strain every nerve to bring about a change by other means. That is what we did.

Prosecutor: Those measures you mention were to imprison and ultimately execute members of the old government most opposed to the abolishment of the republic?

Sandrop: Concerning the measures that Harris took to resist the opposition, I should like to describe the possibility of doing this as follows: Of itself—

Prosecutor: Can you answer my question? Time may not mean quite as much to you as it does to the rest of us. Can't you answer yes or no? Did you then know, at the same time that you knew that Harris intended to abolish the republic that Harris also intended to imprison the opposition? Can't you tell us yes or no?

Sandrop: I can say that I knew that, at that time, it was possible.

Prosecutor: And after that time, it was well known to you that the major political opposition was indeed imprisoned and subsequently executed, and this was affected solely to prolong the Committee for the Continuance of Government's hold on power?

Sandrop: I believe you're mistaken. This was all Mandy Ford. If I had had knowledge of this at my disposal, at the time, of course, I should have countered this action.

Prosecutor: Yet we have the records of you having voted for this in the Committee, indeed your arguments in favor of imprisonment and execution? Was there any opposition to these executions by the Committee?

Sandrop: Thank God, we really didn't understand what we were voting for. I have just said that, it was all Ford and Harris.

Prosecutor: And there was no way to prevent this?

Sandrop: As long as Harris was the Chairman of the Committee, he alone decided whether the imprisonment was to go on. As long as he was Chairman, he alone decided, and his demands were absolutely unconditional in that there would be no factionalism on the Committee, because there's nothing more detrimental to success than factionalism, except perhaps treason.

Prosecutor: Well, the Americans who thought it was time that the slaughter and starvation should stop had no means to stop it except revolution, did they?

Sandrop: A revolution always changes a situation, if it succeeds. That's a foregone conclusion.

Prosecutor: That's an inane answer, Mr. Sandrop.

Sandrop: Unfortunately, yes, but is the only answer I will give you to that question.

Prosecutor: It was voted on three separate times to deny weekly rations to Cheyenne, Wyoming. You know about that? You voted for that? Your position on the Committee made you responsible for denying those people food?

Sandrop: That's correct.

Prosecutor: And in making this decision, I call your attention to this statement: "Starve them out. If they can't behave, they get no food. Have no mercy on those racists."

You made that statement in the Committee meeting before voting to deny food to Cheyenne the second time, did you not?

Sandrop: I can only answer, I do not know. I do not recall. I neither betrayed the principles of progress, nor did I at that time counter the Committee. This act was originated by Harris and Ford, it's based on an extremely regrettable mistake, and one which grieves me deeply—we had limited tools at our disposal to counter opposition. It was all due to an error in understanding and perhaps a misrepresentation by Ford. I, myself, never thought for a minute of taking away food as a good idea.

Prosecutor: In any event, you voted for it and carried out the action?

Sandrop: That's correct.

Prosecutor: You also voted to take food away from other cities and people?

Sandrop: Yes.

Prosecutor: Now, in tracing the history of the Committee in your previous testimony you have omitted some things as, for example, the execution of Dr. Hubbell. There was a great purge of her department, was there not, in which many people were arrested, and many people were killed?

Sandrop: I don't know of a single case where a person was killed because of the Hubbell arrest, except that of her assistant, Williams. That was all Harris and Ford. Relatively few arrests were made in connection with Hubbell. The arrests that you attribute to the Committee were initiated by Harris and Ford, not the Committee. These arrests, as I have repeatedly stated and wish to emphasize once more, had nothing to do with the Committee.

Prosecutor: You had lists of people to arrest already prepared at the time of the Hubbell arrests, of persons who should be arrested, did you not?

Sandrop: We had always drawn up, beforehand, fairly complete lists of possible opponents who might be arrested. That had nothing to do with the Hubbell arrest.

Prosecutor: They were immediately put to execution—the people arrested, I mean—after the Hubbell arrest?

Sandrop: Harris ordered the arrests immediately. This had the disadvantage, as I said, of precipitating certain matters.

Prosecutor: You and Harris met after the Hubbell arrest, did you not?

Sandrop: That's right.

Prosecutor: And then and there it was decided to arrest all the others that you had listed?

Sandrop: I repeat again that the decision for their arrests had been reached some time before this; it simply meant that on that night they were immediately arrested.

Prosecutor: And the next morning the decision was presented by the Committee to Ford, to execute them all, was it not?

Sandrop: I believe so, yes.

Prosecutor: You voted in favor of the decision to execute them all? In fact, you introduced the motion to execute them all?

Sandrop: I do not recall.

Prosecutor: What was Dr. Ann Hubbell's offense? What exactly did she do to deserve the death penalty without trial or appeal?

Sandrop: I do not recall.

Prosecutor: Perhaps give yourself a moment to recollect?

Sandrop: No.

Prosecutor: Now, it's known to you, is it not, that Hubbell made a statement in the Committee that the virtual reality centers were creating people who could not differentiate between reality and virtual reality? You knew of such a statement, did you not?

Sandrop: I do not know of any such statement by Dr. Hubbell.

Prosecutor: But there was such a statement made by Dr. Hubbell, was there not?

Sandrop: I do not know.

Prosecutor: And, in any event, you argued for her death and made mention of that statement as justification, did you not?

Sandrop: That's not correct.

Prosecutor: Well, she had begun to make statements about virtual reality centers, had she not, and you were generally opposed to her conclusion?

Sandrop: That accusation that I had anything to do with Dr. Hubbell's death came from a certain foreign press much later. That doesn't bother me because it was not consistent with the facts. I had no reason or motive for advocating for the death of Dr. Hubbell. I did regret very much that it occurred.

Prosecutor: Have you ever boasted of being instrumental in the death of Dr. Hubbell, even by way of joking?

Sandrop: No. I made a joke, if that's the one you're referring to, when I said that, after this, I should be competing with Fidel, that was the joke. But the fact was that I was very sad at her fate, which was completely unnecessary.

Prosecutor: Dr. Hubbell compared the Committee to a George Orwell book, did she not?

Sandrop: No. I don't recall what book she referred to. That's an absolute distortion of the truth to imply that I had anything to do with her death.

Prosecutor: Do you remember the dinner where Harris proposed increasing the weekly calories?

Sandrop: No.

Prosecutor: You don't remember that? I will ask that you be shown the affidavit of Mike Moore, the waiter who served you at that dinner, and I call your attention to his statements that may refresh your recollection. Tiramisu does not jar your memory?

"I wouldn't think so; the resistance would use additional calories to build a reserve and use that against us. The heart of the resistance is male capitalist, supremacist. Increasing calories won't alter that."

That's the relevant portion. You don't recall making that comment?

Sandrop: This conversation didn't take place, and I request that I be confronted with this waiter. First of all, I want to emphasize that what's written here is utter nonsense. Apparently, he has a bad memory. That's the only explanation.

Prosecutor: You know who Hunley is?

Sandrop: Only too well.

Prosecutor: Can you tell us what position he held?

Sandrop: He was regional director of security for the Rocky Mountain zone, and I repeatedly pointed out to Harris, that he would be a problem.

Prosecutor: Now, that word, *problem*, you have left a little indefinite. Problem? What acts did he commit?

Sandrop: Hunley abused his position, and it was intended by Ford to allow him to continue doing so.

Prosecutor: And you had evidence of that fact?

Sandrop: I had sufficient knowledge of that fact.

Prosecutor: But he was never brought to account by the Committee, was he?

Sandrop: That's correct. I wanted to bring about a change and therefore attempted to get Harris to consider it, but Ford blocked me.

Prosecutor: All around nice guy, aren't you?

Sandrop: I believe so.

Prosecutor: Who actually killed Hubbell? Do you know?

Sandrop: I do not know who personally carried out this action.

Prosecutor: Was it Hunley?

Sandrop: That I do not know.

Prosecutor: And who took into custody those who were from Dr. Hubbell's department, and how many were there?

Sandrop: The security agency carried out the arrest. I do not know how many.

Prosecutor: Give me a name?

Sandrop: I do not know.

Prosecutor: You knew the day after Hubbell was executed, did you not? You knew the day after that Hunley had been recalled to Washington specifically for this task and that he took custody of thirty-seven people from Dr. Hubbell's department and that Hunley personally executed Hubbell, and we know you knew because the day after these events occurred, you entered a resolution for the Committee's attention congratulating Hunley for all of this that I have stated.

Sandrop: I say again, I don't know exactly how many were arrested because the arrests, or the arrest of those who were considered as having a part in this, didn't go through me. My action ended, so to speak, in the Committee. I understand Ford a little differently than you, and I sent a note to her in order that it be made clear, that I should curry favor with her, that her department be congratulated. She responded that Hunley was instrumental. That's the way I understood it. But to clarify this statement, you should have to understand, for all I know is what she told me, and I don't know if that's true or not.

Prosecutor: Among those who were killed were Dr. Kirby and his wife. He was one of your political opponents in the government, was he not?

Sandrop: Some might have considered him as such.

Prosecutor: And also, Richard Orozco, who had been in charge of researching virtual reality from a psychological aspect?

Sandrop: Orozco was among those who were shot. Actually, it was Orozco's case which caused me, as I stated previously, to ask Harris to give immediate orders to cease any further action, since, in my opinion, Orozco was quite wrongfully shot.

Prosecutor: All around nice guy, aren't you? Always sticking up for the good guy.

Sandrop: I stand for equality and justice.

Prosecutor: And when it got down to a point where there were only two left on the list yet to be killed, you intervened and asked to have it stopped; is that correct?

Sandrop: No, that's not entirely correct. I made it fairly clear and should like to repeat briefly that not when there were only two left on the list did I intervene; I intervened when I saw that many were shot who were not a threat. And when I did so, two persons were left, and Harris, himself, had ordered that they be shot. Harris was particularly furious with Orozco. What I wanted to make clear was that I said to Harris, "It's better for you to give up the idea of having these two perpetrators executed and put an end to the whole thing immediately." That's what I meant.

Prosecutor: And yet you introduced a resolution to the Committee congratulating Hunley on this matter?

Sandrop: Yes, it was politically expedient to do so.

Prosecutor: And what happened to the two men who were left on the list—were they ever released?

Sandrop: I do not know.

Prosecutor: Now, going back to the time when you met Harris eight years ago; you said that he was a man who had a serious and definite aim, do you recall that?

Sandrop: Please repeat.

Prosecutor: When you met Harris, as I understand your testimony, you found a man with a serious and definite aim.

Sandrop: I think you didn't quite understand me correctly before; for I didn't put it that way at all. I stated that it had struck me that Harris had very definite views of the impotency of deliberation; secondly, that he was of the opinion that equality must be attained. We could not wait any longer. Equality was non-negotiable.

Prosecutor: So, as I understand you, from the very beginning publicly and notoriously, it was the position of the Committee for the Continuance of Government that equality was non-negotiable?

Sandrop: From the beginning, it was the aim of the Committee for the Continuance of Government for America to attain economic, social, and political equality and justice.

Prosecutor: And to do so by murder, if necessary?

Sandrop: We didn't discuss that. We debated only about the condition of equality, that the United States should acquire a different political structure, which alone would enable her to raise the people to a level of equality; this previous one-sided system—people always called it a republic or democracy, whereas we always called it an oligarchy.

Prosecutor: That was the means—the means was the reorganization of the United States, but your aim was to get rid of what you call the oligarchy.

Sandrop: Liberation from the oligarchy can only be attained by an entity more powerful than the oligarchy, and the only potential entity to fulfill that role is the state, which in the long run would make life equitable, and that was the aim and the intention. But we didn't go as far as to say, "We want to murder our enemies and be victorious." Rather, the aim was to suit the methods to the events. Those were the basic considerations.

Prosecutor: And it was for that end that you and all of the other persons who became members of the Committee and gave to Harris all power to make decisions of life and death for individual citizens, and agreed, to give him obedience in the cause of avoiding factionalism?

Sandrop: Again, here are several questions. Question One: The fight against the oligarchy was, for me, the most decisive factor in joining the Committee. For others, perhaps, other points of the program, which seemed more important, may have been more decisive. Giving Harris powers was not a basic condition for getting rid of the oligarchy, but for putting into practice our conception of equality. To give him cooperation before he became the head of the Committee was, under the conditions then existing, a matter of course for those who considered themselves members of his select leadership in the pursuit of equality. I can only tell you what I, myself, did. After a short period of time, when I had acquired more insight into the goals of the Committee, I gave him my unconditional cooperation.

Prosecutor: If you would answer a few questions for me yes or no, then I would be quite willing to let you give your entire version of this thing. In the first place, you wanted a strong central government, a dictatorship, to overcome the oligarchy and institute what you define as equality.

Sandrop: We wanted a strong government anyhow, to counter the oligarchy; but in order to get rid of the oligarchy, the Committee had, first of all, to be strong, for a weak government would never make itself heard in the chaos that existed; that we knew from experience.

Prosecutor: And the dictatorship you adopted because you thought it would serve the ends of abolishing the oligarchy?

Sandrop: Correct, though I would not use the word dictatorship. We intended to call elections when the opposition to equality had been swept away.

Prosecutor: And this aim, one of the aims of the Committee for the Continuance of Government, was to call elections only after your political opposition had been killed or imprisoned and in your mind that constituted a valid electoral process? Something other than dictatorship?

Sandrop: The power of the oligarchy is such that every American, in my opinion, could not help being influenced to vote against their own interest.

Consequently, you can't have valid elections until you destroy all remnants of the oligarchy and those who advocate for the oligarchy.

Prosecutor: You have no doubt in what you believe to be true, do you?

Sandrop: I'm absolutely certain about that.

Prosecutor: Now that you're out of power, you believe the oligarchy will again rise?

Sandrop: I'm not absolutely certain of this. I have no proof. I do not know, but I assume so unless it's actively opposed by a superior power.

Prosecutor: You don't find the votes of the American people to be a superior power?

Sandrop: The influence exerted by the oligarchy at different times in different ways, inevitably deceives the voter. The chief influence on the voter, at least up till the collapse, if one can speak of voters at all, was exerted by the one percent. This influence wavered from time to time and increased greatly in the last years of the old government, for it was easy to win influence by means of money. When the Committee came to power and during the two years immediately following, we abolished the influence of the oligarchy. The most decisive influence on the Committee was the pursuit of equality.

Prosecutor: You don't believe that Americans will vote in their own self-interest?

Sandrop: I have explained that.

Prosecutor: You believed that you could decide for Americans in a superior manner than they could decide for themselves, did you not?

Sandrop: No; only until the oligarchy was destroyed could we decide in a superior manner than the people.

Prosecutor: Was John Tribell part of the oligarchy?

Sandrop: I had nothing to do with Tribell.

Prosecutor: Why was Tribell killed?

Sandrop: That was Mandy Ford. I had nothing to do with that.

Prosecutor: Please, Mr. Sandrop, don't be so modest. You had voted and argued in favor of and made motions to kill malcontents. You had a great deal to do with the murder of John Tribell. Was John Tribell part of the oligarchy?

Sandrop: Tribell was part of the liberty movement, a movement that used the concept of liberty to mask racism, inequality, and promoted all of the advantages in favor of the oligarchy.

Prosecutor: Tribell spent most of his life arguing in favor of equality, but to be attained in a different manner than the methods of the Committee. You claim the Committee was guided by the pursuit of equality, but John Tribell was also guided by the pursuit of equality; yet you killed him for his beliefs. Is it fair to say that the Committee was less interested in equality than in perpetuating its own continued existence and that the only methods it would accept were the narrow views of you and the other members?

Sandrop: No, that would not be fair. Tribell was a pawn for the oligarchy, even if he was perhaps unaware of that.

Prosecutor: So, in the end, the only methods for attaining equality that would not get you killed were the methods that originated in the Committee?

Sandrop: That is not true.

Prosecutor: How was that not true, pray tell?

Sandrop: We spent years planning exactly how to create an equitable society, and we acted on those plans when we had the opportunity. People like Tribell were no more than anarchist wanting to torch all that we had accomplished and planned.

Prosecutor: So, you planned to create the Committee for many years before the credit crisis or war with China?

Sandrop: I already refuted that.

Prosecutor: Ah ha. You had a good deal of difficulty with James Ramsey, did you not?

Sandrop: That is correct. Ramsey didn't strive to get the country to a place of absolute equality. Ramsey believed that we were moving too quickly, too radically. But the decisive control was ultimately held by Harris.

Prosecutor: You have listened to the evidence of the Prosecution against all of the defendants in this case, have you not?

Sandrop: Yes.

Prosecutor: Is there any act of any of your co-defendants that you claim was not one reasonably necessary to carry out the plans of the Committee for the Continuance of Government?

Sandrop: At present those are only assertions by the Prosecution; they're not yet facts that have been proved. In these assertions, there are a number of actions that would not have been necessary.

Prosecutor: Will you specify which acts, of which defendants, you claim, are beyond the scope of the plans of the Committee?

Sandrop: That's a very difficult question that I can't answer straight away and without the data.

Defense: I object to this question. I don't believe that this is a question of fact but rather of judgment, and that it's not possible to give an answer to such a general question.

Judge: Prosecutor, the bench thinks that the question is somewhat too wide.

Prosecutor: You have said that the program of the Committee for the Continuance of Government was to rectify certain injustices that you considered inherent in the United States; and I ask you whether it's not a fact that your program went considerably beyond any matter that dealt with seeking redress for that injustice?

Sandrop: Of course, the program contained a number of other points that had nothing to do with the historical injustices.

Prosecutor: I call your attention to a statement of Ted Harris to the Committee as follows:
"The boundaries of the constitution do not mean anything for the future of this nation. They didn't constitute a defense of the past nor do they constitute a path to the future. They won't give to the people hope or ensure that they eat or have medical care or housing or income. We must rid ourselves of not just the document but of all those who advocate for the constitution."

Sandrop: This is the text of a speech and not the Committee program.

Prosecutor: The Chairman was not to be opposed in the Committee, or so you have testified? Factionalism and all of that? If so, how was this not the program of the Committee?

Sandrop: For this very reason, this point was distinctly separated from the program. Harris is directly connected with the Committee only insofar as the leader, as proclaimed, was most listened to; for the Committee decided on the program. Harris was voicing his opinion.

Prosecutor: Which is it? Either you were responsible for the murders and starvation that you have excused as merely comity for the sake of opposing factionalism because Harris and Ford decided it all, or the Committee decided on the program.

Sandrop: Either at different times.

Prosecutor: You still haven't answered my question.

Sandrop: Yes, I did.

Prosecutor: You have testified, have you not, on direct, that it was Harris's opinion that the United States would never recover from the war, even if you were completely successful in the Committee's program, and that he counted on the corporations to produce a minimal amount of food and fuel for the infinite future?

Sandrop: That is entirely incorrect. That's the very reason why I refused from the beginning to give my oath to these interrogations. Now, as far as this statement is concerned, I should like to put it right. I said that, at first, Harris didn't believe that America would return to capitalism and that he was confirmed in this belief by the attitude of the foreign press and the feedback we received from Giles. Such nonsense—I hope you will excuse me—as to say that America would not ever recover from the war even if we were successful, you will understand that I could never have uttered or embraced, because, I believed in the program of the Committee.

Prosecutor: But did Harris say it?

Sandrop: No.

Prosecutor: You talked with him about this subject, did you not?

Sandrop: About the subject of America's recovering from the war, I could very well have talked with him; it's even probable.

Prosecutor: You told him that a democracy could not mobilize its economy as efficiently as a socialist dictatorship, did you not?

Sandrop: I didn't tell him any such nonsense, for we had no reason to debate history when we owned the future.

Prosecutor: You have testified on direct, if I understand you correctly, that there were at all times two basic ideas in Harris's mind, either to ally himself eventually with China and seek an increase in trade through the submission to Beijing or to keep the United States closed to international commerce. But in view of his orientation, he would very much have preferred to ally himself with China, is that true?

Sandrop: That is mostly correct. The dependency was on China agreeing to keep the Committee in place and in power.

Prosecutor: Harris was willing to commit the United States to being a vassal state of China as long as he got something out of the deal?

Sandrop: That is not correct.

Prosecutor: All right; tell us in what manner that is incorrect.

Sandrop: Shortly after the war, Harris made several proposals for cooperation; but, since these were not taken seriously by China, he ordered a complete closing of international trade, not that there was much trade at that point. But it had nothing to do with Harris' personal future. China had little interest in talking.

Prosecutor: What do you mean by that, little interest in talking?

Sandrop: China had no interest in negotiating with the Committee about anything.

Chris Malone glanced at the clock and saw that it was 2:00 AM. He turned the television off and thought to himself, *Lots of history left to write*.

Glossary

16th Amendment

Empowered the Federal government to collect income tax from individuals. Text: The Congress shall have power to lay and collect taxes on incomes, from whatever source derived, without apportionment among the several states, and without regard to any census or enumeration.

17th Amendment

Provided for the direct election of US senators by the people. Prior to that, they had been selected by the state legislatures. Text: The Senate of the United States shall be composed of two Senators from each State, elected by the people thereof, for six years; and each Senator shall have one vote. The electors in each State shall have the qualifications requisite for electors of the most numerous branch of the State legislatures.

Aristocracy

Government by the best individuals or by a small privileged class.

Casus belli

An event or action that justifies or allegedly justifies a war or conflict.

Comity

Friendly social atmosphere or social harmony.

Free Market

In the context of *Our Dogs Did Not Bark*, a free market is one in which no one is required to buy or sell; no one is prohibited from buying and selling; and price determination, quantity, and terms are a completely voluntary agreement between the buyer and seller. In a free market there's no government compulsion or prohibition, and government is not engaged in directly or indirectly controlling commerce or prices.

Intersectionality Theory

The complex, cumulative way in which the effects of multiple forms of discrimination (such as racism, sexism, and classism) combine, overlap, or intersect especially in the experiences of marginalized individuals or groups. For example, as applied in a political manner, a black woman suffers handicaps that a white woman or a black man doesn't.

Liberty

Historically defined as the absence of interference by government or others in personal or commercial affairs. Within the context of natural rights, it's the concept that government exist to defend natural rights and not to engage in the deprivation of natural rights. Examples of Natural Rights would include freedom of speech, freedom of conscience, freedom of worship, freedom of movement, freedom to earn a living, and freedom to defend yourself.

Meritocracy

A system in which the talented are chosen and moved ahead on the basis of their achievement.

Miner's Courts

In the western United States during the 19th century, mining activities often outpaced the reach of formal government. Mining camps would spring up seemingly overnight with no clear governmental jurisdiction and, consequently, no courtrooms and judges. The occupants of the mining camps would, if necessary, conduct a criminal trial or settle a civil dispute, select a jury, and elect an individual to perform the duties of a judge, and then conduct trials without trained lawyers and judges or formal courtroom procedures in order to arrive at a verdict, settlement, or punishment.

NKVD

Narodny komissariat vnutrennikh del, People's Commissariat of Internal Affairs: The Soviet police and secret police from 1934 to 1943: The police from 1943 to 1946 responsible for operating the Gulag system, executions, assassinations domestic and foreign, the starvation of millions, and the imprisonment and torture of probably millions.

Occams Razor

Occam's Razor is a problem-solving principle that the simplest solution tends to be the correct solution more often than not, particularly when explaining behavior.

PLA

Peoples Liberation Army, the overarching military infrastructure of the Peoples Republic of China.

Privilege Theory

Privilege theory argues that each individual is embedded in a matrix of categories and contexts and individuals will be in some ways privileged and other ways disadvantaged, with privileged attributes lessening disadvantage, and membership in a disadvantaged group lessening the benefits of privilege. The most commonly referenced context is that of "white privilege", an accusation that moral structure, social structure, government structure, commerce, and culture in the United States are essentially European and work to the advantage of those of European descent and to the disadvantage of those not from European descent. For example, as applied in a political manner, a white heterosexual male would rank at the bottom of the list of those whom had been marginalized while, for example, a Hispanic lesbian might rank near the top and consequently would receive compensation or preference.

Realpolitik

Politics based on practical and material factors rather than on theoretical or ethical objectives

Rearmament

To arm a nation, a military force, or other again with new or better weapons.

Rurik

Rurik is generally considered the first ruler of what would eventually become Russia, creating a hereditary dynasty in the 9th century. Rurik is perhaps best known for having allegedly used the skulls of his vanquished enemies as his preferred drinking vessels for consuming alcoholic beverages.

Spoliation

Plundering.

Suzerain

A superior feudal lord to whom fealty is due.

Transylvania and Ottoman's game

For several hundred years, from the late Middle ages until the late 17th century, Transylvania was a pawn and the object of diplomatic intrigue, occupation, and military invasion between Hungary, Austria, and the Ottoman Empire. Transylvania is currently part of Romania.

Unanimity

The quality or state of being without dissent or opposition.

Zeitgeist

The general intellectual, moral, and cultural climate of an era.

Made in the USA
Coppell, TX
19 July 2020

30801670R00157